Movieland

"Goldberg's compelling follow-up to *Gated Prey* is a fast-paced, riveting police procedural influenced by actual events in California. A character-driven series entry that skillfully depicts Hollywood corruption."

—*Library Journal* (starred review)

"The fourth book in Lee Goldberg's series is his most ambitious and best realized yet . . . *Movieland* is crime writing of the highest order. Goldberg's style touches on both Michael Connelly and Robert Crais, in whose company he now squarely belongs."

—*The Providence Journal*

"*Movieland*, Lee Goldberg's fourth novel featuring Ronin, is every bit as good as the first three. The characters, including victims, suspects, and an assortment of lazy, hardworking, honest, and corrupt cops, are quirky and well developed. The depiction of police procedures feels authentic. The writing is vivid and precise. And with startling twists around every corner, the suspenseful tale unfolds at a furious pace."

—Associated Press

"Lee is fantastic at combining clever plotting, humor, and thrills in his stories."

—Boyd Morrison, #1 *New York Times* bestselling author

"LA noir is real; so is Malibu noir, and no one does it better than Lee Goldberg."

—Luanne Rice, *New York Times* bestselling author

"Finished this on the plane home. Typically classy police procedural from Lee Goldberg—giving Michael Connelly a run for his money."

—Ian Rankin

Gated Prey

"The seamy side of California dreaming . . . Goldberg not only ties up . . . but links some of Eve's investigations in ways as disturbing as they are surprising."

—*Kirkus Reviews*

"Lively descriptive prose enhances the tight plot of this episodic crime novel, which reads like a TV show in narrative form. Columbo fans will have fun."

—*Publishers Weekly*

"A great series . . . Eve Ronin continues to dazzle and show her gritty side as she progresses in the Los Angeles Sheriff's Department."

—*Mystery and Suspense Magazine*

"Goldberg finds the perfect balance of treachery and resolve in the strong female character of Eve Ronin. She is a force to be reckoned with that all criminals will hate to come face-to-face with and one that is deserving of the big screen."

—Chris Miller, Best Thriller Books

"Violent crimes and desperate criminals and homicide detectives, oh my! Lee Goldberg delivers an intriguing, fast-paced, satisfying novel in *Gated Prey*."

—Steve Netter, Best Thriller Books

"This is going to be a must-read series for me year after year. Eve is such a badass character who will stop at nothing to see that justice is done."

—Todd Wilkins, Best Thriller Books

"Another suspenseful, fast-paced yarn with engaging characters."

—Associated Press

"I whipped my head back and forth reading *Gated Prey*. So twisty, so funny, and so LA—a few of my favorite things. After zooming through these pages, I'll ride shotgun with Lee any day!"

—Rachel Howzell Hall, bestselling author of *And Now She's Gone*

Bone Canyon

A *MYSTERY AND SUSPENSE MAGAZINE* 2021 BEST BOOK OF THE YEAR SELECTION

"Goldberg follows *Lost Hills* with a riveting, intense story. Readers of Karin Slaughter or Michael Connelly will want to try this."

—*Library Journal* (starred review)

"Goldberg knows how to keep the pages turning."

—*Publishers Weekly*

"Lee Goldberg puts the *pro* in *police procedural. Bone Canyon* is fresh, sharp, and absorbing. Give me more Eve Ronin, ASAP."

—Meg Gardiner, international bestselling author

"Wow—what a novel! It is wonderful in so many ways. I could not put it down. *Bone Canyon* is wrenching and harrowing, full of wicked twists. Lee Goldberg captures the magic and danger of the Santa Monica Mountains and the predators who prowl them. Detective Eve Ronin takes on forgotten victims, fights for them, and nearly loses everything in the process. She's a riveting character, and I can't wait for her next case."

—Luanne Rice, *New York Times* bestselling author

"*Bone Canyon* is a propulsive procedural that provides high thrills in difficult terrain, grappling thoughtfully with sexual violence and police corruption, as well as the minefield of politics and media in Hollywood and suburban Los Angeles. Eve Ronin is a fantastic series lead—stubborn and driven, working twice as hard as her colleagues both to prove her worth and to deliver justice for the dead."

—Steph Cha, author of *Your House Will Pay*

Lost Hills

"A cop novel so good it makes much of the old guard read like they're going through the motions until they can retire . . . The real appeal here is Goldberg's lean prose, which imbues just-the-facts procedure with remarkable tension and cranks up to a stunning description of a fire that was like 'Christmas in hell.'"

—*Booklist*

"An energetic, resourceful procedural starring a heroine who deserves a series of her own."

—*Kirkus Reviews*

"This nimble, sure-footed series launch from bestseller Goldberg . . . builds to a thrilling, visually striking climax. Readers will cheer Ronin every step of the way."

—*Publishers Weekly*

PRAISE FOR LEE GOLDBERG

Murder by Design

"*Murder by Design* is original and fresh, amusing and cheeky, deadly and thrilling, and completely engrossing. The kind of book that you read in one sitting, sleep be damned, because it's so relentlessly entertaining and captivating that you cannot stop until you see how it all ends. Lee Goldberg has outdone himself, delivering a murder mystery that demands to be read and will end up being ranked at the top of any serious list extolling the best books of 2026."

—Steve Netter, Best Thriller Books

"Hilarious and thought-provoking. The mystery itself is complex, and somehow Goldberg balances the humor and drama to perfection. The second book in this series cannot come fast enough, and hopefully a TV series is in the future as well."

—FirstCLUE

"*Murder by Design* is the most ingenious mystery I've read in years, with more twists than a Wetzel's Pretzel. Brain-injured yet supremely confident former detective Edison Bixby and likable but self-absorbed actor—is there any other kind?—Wally Nash make for an unlikely but appealing sleuthing duo. But the real magic of this mystery is the way Goldberg turns environments and objects that we take for granted into clues we never would have noticed but for his deft hand. After reading *Murder by Design*, you will never look at your local mall—or any building, object, et cetera—the same way again."

—Ellen Byron, Agatha and Lefty Award–winning author

Dream Town

"Old bones, paparazzi, rappers, sex tapes, the whole nine yards—topped off with a surprisingly Big Reveal."

—*Kirkus Reviews*

"Fans of fast-paced police procedurals will enjoy Goldberg's trademark humor and his insight into the entertainment world (following *Movieland*)."

—*Library Journal* (starred review)

"Goldberg overtly offers sly, knowing commentary on the state of today's media, even as he spins an engaging and exciting police procedural."

—*Deadly Pleasures*

"Lee Goldberg consistently writes entertaining and engaging stories with relatable characters and plots that feel recognizable yet fresh. *Dream Town* is the perfect continuation of the Eve Ronin series—an equal mix of Hollywood theatrics, personal/family drama, criminal mayhem, and investigative prowess."

—Steve Netter, Best Thriller Books

"Goldberg has created a terrific character in Eve Ronin, and he knows how to write a fast-paced thriller mixed with humor and inside jokes with no fluff."

—FirstCLUE

"The first book in what promises to be a superb series—it's also that rare novel in which the formulaic elements of mainstream police procedurals share narrative space with a unique female protagonist. All that, and it's also a love letter to the chaos and diversity of California. There are a lot of series out there, but Eve Ronin and Goldberg's fast-paced prose should put this one on the radar of every crime-fiction fan."

—National Public Radio

"This sterling thriller is carved straight out of the world of Harlan Coben and Lisa Gardner . . . *Lost Hills* is a book to be found and savored."

—BookTrib

"*Lost Hills* is Lee Goldberg at his best. Inspired by the real-world grit and glitz of LA County crime, this book takes no prisoners. And neither does Eve Ronin. Take a ride with her and you'll find yourself with a heroine for the ages. And you'll be left hoping for more."

—Michael Connelly, #1 *New York Times* bestselling author

"*Lost Hills* is what you get when you polish the police procedural to a shine: a gripping premise, a great twist, fresh spins and knowing winks to the genre conventions, and all the smart, snappy ease of an expert at work."

—Tana French, *New York Times* bestselling author

"Thrills and chills! *Lost Hills* is the perfect combination of action and suspense, not to mention Eve Ronin is one of the best new female characters in ages. You will race through the pages!"

—Lisa Gardner, #1 *New York Times* bestselling author

"Twenty-four-karat Goldberg—a top-notch procedural that shines like a true gem."

—Craig Johnson, *New York Times* bestselling author of the Longmire series

"A winner. Packed with procedure, forensics, vivid descriptions, and the right amount of humor. Fervent fans of Connelly and Crais, this is your next read."

—Kendra Elliot, *Wall Street Journal* and Amazon Charts bestselling author

"Brilliant! Eve Ronin rocks! With a baffling and brutal case, tight plotting, and a fascinating look at police procedure, *Lost Hills* is a stunning start to a new detective series. A must-read for crime-fiction fans."

—Melinda Leigh, *Wall Street Journal* and #1 Amazon Charts bestselling author

"A tense, pacy read from one of America's greatest crime and thriller writers."

—Garry Disher, international bestselling author and Ned Kelly Award winner

MURDER BY DESIGN

OTHER TITLES BY LEE GOLDBERG

Calico

Crown Vic

Crown Vic 2

King City

The Walk

Watch Me Die

McGrave

Three Ways to Die

Fast Track

The Sharpe & Walker Series

Malibu Burning

Ashes Never Lie

Hidden in Smoke

The Eve Ronin Series

Lost Hills

Bone Canyon

Gated Prey

Movieland

Dream Town

Fallen Star

The Ian Ludlow Thrillers

True Fiction

Killer Thriller

Fake Truth

The Fox & O'Hare Series (coauthored with Janet Evanovich)

Pros & Cons (novella)

The Shell Game (novella)

The Heist

The Chase

The Job

The Scam

The Pursuit

The Diagnosis Murder Series

The Silent Partner

The Death Merchant

The Shooting Script

The Waking Nightmare

The Past Tense

The Dead Letter

The Double Life

The Last Word

The Monk Series

Mr. Monk Goes to the Firehouse

Mr. Monk Goes to Hawaii

Mr. Monk and the Blue Flu

Mr. Monk and the Two Assistants

Mr. Monk in Outer Space

Mr. Monk Goes to Germany

Mr. Monk Is Miserable

Mr. Monk and the Dirty Cop

Mr. Monk in Trouble

Mr. Monk Is Cleaned Out

Mr. Monk on the Road

Mr. Monk on the Couch

Mr. Monk on Patrol

Mr. Monk Is a Mess

Mr. Monk Gets Even

The Charlie Willis Series

My Gun Has Bullets

Dead Space

The Dead Man Series (coauthored with William Rabkin)

Face of Evil

Ring of Knives (with James Daniels)

Hell in Heaven

The Dead Woman (with David McAfee)

The Blood Mesa (with James Reasoner)

Kill Them All (with Harry Shannon)

The Beast Within (with James Daniels)

Fire & Ice (with Jude Hardin)

Carnival of Death (with Bill Crider)

Freaks Must Die (with Joel Goldman)

Slaves to Evil (with Lisa Klink)

The Midnight Special (with Phoef Sutton)

The Death March (with Christa Faust)

The Black Death (with Aric Davis)

The Killing Floor (with David Tully)

Colder Than Hell (with Anthony Neil Smith)

Evil to Burn (with Lisa Klink)

Streets of Blood (with Barry Napier)

Crucible of Fire (with Mel Odom)

The Dark Need (with Stant Litore)

The Rising Dead (with Stella Green)

Reborn (with Kate Danley, Phoef Sutton, and Lisa Klink)

The Jury Series

Judgment

Adjourned

Payback

Guilty

Nonfiction

The Best TV Shows You Never Saw

Unsold Television Pilots 1955–1989

Television Fast Forward

Science Fiction Filmmaking in the 1980s (cowritten with William Rabkin, Randy Lofficier, and Jean-Marc Lofficier)

The Dreamweavers: Interviews with Fantasy Filmmakers of the 1980s (cowritten with William Rabkin, Randy Lofficier, and Jean-Marc Lofficier)

Successful Television Writing (cowritten with William Rabkin)

The Joy of Sets: Interviews on the Sets of 1980s Genre Movies

The James Bond Films 1962–1989: Interviews with the Actors, Writers and Directors

MURDER BY DESIGN

A THRILLER

LEE GOLDBERG

THOMAS & MERCER

Published by Thomas & Mercer, Seattle

www.apub.com

EU product safety contact:
Amazon Media EU S. à r.l.
38, avenue John F. Kennedy, L-1855 Luxembourg
amazonpublishing-gpsr@amazon.com

ISBN-13: 9781662533594 (hardcover)
ISBN-13: 9781662533617 (paperback)
ISBN-13: 9781662533600 (digital)

Cover design by Jarrod Taylor
Cover images: © Shabdro Photo / Getty; © logoboom / Shutterstock

Printed in the United States of America
First edition

To Valerie & Madison, beauty by nature and grace by design

PROLOGUE

There are some things you need to know before I start telling you this incredible, improbable, but absolutely true story.

In life, there's the natural world, the built world, and the imaginary world.

The natural world is the earth itself—the land, the sea, the air.

The built world is one designed by humans that we've imposed on the natural world so we can try to exert some control over it and improve our lives.

And then there's the imaginary world, the one that exists in our minds, and that we share with others through the arts.

We all live in the first two worlds, but the third one is my happy place. That's because I'm an actor and a writer. My name is Wally Nash and my passion is telling stories and playing characters. Unfortunately, I haven't been able to make a career out of it yet. This book could change all that.

I've self-published two novels (which were too edgy and literary for mainstream publishers) and I've had roles in *NCIS*, *Grey's Anatomy*, and *The Rookie* (I was a corpse in all three shows, and if you saw them, you know I was able to convey, even in death, the totality of their characters and their unfulfilled dreams), but the combined earnings from those gigs might buy me a week's worth of McDonald's Happy Meals. So, to pay my bills, and still have time for auditions and writing, I work with a temporary staffing agency.

Which was how I met a man who sees the built world with a clarity nobody else does and who would completely change my life.

A man who is, let's face it, the only reason you've read this far:

The sickeningly wealthy, painfully handsome, irritatingly brilliant, outrageously self-absorbed, and infuriatingly manipulative detective—

Edison Bixby.

CHAPTER ONE

The legal term for what I am about to share with you in this first chapter is "hearsay," meaning I didn't witness any of it myself. I've cobbled together this pivotal event in Edison Bixby's extraordinary life from what I was told by people who were there, what I've read on the internet, and what I've imagined. But I assure you it's 99 percent accurate, because I'm an actor with an intuitive ability to create full-bodied characters from the slightest scraps of information.

Like so much in Bixby's life, it all began with a murder.

Let me set the stage, because what happened was like a play that Agatha Christie might have written . . . if she were on crack.

The location was the ballroom of the grand old Belmont Hotel in downtown Los Angeles, where five hundred of the city's elite gathered for a luncheon honoring Grant Murdock—the talented chef, successful restaurateur, hard-partying metrosexual playboy, and unapologetic narcissist—as businessperson of the year due to the extraordinary success of Slop, his new Michelin-starred restaurant.

But they never got the chance. Murdock dropped dead at the table of honor after taking one sip of his gumbo, which, to add insult to fatal injury, was his own signature dish, though I'm sure fast-acting poison wasn't in his recipe.

The Belmont's savvy manager, who'd dealt with plenty of celebrity overdoses, suicides, and murders in the hotel over the years, immediately ordered the entire property sealed off by armed security guards.

Not a single person, employee, napkin, or spoon was allowed to leave the building.

The first LAPD detective on the scene was Bridget McGregor, wearing the same off-the-rack pantsuit and blouse that she'd worn the day before and sporting a carefree hairstyle created by her bed pillow. It didn't take her long to establish the facts of the murder and to assess the tricky context in which it had occurred.

Some of the most politically connected people in Los Angeles were in that ballroom, four of them at the table where Murdock was face down in his soup. They were important, angry, and demanding a quick solution to the murder. And, to her credit, McGregor knew that she couldn't give them one.

But she knew someone who could.

McGregor took out her phone and reluctantly called Edison Bixby, the LAPD's top homicide detective, who undoubtedly would've been assigned the case if it hadn't been his day off.

Bixby pulled up to the Belmont thirty minutes later in a matte-black Bugatti Chiron with a flashing red bubble light stuck on top. It was brash and ridiculous, with a touch of self-deprecation, designed to make Bixby come across as charming rather than obnoxious, which wasn't an easy feat to pull off. But, somehow, he did it.

He drove under the hotel's vast portico, past the medical examiner's wagon and the crime scene unit's van, and took the open spot directly in front of the lobby doors.

The Chiron's driver's side door opened and Bixby effortlessly emerged in a perfectly tailored Tom Ford suit, a flower in his lapel and his badge wallet open over the breast pocket of his jacket. He might as well have been wearing a tuxedo. Frankly, I'm surprised that he wasn't, since he was obviously going for a Bruce Wayne vibe. He was thirty-one years old, but looked much younger. He had a smattering of curated stubble on his cheeks and his hair was artfully askew, as if he'd just arrived from the makeup chair at a *Vanity Fair* photo shoot, which, incredibly, was exactly where he was coming from.

Bixby smiled and handed his key to the bewildered valet. "Don't press the wrong button or you'll activate the ejector seat."

The multimillionaire detective, and LA's most eligible bachelor, strode into the lobby with a dancer's grace, as if he might break into song or bust a move at any moment—then he saw medical examiner Rosalind "Rosie" Okamoto and some CSI techs milling around, killing time.

Bixby went up to Rosie, a stout woman in her forties, who was leaning against a pillar and checking her email. She looked up as he approached and he gestured across the lobby to the ballroom doors, where two uniformed police officers stood guard.

"Isn't the body in there?" he said.

"Yes, and I got a quick look at him, but we got shooed out by McGregor. We were told to wait on you before doing our work," Rosie said. "Terrific entrance, by the way. Shame there were no photographers here to see it."

"If you're going to arrive," Bixby said, "you should *arrive*."

"I wish I could, but I don't have a $3 million sports car, a $6,000 suit, and a personal trainer to keep me slim."

He leaned close to her ear and whispered: "It's not the money. It's the attitude."

"What's yours?"

"This job is so much fun and I'm great at it."

"Every day we see dead bodies and meet people experiencing the worst moment of their lives," she said. "What's fun about that?"

"Solving mysteries, fixing problems, and making the world a better place."

Bixby said it without a trace of sarcasm, cynicism, or any *ism*. It was an honest response.

Rosie stared at him. "You can't be for real."

"You have to embrace life, Rosie. But first, tell me why Grant Murdock can't anymore."

"I obviously haven't done an autopsy or any toxicology tests yet, so don't hold me to this, but I'd say he was killed by a fast-acting poison, probably cyanide or strychnine."

Bixby tugged the flower out of his lapel and gently slipped it into Rosie's hair. "Don't get too comfy. I'll only be a few minutes."

"You're awfully sure of yourself."

He winked at her. "Awfully."

Bixby strode to the ballroom, where the uniformed police officers standing guard opened the doors for him like he was royalty. And, let's face it, that's exactly what he was, at least at the LAPD, where he had an unprecedented 100 percent case-closure rate.

His arrival in the ballroom created an immediate buzz. People discreetly slipped their phones out of their pockets or handbags to snap a picture of him as he weaved among the tables toward the table of honor in front of the dais.

I'm sure he noticed the phones because he's a man who sees everything without appearing to be looking at anything. He also noticed the banquet tables, the place settings, the flower arrangements, the chandeliers, as well as minutiae like the knot on someone's shoelaces, a dirty fork on the carpet, fresh crumbs on a tablecloth, and the hairs on a passing fly's ass. I could go on and on, but you get the idea.

He stopped just short of the table of honor, where Murdock lay face down in his soup and the table's four other guests stood near their former seats, radiating their social stature and their withering impatience. Detective Bridget McGregor stood off to one side, interviewing a nervous male server.

Before McGregor could approach Bixby, one of the guests, a middle-aged woman with a Botox-tightened face and collagen-swollen lips who wore more diamonds than most jewelry stores have in stock, cut him off.

"The great detective has finally graced us with his presence," Edith Gotsford said. "How much longer do we have to stand here watching Grant decompose in his gumbo?"

"You could look the other way," Bixby said.

"She can't." This snide comment came from a woman much younger than Gotsford, but also a devotee of plastic surgery. Her name was Lake Blue, but prior to leaving Oklahoma for Hollywood to pursue a career as a supermodel, social media influencer, actress, or, if all else failed, the wife of a very rich man, it was Harriet Glick. She was too thin, thanks to injections of black-market Ozempic, and top heavy, thanks to surgically enhanced breasts, which were very much on display in a low-cut summer dress.

"She's loving it," Lake continued. "I'll bet she already took a selfie with his corpse."

"And I'll bet you've lifted his wallet." Gotsford glowered at her, then shifted her glower to Bixby. "I'd frisk that gold digger if I were you."

Lake smiled at him. "I'd like that. Be thorough. Pro tip: It could be in my cleavage."

Gotsford took a glance at her bosom and sneered. "You could hide a duffel bag between those enormous basketballs. Pro tip: Don't get your boob job at Dick's Sporting Goods."

Bixby ignored them both and walked around the table, shouldering past a man to get a closer look at Murdock's body.

The man was Roger Fitzhugh, the Southern California car dealership tycoon, who smelled heavily of breath mints and alcohol, which he sucked on to hide the smell of everything he'd been drinking, fooling no one. His rheumy eyes, the spider veins on his bulbous nose, and the drops of red wine on his tie were some of the subtle giveaways. I'm sure Bixby spotted even more.

"At least Grant's last meal had a Michelin star," Fitzhugh said. "He would have wanted it that way."

Bixby glanced at Fitzhugh's bowl of soup and the other dishes on the table. It appeared that Murdock's death had ruined everyone's appetites. Nobody had touched their soup, which was totally understandable. I wouldn't have, either. Even the basket of bread hadn't been disturbed.

"It's restaurants that get stars," Bixby said, "not individual dishes."

"It's the dishes that make the restaurant, *monsieur*," said Pierre Delcourt, another of the table guests, who wore a tailored chef's jacket with his name embroidered on it, even though he wasn't cooking anything that day and hadn't been in an actual restaurant kitchen in years, not counting the fake ones on his Fox Network cooking competition shows, of course. The jacket was his brand, like Colonel Sanders' white suit and black bow-ribbon tie, though he'd hate that comparison.

"If you say so." Bixby plucked a piece of bread from the basket and sniffed it. "Mmmm. Sourdough. I love the smell."

Gotsford snorted. "Are you sure you're capable of solving this murder? Frankly, you don't seem up to it to me."

Before Bixby could respond, McGregor grabbed him by the arm and led him away from the table.

"Excuse us," she said, and practically dragged him over to the wall beside the dais.

Bixby turned his back to the table to face her. "What a lovely group of people."

"And they each have a motive for killing Murdock."

"Of course they do," he said, taking a bite of the bread.

"Edith Gotsford was Murdock's first wife. He married her for her money and social contacts, exploiting them to the max to boost his career, while also having an affair with Lake Blue, who is now his second wife, and he's cheating on her with the eighteen-year-old star of a Disney sitcom, if you believe the tabloids."

"They've always been accurate about me."

"Because they lavish you with praise, treating every case you solve like you've achieved cold fusion in your kitchen using Elmer's glue and a bag of ice."

"Do you know what cold fusion is?"

"I don't have the slightest idea."

"You could have fooled me," Bixby said.

She studied his face. "Are you wearing makeup?"

"Just a little," he said. "I didn't have time to wash it off after the photo shoot. Does it make me seem self-absorbed and obsessed with my appearance?"

"No more than the usual," McGregor said. "Getting back to the murder, Chef Pierre Delcourt was Murdock's mentor, who taught him everything. Murdock repaid the favor by stealing his recipes, including the gumbo he died in, to make himself famous. Roger Fitzhugh invested heavily in Murdock's much-hyped frozen-food venture, which bombed because of terrible quality control, by which I mean none at all. People got violently ill eating that shit. Murdock diverted most of Fitzhugh's money into renovating his beach house, which he claimed was the company's headquarters. None of the four are making a dime out of Slop, his wildly successful new restaurant. The place is booked solid for two years. It's easier to get a reservation at Buckingham Palace."

"You will definitely be needing these soon." Bixby reached into his pocket and handed her a set of handcuffs. "You left them locked to the bedpost this morning."

She snatched the cuffs from him and jammed them into her pocket, looking around to see if anyone noticed. Nobody did. "I knew it was a mistake bringing you down here."

"Then why did you do it?"

"Because Grant Murdock was murdered in front of everyone at his table, and hundreds of other people—including most of the Los Angeles City Council, two Oscar winners, and the man most likely to be our next mayor—and I have no idea how it was done."

Bixby glanced over his shoulder at the table, turned back to her, and shrugged. "The murder doesn't seem that complicated to me."

"It's impossible."

"I don't see why."

"The seats at the table were reserved for specific guests, but the actual seats themselves were unassigned, so nobody could have known ahead of time which seat Murdock would take or which bowl he would eat his soup from," she said. "Moreover, the guests at the table had no way of knowing which server, or which tureen of soup, would be used at that table. Not only that, but the server couldn't have poisoned him, because none of the other people he served at that table, or any previous table, from the same tureen were poisoned. On top of that, the server doled out the soup before the diners at the table were all seated."

While she was telling him all those important details, Bixby ate his piece of bread and studied the ceiling, which she found very distracting.

"Did you hear a word that I just said?" she said.

"I heard you say 'soup' a lot." Bixby shifted his gaze from the ceiling to her. "Isn't gumbo more like a stew than a soup?"

"I think you're missing the point."

"I haven't missed anything."

She knew that was probably true, which was why she'd called him, so now she studied the ceiling, though she had no idea what she was looking for. "What do you see up there?"

"Get the hotel manager over here right away."

"You think the poison was dropped into Murdock's soup from the ceiling?"

"Go," he said urgently, then turned his back on her and studied a row of identical light switches on the wall.

She left to find the manager and, as soon as her back was to him, Bixby took a black Sharpie out from inside his jacket and began drawing a big square on the wall above the row of light switches. He then put X's in each interior corner and two in the center. He was still working on it when McGregor returned with the hotel manager.

"Detective Bixby, this is the Belmont's manager, Jack Porter."

Porter was short, with an epic comb-over that drew long hair from the sides of his head that would have otherwise entirely covered his hobbit-like ears and hung down to his shoulders. "Are you drawing on my wall?"

Bixby pointed his Sharpie at the row of light switches. "Do you know which of these switches controls the chandeliers?"

McGregor groaned to herself.

"No, I don't," Porter said. "But I could get our tech guy down here."

Now it was Bixby's turn to appear incredulous. "You're the manager of the hotel and you're telling me that you don't know how to operate the ballroom lights?"

"It's not my job," Porter said.

"Your job is to assure that your guests have a pleasurable experience in your hotel."

"It's just the lights—"

Bixby interrupted him. "Lights are crucial, and how to turn them on and off should be obvious to anyone, including you or a guest, without having to call 'the tech guy.' But it's not. It's totally unclear from this row of switches which one controls which light."

McGregor spoke up, her impatience giving her voice an edge. "What do the light switches have to do with the murder?"

"They are the only thing in this ballroom that's impossible to understand." Bixby tapped his Sharpie against his drawing on the wall. "This is a map of the chandeliers on the ceiling. Install a light switch where each X is—that way anybody who walks in here will instantly know which switch controls each chandelier. Problem solved."

McGregor had to practically grit her teeth to keep her anger in check. "The lights aren't the problem you're here to solve, Bixby. *It's the murder.*"

He waved off her objection. "Oh, I did that the instant I walked in the room."

"You *did*?"

"The answer is in the design."

"You always say that."

"Because it's a fact of life." Bixby glanced at Porter. "Don't go anywhere. I'm not finished with you yet."

And then Bixby went to the dead man's table, McGregor and Porter following along. He addressed the four guests, who still stood impatiently by their seats at the table.

"The layout of the room, the arrangement of the tables, the placement of the dishware, and the system for serving food are all designs that combine to determine what can and can't be done in the space. Unless you are very smart and figure out a way to use the design against itself. But that didn't happen this time. This murder was stupid."

McGregor said, "Are you saying I'm dumb?"

"I'm saying they are." Bixby swept an arm toward Edith Gotsford, Pierre Delcourt, Lake Blue, and Roger Fitzhugh. "They killed him."

Everyone except Bixby appeared to be stupefied by the pronouncement, but it was McGregor who asked the obvious question.

"How did they do that?"

"Look at the table," Bixby said, and McGregor did. "None of the guests touched their spoons or tasted their gumbo. That's because each spoon is coated in poison."

McGregor nodded, the pieces fitting together for her now. "Since they didn't know which seat Murdock would take at the table, they simply poisoned every spoon."

"Simple, but stupid." Bixby looked right at Gotsford. "Not exactly the work of a criminal mastermind, is it?"

And with that, he was done and shifted his attention to the astonished hotel manager. "Come with me, Mr. Porter. I want to see your hotel rooms. I'm sure the switches in there are a mess, too."

Bixby turned his back to Gotsford and started to walk away, the murder and the killers already forgotten. The light switches were more important to him.

"Don't you dare turn your back on me," Gotsford shouted.

Bixby looked over his shoulder at her, a bemused grin on his face. "Who are you again?"

"You sanctimonious prick." She thrust her hand into her Birkin bag, yanked out a small gun, and shot Edison Bixby in the face.

That should have been the end of his story.

But it wasn't.

It was only the beginning.

CHAPTER TWO

Four years later, in a very nice French restaurant, a young man, let's call him Casey, sat across a table from a beautiful woman. He was a decent, warm, caring person, a poet desperate to love and to be loved—and he believed that this woman could be the answer to his dreams. But there was a huge obstacle to overcome first.

Unlike everybody else in this elegant restaurant, Casey didn't sit on a fine leather-upholstered chair.

He sat on a bright white ceramic toilet.

She smiled at Casey, her eyes radiant, and then he felt that familiar roiling spasm in his stomach, and with it the agony of all his crushed dreams, the impossibility of ever finding lasting love. He clutched his stomach with one hand, pounded his fist against the table with the other, and sobbed, deep and wounded, a man suffering the death of his soul, of his—

"Cut!"

A bell rang in the soundstage, breaking me out of character, but I could still feel the sting of Casey's tears in my eyes as I sat on that toilet at the table.

Josie Boland, the actress sitting across from me, swore to herself and shook her head. She was clearly blown away by my searing performance.

Harry Hibler, the rangy twentysomething director of the commercial, came over to the table. His nose, lip, and ear were pierced. I'm sure plenty more of his body was pierced, too, and it made me cringe just thinking about it.

"What the hell was that?" he said.

I thought it was obvious. "Casey feeling his bowels churning at the worst possible moment."

"Who is *Casey*?"

Again, an obvious question, but I tried hard not to sound like I was patronizing him with my answer. "The character I'm playing."

"He doesn't have a name in the script."

"He needs to be a full-bodied human being if people are going to emotionally invest in his plight," I said. "And people have names."

Hibler sighed. "Okay, fine. He's Casey. But why were you sobbing?"

I looked at Josie and out at the crew to see if any of them were as dumbfounded by the question as I was, but they were all checking their phones. Clearly, they were as embarrassed for Hibler as I was and didn't want to show it. I was buoyed by their silent support.

I faced him. "Wouldn't you be sobbing if you were on your first date with the woman of your dreams, and your seat at the dinner table *was a toilet*? It's horrific."

"He's not actually sitting on a toilet," Hibler said, in as patronizing a tone as it's possible to have without actually saying *I'm patronizing you*. "It's metaphorical."

"I know that, but it's brutally real to Casey," I said. "This is his living nightmare. He's a prisoner of his toilet. He can't ever escape it."

"Yes, he will, by taking Tremvoya, a new prescription medication for treating Crohn's colitis." Hibler took the prop bottle of pills out of one of the dozen pockets on his cargo vest and held it up. "That's what we're advertising in this commercial."

"But Casey doesn't know yet that his blessed salvation is coming," I said. "This is his psychological and spiritual low point, beaten down by his turmoil, his crushed dreams, and his devastating shame. The only way out he sees now is suicide." I pointed to the steak knife on the table. "He's fighting the urge to plunge that knife into his throat and bleed out right here on this white tablecloth."

The director stared at me for a long moment, moved by the raw intensity of my connection to this character.

"Let's do it again, but without the sobbing." He snatched the knife off the table. "Or the suicide."

"Got it. I'll take the intensity down a notch."

"Take it down thirty-six thousand feet." Hibler went back to his seat behind the bank of camera monitors.

I felt sorry for him. He didn't realize this was more than just a drug commercial—it was a character study, an intense human drama, and engaging an audience emotionally was what ultimately would sell the product, while also raising this from a mere commercial into a genuine work of art.

"Action," Hibler said.

And then I was Casey again, looking across the table at this radiant beauty of a woman, and seeing their wonderful future in store for them. Marriage, children, their fiftieth wedding anniversary. And then he felt the cursed spasm in his belly, the sour disappointment that inhabited his bowels and crushed all his hopes.

Casey clutched his stomach, trying to contain the horror, but he knew it was impossible. He saw the revulsion in her eyes and the death of his dreams . . .

"Cut!" Hibler shouted.

I turned to look at him.

Hibler, rubbing his temples, got up from his seat and shambled back over to me. "Why were you clutching yourself in agony?"

I tried not to sound patronizing when I answered his question. "Casey has Crohn's colitis."

"He's feeling a twinge in his stomach," Hibler said. "That's it."

"That twinge is so much more," I said.

"No, it's not. Let's do it again. Just touch your stomach, that's all. The toilet sells the rest."

We tried it fifteen more times before we hit a creative impasse and Hibler decided that my talent, my deep understanding of this tormented character, exceeded his filmmaking ability to capture all of those emotional shadings with his camera. Perhaps someday he'd acquire the skills necessary to achieve that level of acting excellence.

But it wasn't that day.

Instead, the director settled for mediocrity, dropping me in favor of a lesser actor, a mere background extra in the scene, who wouldn't push him to achieve something truly meaningful, something that would deeply move viewers, provoke sympathy for Crohn's colitis sufferers everywhere, and ignite prescriptions for Tremvoya.

Hibler let *the toilet sell it*, which tells you all you need to know about him as a director.

It was Tremvoya's loss.

And, to some degree mine, too, since I wouldn't be getting a paycheck for my work. Alas, while I hadn't filled my larder, I'd fed my soul. I had the pleasure of the performance to carry back with me to my one-bedroom apartment in Canoga Park, with its enchanting view of the Home Depot loading dock.

Casey would live in me forever, but I was facing eviction. I was two months behind on my rent.

I was sitting in my apartment, eating a microwaved Lean Cuisine, when I got a text from the temp agency, informing me that they'd found another boring, demeaning, nonacting job for me the next morning at Triax Global Insurance if I was available.

I was thankful for the paycheck, though I dreaded the prospect of earning minimum wage in yet another knockoff Herman Miller chair, answering phones or filing or doing some other dreary, monotonous administrative task.

But I'd suffer through it and find a way to use the experience as character research for a future role, just like I had with so many other dead-end jobs, biding my time until I finally got my big break.

I didn't know it then, but it had just happened.

The Los Angeles headquarters of Triax Global Insurance was in a Santa Monica office park, so technically it should have been called their Santa Monica headquarters, but that kind of address fudging is done all the time. As long as you're in Los Angeles County, it's considered fair game to say you are located anywhere within its borders.

That's especially true with Hollywood and any entertainment industry–related business. If you're a production company or a casting agency, you've got to say your office is in Hollywood, even if it's actually a PO box in West Covina or Duarte, because it's more of a fantasy than a place, even though the actual Hollywood—the place, not the fantasy—is a drug addict–infested, gang-ridden hellhole where nobody wants to be unless they are shopping for crack or a hooker.

Triax was also situated in a loosely defined area known as Silicon Beach, because so many tech companies were there and because Los Angeles, West Los Angeles, Santa Monica, and Hollywood didn't have the right cachet associated with their names.

So there were at least four or five different places, geographically or virtually, where Triax could get away with saying they were located, depending on the image they wanted to project. The name of a place had become like an actor's wardrobe, something you wore to convey character, and could add or discard just as easily.

I was thinking about that as I sat in Triax's eighth-floor lobby, waiting to be called in to see Melissa Priddle, their senior VP of investigations.

She came out to greet me herself, and she turned out to be a beautiful woman in her early thirties with the sexiest British accent I'd ever heard and the body of a ballet dancer. I would have gladly answered her phone or attended to any other request she had, no matter how dreary or monotonous, just to hear her speak or to get another chance to look into those radiant blue eyes.

Melissa took me into her office, gestured to one of her two guest chairs, and sat behind her orderly desk, where she broke the sad news to me that I wouldn't be working for her. The opening I'd be filling was for the paperwork-shuffler, researcher, occasional driver, and all-around legman for her top investigator, who'd specifically requested either an actor or a writer for the thankless task.

"You tick all of those boxes," she said.

It was her boxes that I wanted to tick.

She went on to say, "But your primary responsibility will be to run interference, to stop him from saying something that offends everybody around him. And if you can't do that, at least try to smooth things over afterwards."

It seemed to me there was an easier way to handle things. "Why doesn't he just think before he speaks?"

The stern expression on her face made me wish I'd followed my own advice.

"Because he can't," Melissa said. "He suffers from traumatic coprolalia, a rare disability caused by a serious injury to the prefrontal cortex, the portion of the brain that deals with impulse control. As a result, he can't always stop himself from saying whatever crosses his mind. Imagine if you couldn't keep your inappropriate observations or thoughts to yourself?"

It's your boxes I'd like to tick. Saying that thought aloud would have been mortifying.

"I can see the problem," I said.

"It cost him his career as an LAPD homicide detective," she continued. "He's brilliant, but after his injury, the things he blurted out to suspects, coworkers, and anybody else he encountered were so inappropriate, racist, sexist, and insulting that it jeopardized the prosecution of cases. It exposed the city to lawsuits and cost them millions of dollars in settlements. I know, because that's why we canceled their insurance policy."

"And then you hired the same guy as an insurance investigator?" I said. "That's insane."

I couldn't believe I'd said that. It came out before I could stop myself, and I didn't have traumatic corpo-whatever as an excuse.

But Melissa wasn't offended. She actually seemed amused.

"You aren't the first person to say that. But we aren't a law enforcement agency. We don't operate under the same regulations or face the same risks and liabilities. And our priorities are very different. The LAPD wants to prosecute cases."

"You want to make money."

"We already do that quite well," she said. "What we really want to do is keep it. In other words, we'd like to pay as few claims as possible and for the least amount of money. He helps us determine if some potentially expensive claims are legitimate or not."

"How does that work with an insurance investigator who offends everybody he meets?"

"He has an amazing ability to see the designed world around us, and to use that unique perspective to determine the cause of accidents and solve crimes, from fraud to heists, kidnappings to murder, saving us tens of millions of dollars in claims. So the benefit far outweighs any risk he poses with his behavior."

"What's his name?" I asked.

"Edison Bixby."

I remembered him. His name was regularly in the news when I'd first arrived in Los Angeles from Owensboro, Kentucky, to pursue my acting dreams. The last I'd heard, he was shot in the face at some luncheon. Now his traumatic corpo-whatever made sense.

"Isn't he a zillionaire?" I asked.

"He is."

"So why does he need to work for you or anybody else?"

"Because it's what he lives for," she said.

I could understand that. I've always loved acting. I started in preschool plays, worked my way up through high school and community college productions, and finally became a star in the local Owensboro theater scene, where there were no trained, working actors on the stage, just ordinary people moonlighting from their real jobs. But I wanted to make acting my life, so I went where that dream was possible. I moved to LA, where I had to compete against professional actors for roles instead of a grocery store cashier, or a tree trimmer, or a pharmacist who did it as a hobby. It was a constant struggle, one I knew I could never walk away from, no matter how hopeless it sometimes seemed.

But it's not me you want to read about, is it?

You're here for Edison Bixby.

Melissa told me that he was the only child of Arlo and Uma Bixby. Arlo was an eccentric inventor of all kinds of household devices, like the Banana Peeler, the Neck-tier, the Laundry-Folder, and the Lawnmowerbot. People loved to hold and behold his machines, even if they weren't very practical. They were crazy works of art that made people smile.

Uma was a renowned and controversial architect who believed that how we behave can't be divorced from design or vice versa. To her, a building was more than four walls and a roof. It was a reflection of someone's needs, desires, and dreams and, like a person, it would influence the behavior of other people. Her emotional-design philosophy led to some very quirky LA homes and buildings that somehow seemed alive, to have actual personalities, and while it didn't get her many building commissions, it did make her a sought-after movie production designer.

When Bixby was sixteen, his parents were driving home from a dinner party on the northbound 405 freeway and slammed head-on into the wedge-shaped concrete divider between the dual on-ramps to the westbound and eastbound 101. Arlo's blood alcohol level was 0.07 percent, just 0.01 percent shy of driving under the influence, and his "practical intoxication" was blamed for their deaths.

Edison didn't believe his father was responsible. So, he took what he'd learned from his parents and put it to work. One of the lessons that Uma Bixby taught him was this:

"We move through spaces created by someone else's vision, unconsciously shaped by their choices and intentions, their decisions shaping our actions like invisible currents in a stream. The guidance is so subtle, we mistake it for our own direction, following a path we never consciously chose."

With that in mind, Bixby studied the design of the freeway interchange, specifically the merge corridor, the point where cars coming off the northbound 405 not only had to cross the traffic speeding toward the east and west 101 on-ramps but also cross in front of cars coming onto the 405 freeway from the street. Those incoming cars had to merge into the 70 mph flow of the northbound 405 as well as into the two directions of the 101. It created a traffic whirlpool.

But Bixby didn't stop with the freeway. He went back to something Arlo Bixby taught him about devices:

"Most accidents are blamed on human error, but that's an outright lie. The device is *always* responsible. Because if it was designed properly, the bad result couldn't have happened."

So Edison studied the design of the Monarch Zephyr, the boldly styled car that his parents were driving, and zeroed in on the terrible sight lines from the sharply raked back windows.

And from those two investigations, he came to an inescapable conclusion.

His parents were murdered.

The California Department of Transportation and Monarch Motors killed them.

He took his case directly, without a lawyer or any other representation, to a closed-door joint hearing of CalTrans, the US Department of Transportation, the County of Los Angeles, and the National Transportation Safety Board.

And, incredibly, he convinced all those bureaucracies that he was right.

The State of California paid Bixby a $15 million settlement and agreed to demolish, and completely redesign, the 405-101 interchange based on his recommendations. Which they did. It's the interchange that exists today.

Then he confronted Monarch Motors, at a closed-door board meeting in Detroit, with the glaring design failures of the Zephyr that were largely responsible for his parents' deaths.

Facing the likelihood of a successful class action lawsuit, and humiliation on a historic scale not seen since Ralph Nader branded the Chevrolet Corvair as "unsafe at any speed" in the 1960s, the chagrined board immediately wrote him a check for $25 million and took the car off the market.

Publicly, Monarch Motors said the Zephyr car line, like so many models before it, "had simply run its course." But they also secretly bought up every used Zephyr they could find and crushed them into scrap to avoid any future liability or embarrassment. Which is why you're in deep shit if you own a Zephyr today that breaks down and you need a replacement part. There aren't any.

At seventeen years old, Bixby was a multimillionaire and a proven genius, a prodigy who could clearly see how the design of the natural, built, and even imaginary worlds could be used to understand and influence human behavior.

"He was so rich that he never had to work," Melissa concluded. "But he'd found his calling or, more accurately, his intellectual and emotional obsession: saving people from bad design. So he became a cop."

That didn't seem like a natural progression to me at all. Why not become an engineer, an architect, an interior decorator, or the host of a reality show that identified and fixed bad design in everything?

I asked, "What does design have to do with crime?"

"Everything." She opened the credenza behind her, removed a huge binder from it, and set it on her desk in front of me. "Here's all you need to know about how to manage his disability. But it's not me you have to impress to get the job. It's him. I just do the initial screening."

What she was asking me to do was perform a role, to be the quirky detective's grounded assistant, to be the Dr. Watson to his Sherlock Holmes. The Archie Goodwin to his Nero Wolfe. The Sharona to his Adrian Monk.

I was confident that I could do that and bring my own spin to the timeworn, formulaic character. But I wanted to achieve more with the role than simply convince Bixby to hire me.

"What would I have to do to impress you, Miss Priddle?"

She gave me a big smile and I felt my heart flutter. "Make it through the week without getting fired or quitting in tears."

"That seems like a low bar."

"Nobody has impressed me yet," Melissa said.

I was determined to change that.

CHAPTER THREE

Melissa told me what my salary would be, which was higher than I'd expected but lower than a living wage for Los Angeles, unless you're living in a van and moving it each day from one Walmart parking lot to another. That was what I'd soon be doing in my old Hyundai Sonata if I missed another month's rent and didn't work out a payment plan for what I still owed.

She had me sign a nondisclosure agreement, then gave me a Triax gym bag that contained the binder on Bixby's disorder, another binder containing the company's rules and regulations, a fat case file on the next claim that she wanted Bixby to investigate, and a complimentary Triax ballpoint pen. Finally, she wrote down the address to Bixby's home on a Post-it note, slapped it on the bag, and sent me on my way.

I went to my car, which I'd left on the street in case Triax didn't validate parking, and sat in the driver's seat to prepare myself for meeting Bixby. I browsed through the binder on strategies for dealing with traumatic coprolalia, which didn't seem very useful, and then I googled Edison Bixby on my phone.

The first search result that came up was the *Vanity Fair* article, which was headlined Meet LAPD's Millionaire Detective and featured an Annie Leibovitz photo spread, the last picture taken of Bixby before he was shot in the face that same day.

Bixby wore a Tom Ford suit, his tie casually loosened at his collar, with a flower in his lapel and his arms crossed under his chest. He leaned casually against his Bugatti Chiron, a police bubble light on top of the car. It was a cheeky shot, one I thought was cleverly staged to sum up the man in a single image. I didn't discover until later that was actually his ride and how he dressed. No staging had been necessary.

He was movie-star handsome, like me and Paul Newman, not character-actor handsome, like Gene Hackman or Matt Damon. In fact, if you'd asked AI to generate a face using the best aspects of Brad Pitt, George Clooney, Glen Powell, Leonardo DiCaprio, and the three Hemsworth brothers, the result would be Edison Bixby. (I know because I tried it, which is why I said "in fact.")

But his defining features were the sparkle of playful mischief in his brown eyes and the easygoing smile that belied his fate. The knowledge of what was about to happen to him gave the photo spread a haunting, emotional resonance that Annie couldn't have anticipated.

I set down my phone and considered how I should approach this audition for the role of Bixby's assistant. There wasn't a script, so I would have to create the character myself.

To create a contrast and yet strike a balance with Bixby, his assistant should be scrappy and tough, more streetwise than his flamboyant and wealthy boss. My character should also be inquisitive, brash, and impetuous. Someone who lives not by any design, but by instinct. I naturally embodied most of those qualities, so I wouldn't have to reach too deep for my character. I would be a heightened version of myself.

Bixby was smart, self-confident, and had a strong personality. I figured that he would probably be irritated by someone who cowered in his presence or constantly stroked his ego. So, as much as I needed this paycheck, I decided that I'd have to risk standing up to him or I'd be crushed in seconds. I didn't believe that he'd enjoy being around someone he could so easily destroy.

I started the car and headed to my second interview.

Edison Bixby lived in Topanga Canyon, a community in the Santa Monica Mountains that was known in the 1960s and '70s as a woodsy, secluded haven for "hippies," artists of all kinds, social activists, religious zealots, and anyone else who wanted to just be left alone to do their own thing.

But that Topanga was mostly a memory now, ancient history kept alive as a fashion, a sort of domestic cosplay performed by the privacy-seeking, wealthy celebrities who destroyed the rustic original bungalows that characterized the community and built massive, garish mansions behind gates where they could let their underarm hair grow, wear designer T-shirts, skip a shower or two, and pretend their substance abuse was a creative pursuit.

The only authentic vestiges of historic Topanga that still survived were embodied by the dwindling number of longtime residents, who'd clung to their land and their culture despite the onslaught of mansion development, floods, wildfires, and landslides.

As I drove along the narrowing, winding roads off Old Topanga Canyon, I was sure that I heard wind chimes in the pleasant cacophony of rustling leaves, chirping birds, and burbling creeks and smelled whiffs of marijuana and scented candles amid the natural aromas of oak, dirt, and a hint of wildfire ash carried in the breeze.

But it was probably just my imagination, mixed with more than a little wishful thinking.

Bixby's house wasn't visible from the road, but his wooden mailbox was impossible to miss. It looked like the open-mouthed head of an enormous snake that was curled up and around a post.

I turned onto the flagstone driveway, following it as it curved around the tall trees that hid the house from view.

As I rounded the turn, I expected to see one of those grandiose and garish mansions, full of Doric columns, huge porticoes, and all the other ridiculous architectural flourishes that the wealthy use to convey their money and power. Instead, I felt like I'd driven into the pages of a children's storybook, one written by J. R. R. Tolkien and illustrated by Dr. Seuss.

The house was sprawling, enchanting, and whimsical and appeared to have been lovingly hand-built over decades from whatever the land itself provided. The lopsided white plaster walls were distressed with age, revealing glimpses of the stone underneath.

The front entrance was a round-topped door at the bottom of a tall, circular turret, with an ascending spiral of distorted windows winding around it up to a conical top. The roof sagged along its spine, but elsewhere it rolled over the house like a wave that swept up high along the three steeply pointed, crooked gables, each with a fancifully misshapen dormer window at its peak. The stovepipes were curled and the chimney looked like it was built in stages, each with a different kind of stone or brick, and might topple at any moment. I wouldn't want to be standing near it during an earthquake or even if somebody sneezed very hard.

I got out of the car with the Triax bag slung over my shoulder and a big, goofy smile on my face. I couldn't help it. There was something wonderfully magical, charming, and inviting about the house.

I ambled up to the massive front door, which had far too many crisscrossing battens and two enormous iron-strap hinges, as if it might have to withstand an attack from rampaging Vikings. I grasped the knocker, a brass ring held in a gargoyle's mouth, and rapped it against the door to announce my presence.

Edison Bixby opened the door almost immediately, as if he'd been standing behind it, watching me through the peephole, and greeted me in black silk pajamas and a red velvet smoking jacket that he must have stolen from Hugh Hefner's grave.

He had the same mischievous glint in his eye, and the casual smile, that I saw in the Annie Leibovitz *Vanity Fair* photo of him, but now there was also an ugly, puckered scar above his right eye. The injury hadn't diminished his stunning good looks one bit. If anything, it added character, like the scar on Harrison Ford's chin. I wondered if getting a scar would help my career.

"You don't look like a Girl Scout, a Realtor, or a Jehovah's Witness," Bixby said. "Let me guess: You're selling magazine subscriptions so you can win a new bicycle."

"Triax sent me to be your new assistant. I'm Wally Nash."

"Ah yes, the failed actor."

That stung, but I figured the remark was a symptom of his brain injury.

"I'm a talented actor who hasn't played a role yet that's earned me wide recognition and financial security. That's not failure."

"It's worse," he said. "It's self-delusion."

That was just mean. "At least I don't have an ugly hole in my head."

That was even meaner and, if I'd misjudged Bixby, it would probably be the end of my job interview, right there on his front step.

Bixby touched his scar, as if he'd forgotten it was there. "It's a miracle I'm alive. The bullet hit my forehead at an angle, traveled around the outside of my skull, then exited out the back of my head. Everybody thought I was a dead Kennedy."

"Was that Kennedy remark an example of your traumatic coprolalia?"

"It was wit. Sorry if I offended you. I didn't realize you were a Kennedy."

I looked past him at the foyer and the serpentine staircase beyond that wound around the central turret. The interior was every bit as charming as the exterior, with arched doorways, distressed beams across the ceiling, and wrought iron sconces on the bulging stucco walls.

"I understand that singing a song, like 'Supercalifragilistic-expialidocious,' or counting to twenty can stop you from saying stuff you don't want to." I held up the gym bag with the Triax logo. "It's one of the many prevention strategies in the fat binder that Miss Priddle gave me."

"You should have tried one of them yourself before mentioning the ugly hole in my head."

"I guess now you know what it's like to be on the other side of your situation." I waved my hand in front of him to encapsulate it all. I decided I might as well go for broke, which was no great risk, since I was already broke. "What's with the silly smoking jacket?"

He cocked his head, apparently confused. "I'm Edison Bixby. Isn't this what you expected to see?"

"I'm sure you are a lot of things," I said, "but a cliché isn't one of them."

"What cliché is that?"

"The rich playboy detective."

"I *am* a rich playboy detective."

"But not like this," I said. "It's too on the nose and cartoonish."

Bixby tugged at his silk sleeves. "I thought that you, as an actor, would appreciate me playing the part."

"Acting is more than wearing the costume. You have to embody the character. But you can't help being you."

"That's the story of my life," Bixby said. "At least lately."

"Do you always dress up in costumes to conduct job interviews?"

"I wanted to have some fun and to see how you'd react."

"Did I pass the test?"

Bixby smiled. "Most people can't look past what they expect to find or what they want to see. But you did. That ability is a big part of this job." He stepped outside, closing the heavy door behind him, and edged past me. "Come with me, Wally."

There was a jolly spring in his step, and I half expected him to do a somersault, like Gene Wilder's entrance as Willy Wonka, and perhaps start singing "Pure Imagination."

And that's when I instinctively realized, without him even telling me, that this was his childhood home, and that in many ways, he *was* Willy Wonka, a rich, eccentric man-child living in a dreamworld of his own creation. Except when he ventured out of it to solve crimes and needed someone to hold his hand.

We followed a path around the side of the house into the lush, densely landscaped backyard, where a delightfully arched bridge crossed a rippling creek that snaked across the property.

"This was my childhood home, every detail of the structures and landscaping designed by my parents to produce happiness and serenity.

In many ways, it was a living, ever-changing laboratory for their theories of design."

"It's like an amusement park," I said. "Or a movie set."

"And it's every bit as premeditated and manipulative as those are. Don't let the whimsy fool you," he said. "But that doesn't mean you shouldn't give in and enjoy it. I certainly do."

Bixby led me to a barn, with the same pointed gables as the house, but it also had a teetering grain elevator made out of stacked stones and bricks of all sizes and shapes.

"That's the garage, where I keep my collection of cars, and where my father had his workshop," he said. "It's still there, untouched since the day he died."

We kept on going down the path, arriving at a cabin that looked like it came right out of the old Candyland board game I played when I was a kid. The stucco walls were swollen like a baked cake with a white roof that looked like frosting that seemed to drip off the rounded eaves of the single tall, crooked gable in the center.

"This is the guesthouse. It was originally designed as a playhouse for me, but I moved into it when I was a teenager," Bixby said. "Now it's yours."

I wasn't sure what he meant by that. "You mean it's my office?"

"I mean this is your home."

I couldn't believe what I'd heard. "You expect me to live here?"

"I get called on cases 24/7 and I have to move fast," he said. "I can't wait around for my assistant to show up here, or at the scene, or at the airport."

"The airport?"

"The company we work for is called Triax *Global* Insurance for a reason. Not every case is in Southern California."

"I don't think you understand," I said. "This is a temp job, not my life. I'm an actor."

"But you aren't making a living at it."

"Yet," I said. "These temp jobs broaden my acting range and they'll make colorful anecdotes I can share in interviews when I become a big star."

He opened the front door. The ceiling was high, with light coming in through the dormer window. A huge stone fireplace dominated the single main room, with kitchen cabinets that looked hand-carved and appliances that were vintage art-deco designs that were both simple and stylish. I imagined the bedroom was just as warm and appealing.

"This house is fully furnished and rent-free, all utilities included," he said. "When we aren't in the middle of an investigation, your time will be your own. You can come and go as you please or have people over, if you like."

He had me at "rent-free" and "utilities included." But I didn't want to seem easy or desperate. "What if I land a commercial, a guest part on a TV show, or a role in a movie?"

"I'm brain damaged, Wally, not brain dead. I can get along on my own while you're playing a corpse on *NCIS* or a man who needs new medications for uncontrollable flatulence."

He'd obviously seen my work, or at least browsed my résumé on IMDb, before I'd shown up at his door, and he wasn't impressed by any of it.

"Neither of those parts is easy," I said. "There's an entire life behind those tragic characters that has to be conveyed in seconds, without words."

"I respect that," he said.

"It doesn't seem like it."

"It's why I want an artist for this job and not an aspiring criminologist, social anthropologist, or environmental psychologist."

"What's wrong with them?"

"Creative people are great at this kind of work. They aren't rigid thinkers. They have vivid imaginations. Actors and writers, in particular, can see the world through someone else's eyes. That's a skill I don't have and that I need."

I was impressed. Even though he'd called me a failure, he still looked at me and saw an actor. A creative person. That was something my parents, who truly loved me, still couldn't see. They wanted me to go into the furniture business.

"How many assistants have you gone through?"

"Eleven," Bixby said. "Twelve if you include the ventriloquist and her dummy."

"Why didn't they work out?"

"They couldn't stand how much smarter, richer, and better looking I was than they are," he said. "And neither could I."

"Did you think before saying that?"

He shrugged. "I'm not sure. Do you want the job?"

I did. I reached into the gym bag, pulled out the file, and handed it to him.

"Miss Priddle gave me a new case for you to investigate. It's a life insurance claim on Lawrence Keefer, a sixty-seven-year-old widower, who was killed a few nights ago in a home invasion burglary. Someone from the LAPD will meet us at the house to release the crime scene to you."

He opened the file, took a quick look at the cover sheet, and smiled. He handed the file back to me. "Let's go. You can call me Bixby."

I gestured to his smoking jacket. "Don't you want to change first?"

He glanced at himself and smiled. "I'm getting to like this."

And in that instant, the smoking jacket looked perfect on him. Now he was wearing it for fun, not as a statement or an act, but as a reflection of his true personality. It wasn't a costume anymore. It was him.

I'm sure he knew that, too. He was a much more complicated man than he seemed and yet, at the same time, more self-aware than anybody I'd ever met.

Perhaps that's what made the simplicity, the ease, with which he made that jacket his own so impressive. He did it effortlessly, with just a smile and an almost imperceptible change in his body language in how he wore it. As an actor, I admired the instant transformation. I needed to learn how to do that.

He led me back to the garage while he made a quick call to the LAPD detective to say that he was on the way and arranged to meet her there. We went inside, and I saw his immaculate collection of about two dozen cars.

I'm not a car guy, but I recognized a few. There didn't seem to be a theme to his collection. There were domestic and foreign, new and old cars. Some highly stylish, some ordinary.

Bixby picked a red 1959 Cadillac convertible with a white interior and enormous tail fins. I thought he would toss me the keys, but he didn't. He must have noticed the look on my face.

"I don't need a chauffeur, Wally. After my head injury, I learned evasive driving at Quantico and raced my Porsches at Nürburgring."

We got into the car. It was in perfect condition, as if it had just rolled off the assembly line. "You have more than one Porsche?"

"I also have more than one tie."

Bixby slipped on a pair of Ray-Bans and we sped out.

CHAPTER FOUR

The Cadillac was like a yacht, and Bixby sailed it smoothly and assuredly northbound on Topanga Canyon Boulevard, out of the Santa Monica Mountains, and clear across the San Fernando Valley to the 118 freeway, which ran just below the foothills of the Santa Susana Mountains. Bixby seemed to be in no particular hurry to get where we were going, clearly enjoying the ride.

I liked it, too.

I lowered the window, rested my arm on the door, sank back into my seat, and basked in the sunshine. The only thing that could have made the ride more like everybody's image of the California dream would have been if we were cruising down the Pacific Coast Highway and listening to the Beach Boys on the radio. Sure, it was a cliché, but I loved that I was almost living it. I was probably humming "California Girls."

We headed east on the 118 for a few miles before getting off at the Reseda Boulevard exit and heading north, up into a 1960s-era tract home community that straddled the border of Porter Ranch and Granada Hills.

We arrived at Lawrence Keefer's rambling one-story ranch house on a ridge overlooking Aliso Canyon Park. A woman wearing a pantsuit and holding an iPad under her arm leaned against an unmarked police sedan in the driveway, waiting for us. She had a strange, conflicted look on her face, like she was both happy and irritated to see us arrive.

Bixby coasted the car to the curb. I grabbed the case file and we got out, meeting the woman at the house's front porch.

She nodded at Bixby, without reacting at all to how he was dressed, and then introduced herself to me. "I'm Bridget McGregor, LAPD."

"I'm Wally Nash. Mr. Bixby's new assistant."

"You look familiar," she said. "Have I arrested you before?"

"You've probably seen me on *NCIS*. I've been a featured corpse three times."

I listed it as a "recurring role" on my acting résumé, even though it wasn't a speaking part or even the same corpse each time.

She shook her head. "That's not it. I have a great memory for faces. It will come to me."

McGregor turned her attention to Bixby, who looked past her at the smelly pile of unopened meal-delivery boxes on the porch, the rotting food inside them leaking out through the stained cardboard, drawing a line of ants. Someone forgot to cancel Keefer's standing orders after he died. I actually considered returning there later, cleaning up the mess, and then helping myself to the fresh deliveries that arrived until someone finally canceled the subscription. That was how desperate I was.

"I didn't expect to see you on this one," McGregor said to Bixby. "I thought Triax saved you for the really tricky cases."

"The trickiest are the ones that seem mundane but really aren't."

"I'm not easily fooled."

"Your breasts look great today."

I was shocked by the comment and fumbled for a way to deal with it.

"He didn't mean that," I sputtered.

She gave me a cold look. "Are you saying I don't have a great rack?"

Bixby said, "They really are very nice, Wally."

"What he means, and what I mean," I said, "is that you're defined not by your appearance but by who you are as a complex human being, and as a law enforcement professional, and we both deeply respect that while also appreciating your beauty."

They both stared at me. I knew I'd fumbled it. But they were obviously having some fun with me, and their easy comradery suggested that they were more than casual acquaintances. I wondered if this was another test of some kind.

McGregor looked back at Bixby. "I miss the ventriloquist."

"Only because her dummy kept insulting me."

"You deserved it."

She unlocked the front door and led us into the house. The living room was orderly, almost untouched, but the furniture was decades out of date, and it didn't seem to me it was because they were antiques. My guess was that they had been bought new in their day and hadn't been used much.

We followed her across the living room and on into the den, which had been converted into an office. I came to that conclusion because of the big stone fireplace that dominated the room. It was also where Lawrence Keefer had fought for his life.

The signs of both a ransacking and a struggle were everywhere. The drawers were open on the desk and credenza, and the floor was littered with books, broken glass, toppled furniture, scattered papers, and fallen lamps. The most unsettling sign, though, was the large, brownish-red bloodstain in a clear spot on the floor amid the debris. That was where Keefer died.

Bixby began moving around Keefer's office, careful not to disturb anything, his gaze traveling like a searchlight over every corner of the room.

I didn't need to be an expert in deduction to know that Keefer was a crime novelist and screenwriter. The lurid paperback covers of two of his novels were framed on the wall, and so were screen-capture photos of his "written by" credits from several old TV shows, including *Nash Bridges* and *Diagnosis Murder*. The bookcases in the room were overflowing with mystery novels and thrillers. He'd indirectly paid a few monthly utility bills for Michael Connelly and Robert Dugoni.

On the right side of the study was a large wooden desk, covered with manuscripts, stacks of books, and several coffee mugs filled with pens, pencils, scissors, highlighters, and letter openers. A laptop computer was on the coffee-stained blotter, and a single pearl earring lay beside it.

McGregor turned to me. "You should get a dummy. That way you'll have a socially acceptable way to say whatever you want to Bixby."

Before I could answer, Bixby spoke: "Maybe I should get the dummy. Then Triax wouldn't have to worry about what I say."

Then I wouldn't have a job. So I said, "A dummy might give you an excuse to be objectionable onstage, but not in real life."

"The world is a stage, Wally." Bixby leaned over to look at a tape measure and pencil on top of the credenza.

I noticed the glass was shattered on one of the framed photos on the wall near Keefer's desk. As I stepped closer to examine it, I saw bloodstains on the shards of glass that still protruded from the frame and on the photo itself, which was actually a clipping of an *LA Times* review of one of Keefer's books. I was able to make out a paragraph:

> The novel reads as if Keefer challenged himself to write a book made up entirely of clichés in plot, character, dialogue and description. If that was his crazy, subversive intent, then he succeeded brilliantly. However, if the paucity of a single new idea was intentional, a risky and subversive comment on the formulas and tropes that are the foundation of the genre, then this may be the worst mystery novel ever written. It might be either way.

Writing a novel that bad must have been Keefer's shrewd conceit. Otherwise, I couldn't see why he'd want to see that blistering review on the wall every time he sat down to write. I looked back at his desk, imagining him seeing that review, and that's when I noticed the floor safe that was open beside his chair.

"You can think of this room as a set," Bixby said. "Like one on a stage."

I turned and saw him standing to the left of the ash-filled fireplace, studying some framed photos on the wall between the credenza and the fireplace. On the floor beneath the photos, to the edge of the mantel, was a collection of candlesticks caked in melted wax.

"Why would I do that?" I asked.

"Because almost everything around us is man-made or shaped by human design to influence our behavior," Bixby said. "We're all actors following a script we didn't write on a set made by someone to serve the story."

McGregor sighed. "I'd love to stay for another thrilling design lecture, but I have actual police work to do. Take out your phone and I'll give you the crime scene photos."

Bixby produced an iPhone from the pocket of his smoking jacket. She held her iPad next to it and I heard the whoosh and buzz that indicated she'd AirDropped the photos to him. It was a revealing moment of technological intimacy. They were contacts. It made me wonder how close they were in other ways.

"What happened here is simple," McGregor said. "The burglars broke in through the French doors in the kitchen and were ransacking Keefer's office when he walked in on them. He fought with one or more of the guys and got stabbed in the chest with an ice pick."

Bixby leaned close to her side to look at the images on her iPad screen instead of his own, perhaps because hers was larger. But I noticed she didn't seem to mind the closeness. I came up on her other side, but not as close as Bixby did, so I could take a peek at the photos, too.

Keefer looked his age, maybe even older, with a dusting of gray in his hair, dressed in blue pajamas, lying on his back in a puddle of blood, an ice pick in the center of his chest. His arms were at his sides, as if he wasn't just dead but formally deceased, presenting himself for autopsy and burial. The fingers of his left hand were bloodied, like those of someone who'd been in a fistfight.

Bixby pointed at the ice pick. "Where did that come from? There's no bar or liquor cart in here."

McGregor said, "The ice pick was a Finnish mystery-writing award that Keefer won twenty years ago for the translation of one of his paperbacks. His son told me he kept it as a paperweight on his desk. It was the only artistic recognition Keefer ever got for his books."

Bixby shifted his gaze to her. "You're thinking Chilean burglary tourists did this."

What the hell were those?

She nodded, like his comment made sense. "They've hit six houses on this street in the last two months."

I asked, "There's a tour group for thieves?"

"Not literally," McGregor said, looking at me like I was the dumbest person she'd ever met. "But there might as well be."

Bixby took pity on me, patiently explaining: "They're men in their teens or early twenties who come to LA for a few days to break into homes that border open space. This entire street and an adjacent cul-de-sac are above a park. They grab whatever valuables they find that they can fit into a backpack, sell the stolen goods within hours, wire the money home, get a burger and a selfie at In-N-Out, then take the next flight back to Santiago."

McGregor walked out of the office into the kitchen and we followed her. Plywood covered the shattered windowpane on the left side of the French doors that opened out to the backyard. A paver lay amid the shards of glass all over the kitchen floor.

She opened the French doors, revealing a built-in barbecue, a picnic table, and chaise lounges on a patio that offered a nice view of Aliso Canyon Park and a tract home community on the opposite ridge.

"The patio out here is made up of interlocking pavers. Keefer kept two spares right outside these doors to use as doorstops, and there is another paver on top of the barbecue cover to keep it from blowing off. He might as well have left a sign for intruders inviting them to use the pavers to break in." McGregor looked back at Bixby, who was examining some pill bottles by the kitchen sink. "There's no mystery here. It's a burglary gone wrong, not a premeditated murder, and the killers are long gone. Case closed. You're not going to make me look stupid again this time."

Bixby raised his hands in surrender. "That's never my intention. I had no idea this was your case."

"Bullshit."

"Triax sent me. They hate to pay life insurance claims on a violent death without at least taking a cursory glance for themselves. That's all I'm doing."

McGregor closed the French doors, shouldered past me, and stepped up to him. "I know you, Bixby. When have you ever taken only a 'cursory glance' at anything?"

"A moment ago at your breasts."

"That was *gaping*, not glancing. The house is all yours. Lock up when you go." She handed him the keys and started to walk away, slapping him on his buttocks as she passed. "Great ass. Are those pajamas silk?"

"Spun in the mountains of Suzhou by arthritic Chinese monks from the cocoons of *Bombyx mori* moths that were hand-fed mulberry leaves by virgins."

"Must feel nice on the skin. Is that why you're going commando today?"

"I knew I forgot something when I left the house."

She turned her back to him and walked out. Bixby watched her go with a smile on his face.

I said, "Was she shot in the head, too?"

"We have a history."

Which I would learn about later, but I was certain they also had a present. An intimate one.

McGregor came rushing back into the kitchen, startling us, and wagged a finger at me.

"I know you! The stench of the rotting food on the porch just reminded me. You're the explosive farter!"

I felt my face flushing. "It's a condition called aggravated flatulence and I don't actually suffer from it."

"You're the guy who repulses airline passengers and ruins office parties with your loud, smelly farts."

I was glad the harrowing performance made an impression on her, and that I embodied the character so fully that she couldn't see it was just a role. But it created awkward situations like this for me.

"It wasn't me," I said. "Seth was a character I played in a drug commercial, but I'm flattered that my performance resonated with you."

McGregor laughed and turned to Bixby. "Better get yourself nose plugs or you won't survive."

She left again, and I was glad to see her go. I turned and saw Bixby shaking his head sadly at me.

"What?" I said.

"Do you ever get laid?"

Not nearly enough, but not because of the roles I played. It was because I couldn't afford to take a woman out anywhere except McDonald's. But I didn't tell him that. What I said was: "Your question is way out of line."

"It was more of an observation posed as a question."

"You're an HR nightmare," I said. "I can see why Miss Priddle hired me."

"I can't, at least not yet. What can you tell me about Keefer?"

I opened the file and browsed Miss Priddle's cover sheet that summarized the main points. "He made his living as a freelance TV writer, contributing scripts to various cop shows, and wrote a smattering of paperbacks."

Bixby picked up the pill bottles and read the labels. "Tell me something I wouldn't know just by walking through his office."

I skimmed the summary.

"His wife died of Alzheimer's three years ago in a memory-care facility. He has one son, who is married with two children. Keefer was insured by Triax for his home, car, and life insurance. Financially, he was barely getting by on Social Security and a small Writers Guild of America pension. He spent his savings caring for his wife during her long decline."

Bixby nodded. "That's more like it. All good to know."

It was? I said, "Why?"

"It tells me who he was and what he was doing in this house."

"He was living in it," I said. "Isn't that obvious?"

"'Obvious' is a duplicitous, lying vixen who will poison your coffee the instant your head is turned."

Well, that was colorful. But what did it mean?

"You're saying he wasn't living here?"

Bixby sighed. "A house is much more than shelter. It's a very complex environment, a series of spaces designed for certain tasks—a room for cooking and eating, a room for sleeping and sex, a room for grooming and shitting, et cetera. But think of everything else that happens within those walls and what we have to do to make it all possible, to make it a home."

Finally, he'd said something that made sense to me. Whenever an actor steps onto a set, he has to find a way to inhabit both the character and the space if the performance is going to ring true. The set, particularly if it is his home or office, has to feel lived-in and the actor has to appear comfortable in it.

I said, "We have to make it our own."

"That's right, and when you do that, the house isn't just a space anymore. It's a detailed map of your brain."

"What does that have to do with how Keefer got killed?"

Bixby gestured to the backyard with a wave of his hand. "Go outside and do your thing."

"My thing?"

"You say you're an actor. So act."

"Who am I playing?"

"A Chilean burglary tourist. You're wearing a hoodie, gloves, and a backpack to carry your loot, which is whatever you can grab quickly with your hands."

So no TV sets, paintings, or computers. Just cash and jewelry, maybe some credit cards. My character wants to be able to move light.

Bixby went on. "All you've got in your pockets is a burner phone to call for your ride and a flathead screwdriver to pry open things. That's it."

And, I assumed, no ID or passport in case I got caught. "No knife or gun?"

Bixby shook his head. "If you're arrested for breaking into a home while carrying a deadly weapon, then you could be charged with aggravated burglary and locked up for a decade. But if you're arrested for simple breaking and entering, you're only facing a couple of years and low bail. Your gang puts up the cash, you flee to Chile and come back again in a few weeks, maybe to Dallas or Seattle this time, to steal some more."

I nodded. I could work with that to build a character. "Got it."

"I'll be Keefer," Bixby said. "Come back whenever you're ready."

I went outside and crossed the patio to the hillside, which had been recently trimmed of weeds to the naked dirt as a firebreak. About ten yards below was a rusted wrought iron fence marking the property line, and beyond it was a blanket of flowering mustard weeds covering the slope leading to the park.

I slid down the hillside to the fence, then spent a moment getting into the scene and my character.

I was Diego, a pirate in a dazzling land full of riches that were just waiting to be taken, far from Santiago and the filth, despair, and poverty of the barrio, where I was no one. Here I was somebody. Here I could do something to support my frail, broken mother, crushed by a life of hard work and cruel disappointment, and my little brother, who needed a prosthetic leg to replace the one he lost in a motorcycle accident. I was their only hope, and that gave me hope, too. And a sense of purpose.

I scampered up the hill and observed the house, a big treasure chest with windows, for a few moments. No lights were on and there was no sign of activity. If anyone was inside, they were asleep. I saw the kitchen doors, which were little more than windows with hinges, and suppressed a laugh. How was it possible this place hadn't already been robbed a thousand times? And there, beside the door, was a stack of pavers to prop them open on sunny days.

Americans are fat cows, just waiting to be milked.

I scampered across the patio to the kitchen doors and peered through the windowpanes. Nobody was inside.

It was almost too easy.

No, it was more than that.

It was an invitation.

I picked up a paver, pretended to smash it through a pane of glass on the right side, and then I opened the door and slowly crept into the house, moving through the kitchen to the next room.

Just as I stepped through the doorway, Bixby charged at me, screaming wildly, with a fireplace poker held straight out in front of him.

If I didn't move, he was going to impale me.

I recoiled, smacked into the edge of the kitchen island, then whirled away as the screeching madman thrust the poker at my gut. I yelped and scrambled toward the backyard, only to become entangled in the chairs at the kitchen table, tipping them over and falling with them to the floor in my mad panic.

Rolling over, my feet tangled in the chair, I looked up to see Edison Bixby standing over me, the sharp point of the poker nearly touching the tip of my nose.

"Why did you run?" Bixby asked calmly.

"You were running at me with that fucking poker," I said. "I didn't want to get skewered."

"I'm a sixty-seven-year-old man in his jammies," he said. "Why didn't you just take it away from me?"

"Then what? Beat you with it? And what if you impaled me instead?" I pushed the poker away from my face and sat up on the floor. "There are other houses, empty ones. Diego doesn't need this shit."

"No, he doesn't." Bixby used his free hand to lift the chair, put it back into place at the table, and then study it for some reason. "That's a very good point."

"Diego loves the gangster lifestyle, and the foreign travel, but he also has obligations to think about, like his little brother who needs a prosthetic leg."

Bixby shifted his gaze from the chair down to me. "What did you say?"

"If Diego doesn't come back and the money dries up, poor Santo will be hopping on one foot begging for tortillas for the rest of his life to feed himself and his toothless mother."

Bixby broke into a smile. "That's it, Wally. That's the missing piece."

"Of what?"

"Everything that happened here, which you blatantly ignored, starting with using the paver to break in through the French door on the *right* instead of the one on the *left* that the killer used."

"It's what felt natural to me," I said. "I don't know why."

"I do," he said. "It's because you are right-handed. The killer wasn't. And then you ran out of the house before you were barely inside, so we didn't fight, either."

I didn't appreciate the criticism.

"That's because of your lousy directing. You told me to act, not to mimic McGregor's report. Next time, if that's what you want, say so and I won't improvise."

I made a big leap believing there would actually *be* a next time after that, but he wasn't being fair, and that pissed me off.

"On the contrary, Wally, you did exactly what I wanted. You put yourself in the intruder's mind." He gave me his hand and helped me to my feet. "Thanks to you, everything makes sense now."

"Really? Because until now, I wasn't confused about anything."

"While you were out here getting into character, I tried to follow the moves of the struggle in the office by the wreckage it left behind and I couldn't. Now I know why."

I thought about it for a moment and then I understood. "Because it didn't happen. There wasn't a burglar or a fight."

"That's right. If Keefer confronted him, the burglar would have run out of the house just like Diego did. You just proved that this wasn't a home invasion robbery."

It was an exciting moment, one that felt like the beginning of a grand adventure, our hunt for the real killer, the mastermind who'd engineered this deadly, clever charade.

The game is afoot, Watson!

"This was a premeditated murder," I said, "meticulously staged by a criminal genius to look like a home invasion robbery."

Bixby leaned on the poker like it was a cane. "It wasn't that, either."

"Then what else could it be?"

"A suicide," he said.

WTF?

CHAPTER FIVE

There was no way Bixby could be right.

I wasn't a detective, but I was a reasonably intelligent guy with some life experience. Moreover, I was an actor, someone who routinely and easily saw things through the eyes of a wide array of diverse characters.

"The ice pick was buried to the hilt in Keefer's chest," I said. "Who has the strength and the sheer, iron-balled resolve to do that to themselves without flinching?"

"Nobody," Bixby said. "Certainly not Keefer. He was a frail old man."

"But you just said he did."

"I'm impressed, Wally. You noticed it, too."

"Your contradiction?"

"That the ice pick was sticking straight out of Keefer's chest. If he was stabbed while struggling with his killer, the pick should have been at an angle. It was too precise."

I thought about it, picked up an imaginary ice pick, and acted it out for myself and for Bixby.

I tried to stab myself, but I immediately felt an invisible set of hands pulling my arms away from my chest. It was my natural instinct for self-preservation wrestling against my intellectual will to end my life.

But I struggled against it, bringing the sharp point of the pick to my flesh. The instant the blade broke through my skin, and I felt the searing pain and oozing blood, I pulled the pick away.

I would have to do this fast, or I wouldn't be able to do it at all. I took a deep breath, held the pick with both hands, and with a scream, jammed the ice pick hard and fast into my chest, curled over it in agony, and felt my lifeblood drenching my hands until the final beat of my lacerated heart brought me to my knees, never to rise again.

I dropped the imaginary ice pick and looked up at Bixby. "He couldn't have stabbed himself."

"Why not?"

I got to my feet. "He would have been at war with himself while he did it, his instinct to live battling with his determination to die, so the wound should be much more raw and ugly, reflecting that struggle, and it's not."

"Brilliant!" Bixby broke into a big smile. "Is that all?"

No, it wasn't.

"Keefer's hands and arms would be drenched with his own blood and they aren't."

"Bravo!"

"So you agree," I said. "It couldn't be suicide."

"Exactly," Bixby said. "That's why everyone was fooled, except us."

What he was saying made no sense at all. "I still am."

"If it makes you feel better, it also took me a minute to understand exactly what happened."

"A minute? That's all?"

"I was being generous," Bixby said. "Maybe it took me ten seconds. But that's because I didn't have to do any thinking. Lawrence Keefer did it all for me."

"What does that mean?"

"Come with me." Bixby went back to Keefer's office and I followed him. He stopped in the doorway and surveyed the scene. "The way you arrange your space reveals what you are trying to accomplish within it, mostly because we have lousy memories and we're lazy. So we leave clues for ourselves, reminding us of what we need to do. And to make things even easier for our feeble minds, we place the objects that are necessary to complete those tasks close to where they will be used."

"That's what you saw in thirty seconds?"

"That's what I see everywhere all the time. Of course, I instantly knew that Keefer was left-handed."

"Of course? How did you see that?"

Bixby went over to the desk and stood in front of it. "This is where he worked. He organized everything that was important to him and his work to his left . . ."

I surveyed the desktop. The phone. The mug full of pens. His glasses. His notepad. The coffee rings on the blotter. A pair of reading glasses. The "days of the week" plastic pill organizer with individual boxes for each day. They were all placed to the left of his desk chair and laptop.

"And that observation was the key to the rest," Bixby said.

"It was?"

Bixby pointed to the bloodstain on the floor. "That's where Keefer's corpse was, to the *left* of the fireplace from where we are standing now. You'll notice that there is actually a path leading to the hearth. It's the only area of the floor that isn't littered with obstacles from the fight."

Now that he'd mentioned it, I could see it.

There was a clear path to the fireplace.

Actually, it wasn't a straight line.

It veered to the left.

Just like the burglar did at the French doors.

Or, I should say, just like Keefer did. He had his imaginary burglar use the door on the left because that was the one he would have used, the same way I naturally used the one on the right.

What Bixby was saying was that if I started to look at the whole room from the point of view of a left-handed person, I'd see it in an entirely different way.

The way that Edison Bixby did.

"A path is never random," he said. "It's always by design."

I walked over and followed the path from the bloodstain to the hearth and found myself facing not the fireplace but the two framed pictures on the wall. One was a Christmas card photo of a young man, a young woman, and two children, a girl and a boy, both under the age of ten. The girl was in a wheelchair. The other was a recent picture of a grim-faced Keefer and an elderly woman who looked to be his age, presumably his wife, who was sitting in a lawn chair with a vacant expression on her face, staring blankly into space.

Bixby looked over my shoulder. "I assume that's a picture of Keefer's son, daughter-in-law, and grandchildren, and the other is of him with his late wife at her assisted-living facility."

That seemed like a safe assumption to me. "Why would Keefer want such a sad picture of his wife on the wall rather than one of them together from happier times?"

"I asked myself the same question. Now look around for the answer."

I looked to my left and saw a tape measure and pencil on the credenza. I looked down and saw the collection of candlesticks caked with melted wax. I looked to my right and saw a fireplace filled with ashes.

"If there are answers around me," I said, "I don't see them."

"There are two answers. One is from my field of expertise, and one from yours. The first answer is that the picture was a reminder of what he had to do and why. The second is that it was his motivation."

Bixby picked up the tape measure from the credenza, extended the tape, and put the end against the wall. "Look closely where I've stopped and you will see a dot."

I did. And there it was. Made with a pencil. Barely visible to the eye, unless you were looking for it. Bixby then stretched out the tape measure in front of me, holding one end against the wall and the other against my chest. The tape was straight. "The dot is at precisely the same height as your heart and Keefer's."

I tried to wrap my mind around what Bixby was saying, because he was saying it as if the conclusion were obvious, but it wasn't to me.

He must have seen how clueless I was, literally, from the puzzled expression on my face, because he tapped the spot on the wall for emphasis.

"The ice pick was sticking out here, held in place by a glob of wax."

I looked back at the path on the floor, then at the photos on the wall, and was shocked by the answer that came to me. "You're saying that he ran into the ice pick and *impaled* himself?"

Bixby nodded. "And then he fell backward, the deadweight of his body plucking the ice pick right out of the wax, leaving the glob behind, some on the wall, maybe some on the floor." He pointed at the candlesticks. "That's why the candlesticks are there, beside the hearth. Keefer set a roaring fire in the fireplace before he impaled himself. The heat melted the candles, and also the glob, removing any evidence that the ice pick was stuck there and that his murder was a suicide."

That explanation almost made sense, but one thing didn't fit.

"If that was his intention," I said, "then why did he leave the tape measure on the side table?"

"He forgot about it, which brings us to his motivation," Bixby said. "He was in the early stages of Alzheimer's."

"How do you know that?"

"Lots of reasons, but here are three." He held up three fingers, ticking off the list.

"Number one: The medications in the kitchen are for treating memory loss, the dosages divided by day into a pill box on his desk so he'd remember to take them. Number two: the delivery boxes of prepared meals so he'd remember to eat. And number three: the overabundance of clues to remind him of what he had to do to stage this murder and why he had to do it."

Overabundance? I couldn't see even one clue. "What clues?"

"They are everywhere. Like this." He led me to the bad book review in the shattered glass frame stained with blood. "He framed this devastating review because it infuriated him and he hung it here to remind him to punch it, to create the fake defensive wounds on his hand. He placed the pile of pavers by the French doors outside to remind him to break the glass and how to do it. And, of course, there are those." He pointed to the photos on the wall of his family and his institutionalized wife. I got it now.

"He killed himself because he didn't want to end up a zombie in a rest home like his wife."

"It terrified him," Bixby said. "It would terrify me, too."

I was sure that Bixby experienced some of those same fears after he was shot in the face. He probably still did. I would have if I were him or if I were playing him.

"But why stage this elaborate death to avoid his fate? Why not just swallow a bottle of sleeping pills?"

"The one thing I didn't see was the answer to that question," Bixby said. "But *you* did."

"I did?"

"Poor little Santo, Diego's brother who needs a prosthetic leg."

Bixby walked back over to the fireplace and tapped the framed Christmas card. I looked at it and saw the girl in the wheelchair. A closer look revealed that her body didn't sit quite right. There was something physically off about her that suggested this wasn't a temporary injury.

"Keefer's granddaughter is permanently disabled," he said. "I'd guess cerebral palsy. He didn't want his life insurance cashed in to pay for his long-term care. He wanted it to pay for *hers*."

I finally got it all. "This was an insurance scam."

Bixby nodded. "An ironic coda to his life. Keefer was a crime writer whose best plot was the one he wrote to kill himself."

"It certainly was," I said. "Except he didn't get away with it."

"Didn't he? You can't prosecute a dead man."

"But now Triax won't have to pay out anything to his heirs, which is going to make Miss Priddle very happy with you." And, I hoped, with me too, for helping it happen so fast. I'd be sure to highlight my own contributions when I wrote up my report on this case.

"We aren't done yet," Bixby said. "There's one mystery left to solve."

"There is?"

He went back to the desk and pointed to the lone earring on the blotter.

"The story behind that and the open floor safe."

"Isn't it obv—" I stopped myself before I said "obvious." "Keefer wanted you to think he caught the burglars in the act of stealing what was inside."

"That's stupid," Bixby said.

"Isn't stealing things what burglars do?"

"These were smash-and-grab guys, not master safecrackers. That's why they used a paver to break in."

"You don't know that because nobody actually broke in," I said. "Keefer made it all up."

"He was a crime writer," Bixby said. "He'd have known safecracking was out of character for these guys. Do you believe Diego could crack a safe?"

He had a point. "So why do you think the safe is open?"

"Because Keefer emptied it out and forgot to close it."

"Why would he empty the safe if it wasn't part of his scam?"

"That's what we need to find out," Bixby said.

So, in search of the answer to that question, we drove farther north to Santa Clarita, and another tract home community, on the other side of the Santa Susana Mountains, thirty miles outside Los Angeles. That's where Andy Keefer, Lawrence Keefer's son, lived with his family in a modest little house that was virtually identical to every other one on the street.

We drove up to find Andy out front, washing his pickup truck with his two kids while his wife tended to some flowers. His daughter sat in her wheelchair, training a hose on the truck while her father and brother did the lathering with soapy sponges.

Bixby parked at the curb. We got out and approached the driveway.

Andy turned to face us and seemed immediately perplexed by Bixby, which made sense, since he'd probably never had a visitor who wore a silk smoking jacket and pajama bottoms.

"Mr. Keefer, I presume?" Bixby didn't wait for an answer. "I'm Edison Bixby, an investigator with Triax Global Insurance, and this is Wally Nash, my sensitivity coach. I'm investigating your claim."

"I haven't claimed anything," Andy said.

"Oh, okay. Then we'll just keep the $2 million. Toodle-oo." Bixby turned and headed back to the Caddy.

"That wasn't what I meant," Andy said quickly, taking a step toward us. "I didn't know Dad had a life insurance policy or that I was the beneficiary. It's not something I wanted or that I asked for."

I felt sorry for the poor man and said, "Of course not. Mr. Bixby didn't mean to suggest otherwise, and we're truly sorry for your shocking, unbelievably painful loss."

"Thank you," Andy said.

Bixby turned back to us and tipped his head my way. "I told you he was sensitive."

I said, "But unfortunately, we work for a heartless corporation and have to go through the motions of confirming that your father's death met the requirements for the payout."

"It does," Andy said. "He was killed in a burglary."

"You're a liar," Bixby said.

I wasn't sure if that was an uncensored remark or not, so I kept my mouth shut.

Andy dropped his soapy sponge, as if preparing for battle, and glared at Bixby. "Are you suggesting that I killed my father for his life insurance?"

Bixby seemed genuinely surprised by Andy's anger. "Absolutely not. I know you had nothing to do with his death."

"Then I don't understand why you're here."

"I think you do."

I certainly didn't. The girl dropped her hose and rolled her wheelchair over to us, intentionally bumping into Bixby's leg. "I'm Sara."

He looked down at her. "I'm Bixby."

"What happened to your face?"

"Bee sting. What happened to your legs?"

"I was born this way. Why are you wearing pajamas?"

"Because they're comfortable and make people think I'm a relaxed, slow-thinking guy you shouldn't take seriously."

"Are you?" she asked.

"I'm brilliant," he said.

She grinned. "It must be fun to surprise them."

"Fun for me," Bixby said to her, then looked at Andy. "Not so much for them."

Sara considered what Bixby said, then turned to her dad. "I want to wear pajamas to school."

Andy said, "We'll talk about it later. Right now, I have business to discuss with my friends." He waved to his wife, who stood by the flowers, watching this scene warily as it played out. "Jen, can you watch the kids for a minute?"

He didn't wait for an answer. Andy walked down to the Caddy, as if he simply wanted to admire the outrageous fins, and we trailed along with him. But once he was certain he was out of earshot of his kids, he turned and confronted Bixby.

"I don't know what you're talking about."

Bixby said, "Your mother's jewelry and whatever else of value was in your dad's safe."

"The burglars took it, along with his life."

"You have it, Andy. I just don't know whether your dad *gave it* to you before he killed himself or *left it* for you afterwards with a note explaining what he'd done. My guess is after, so you wouldn't try to stop him." Andy didn't say a word, but he was trembling almost imperceptibly and Bixby noticed. "Yes, *definitely* after."

I thought that Bixby was being cruel. Why did he have to make this takedown more painful than it had to be? And why do it in front of the man's kids? He was indulging himself, enjoying the win.

I said, "Maybe we should do this inside, away from the kids."

Bixby ignored me, his eyes on Andy. "The problem is, if anybody ever discovers you have it, you could be arrested and prosecuted for insurance fraud."

"*Could* be?" Andy said.

"I'm going to tell Triax that the police got it right and they will pay the claim."

I was shocked. I'd met Bixby for the first time only a few hours ago, but I couldn't believe that he'd keep the truth to himself or hide a crime.

Bixby continued: "That means you can keep any cash that was in the safe, it's untraceable, but not any tangible items, like jewelry or gold, that were on your father's homeowner's insurance policy. Not even if you're keeping it only for sentimental value. And, of course, you have to destroy the note."

"I burned it," Andy said. "The note was on his desk, under Mom's jewelry, his coin collection, and $5,000 in cash. He was right not to tell me his plan. I would have stopped him. What do you want me to do? Put the stuff back in the house?"

"Of course not, that would be confessing," Bixby said. "I want you to give it to me."

I was stunned by the answer and what it implied. So was Andy.

"So that's what this is," he said. "Blackmail. But it won't end there, will it? You'll want a kickback on the insurance payoff, too, in return for your silence. How much?"

"I don't need your money," Bixby said. "I'm filthy rich."

"He really is," I said. "Google him."

But I was as confused as Andy was. I could see now that confusion would be a regular part of my job if I kept doing this.

Bixby said, "I'm trying to keep you out of prison, Andy. I'll store the jewels and coins in my safe. You or your heirs will get it back when I die."

"Which might not be long, if the past is any guide," I added, trying to be helpful. "Look at his face. He should be dead already."

Bixby glanced at me, amused. "Maybe you need a sensitivity coach."

But Andy did look at Bixby's face, and maybe he saw something in both his expression and his scar. "What will the explanation be for how and why you had them?"

"I'll write in the codicil that I spent years tracking down the loot so it could be used as evidence when I finally caught your father's killers," Bixby said. "But, tragically, it was the one case that I couldn't close."

I cocked an eyebrow at him. "Only one?"

"I want the story to be believable," he said. "The shocking revelation will give my obituary an extra emotional punch."

Bixby didn't seem old enough to me to already be thinking about his obituary and his legacy. But I suppose I'd be a bit fatalistic, too, if I saw a gunshot wound in my face every time I looked in the mirror.

Andy said, "Why are you taking such a big risk? You could go to prison, too, if anybody finds out what you're doing for me."

"I'm not doing it for you. It's for her." Bixby gestured to Sara, who kept watching us with curiosity from her wheelchair on the driveway. "And I don't want your father's sacrifice to be for nothing. But don't worry, nobody is smart enough to catch me."

Andy nodded to himself, making a decision. "I'll go get everything for you."

He went back to the house, disappearing inside, and I turned to Bixby. "Aren't you forgetting something?"

"Oh, yes. The key to Lawrence Keefer's house." Bixby took the key out of his pocket. "I'll give it to Andy when he gets back. Thanks for the reminder."

"That's not it," I said. "There's something enormously significant that you've blithely overlooked."

"I do everything blithely, but I actually am wearing underwear. McGregor was teasing me."

"You didn't ask me if I wanted to be an accomplice to insurance fraud."

He waved off the comment. "It's not necessary."

"What makes you think I won't tell Miss Priddle about this to save myself?"

"Because you're so sensitive. Look at that poor girl. You don't want to take her father away from her."

He was right. But it was also unfair to suggest the blame would be on me if her father suffered the consequences of his own actions.

"Besides," Bixby continued, "you signed an NDA that remains in force until I revoke it or die. So you'll have to wait until then to tell all in your books about our exploits."

His reference to the NDA didn't worry me. I was pretty sure it couldn't be enforced if my silence meant incriminating myself and becoming an accomplice to a felony, not that I had any intention of outing him. I didn't believe what he was doing was a crime. It was an act of tremendous generosity and kindness. I was proud to be an accomplice to that.

What struck me, though, was his use of the word "exploits." It suggested that this was only the beginning of our story. I liked the sound of that. I also liked his idea of writing books about him, even if his assumption was outrageously egotistical. The books could be a way for me to make some real money from this experience. But I tried to act nonchalant about his casual suggestion and, because I am an actor, I am sure that I succeeded.

"What makes you think I'll write about you?"

"Because I'm amazing and you're talentless," he said, his opinion unfiltered. Or perhaps he just had an enormous ego. It was hard for me to tell. "How else will you support yourself when I'm gone?"

"Remember this conversation when I win my first Academy Award. It will be the reason why you aren't thanked in my acceptance speech."

Andy Keefer emerged from the house with a Trader Joe's canvas shopping bag in his hand and came down to us at the curb. He held out the bag to Bixby.

"Here you go."

Bixby took the bag, then gave him the key. "This is the key to your father's house. Case closed. You should get the check in thirty days. Give me a call anytime you'd like to come over and see these jewels. I mean it, Andy. They're yours. I'm only the caretaker."

"I can't thank you enough for this, Mr. Bixby."

"There's one way." Bixby looked over at Sara and smiled. "Let her wear pajamas to school if she wants. She's brilliant."

Andy followed his gaze and smiled, too. "Yes, she is."

We got into the Caddy and Bixby drove off with the jewels and Andy Keefer's gratitude. But that wasn't all that Bixby left with.

He'd also earned my loyalty.

CHAPTER SIX

I moved out of my Canoga Park apartment and into Edison Bixby's incredible guesthouse that same day. It was an easy move. I left behind my shitty furniture (either snap-together stuff from Target or Goodwill finds) and kitchenware. I stuffed everything else—clothes, shoes, books, and DVDs—into my Hyundai, leaving barely enough room for me to fit into the driver's seat, and I sped off like I'd just held up a bank.

I wasn't really worried about the landlord coming after me. She had my security deposit and the last month's rent that I'd paid up front. And now she wouldn't have to go through the aggravation of evicting me.

On the way back across the valley to Bixby's place, I was tempted to stop at a 7-Eleven and buy a lottery ticket or two with my last few dollars since my luck had clearly changed.

Overnight, I went from being fired from an acting role on a toilet to being hired to act as the assistant to a brain-damaged millionaire detective. It was a dream day job until I scored the role that would make me a breakout Hollywood star. Best of all, I didn't have any living expenses besides food. I could bank nearly all of the cash I earned and concentrate on honing my craft, whether it was acting or writing, when I wasn't providing my invaluable assistance to Bixby, who was a fascinating character to watch.

I didn't take me long to unload my car and settle into the warm, inviting, and comfortable little house. There were even a few bottles of port, some jars of nuts, and a couple boxes of crackers in the kitchen. I didn't know whether he'd left them for me as a housewarming gift or if he just generally kept that stuff there for his guests, but I gobbled down a lot of it anyway before heading to bed.

I was on my way to the bedroom when I saw some headlights sweep the window, so I parted the drapes and peeked outside at Bixby's front-yard motor court. I saw Bridget McGregor get out of a Ford Explorer, go to the front door, and let herself in like she lived there. It was nice to know my instincts were right about the two of them. Perhaps I had the makings of a great detective myself. I could certainly play one if the right role came along.

I woke up at around 7 a.m., showered and dressed, then decided to splurge and go get myself a McDonald's breakfast.

I walked out to my car at about the same moment that McGregor came out of the house. She grimaced when she saw me.

"You're still here?" she said on her way to her Explorer.

"It's my job, at least until I'm offered a better part."

She stopped and looked at me. "You see this as a role to play?"

"We're all actors," I said.

"Not me."

"A typical woman could end up playing between six or seven different versions of herself in a day—daughter, sister, lover, wife, mother, friend, partner, or even a homicide detective. That's acting."

She looked at me, but this time it was in a different way. It was as if she saw me, Wally Nash, for the first time instead of Seth, the explosive farter. "Bixby says the world is a stage."

"Shakespeare said it first," I said.

McGregor gave me a little smile. "I think you two might actually be a perfect match."

"What about you two?"

Her smile instantly became a snarl. She took two steps forward, got right in my face, and stared directly into my wide eyes. My testicles went into hiding.

"What made you think that thirty seconds of forced, awkward small talk gave you permission to pry into my personal life? Listen up, Fartman, never go there, do you understand?"

Our noses were practically touching. I could smell the Listerine on her breath.

I nodded. "I'm sorry."

She held the furious stare for a moment longer, then stepped away from me. "Bixby took a bullet in the head. He has an excuse for crossing the line or misreading social signals. You do not."

"You just proved my earlier point," I said. "In an instant, you went from Friendly Woman McGregor to Intimidating Cop McGregor."

"I'm *always* a cop."

She got into her Explorer and drove off. I watched her go and wondered why her anger was so close to the surface. Was she embarrassed about being caught leaving Bixby's bed? It wasn't a secret that I was there. My car was parked in the motor court, too.

I was about to go off in search of an Egg McMuffin when I heard some splashing. Curious, I followed the sound into the backyard, along the creek, and into a lush grove of tropical trees to a secluded pond fed by a waterfall cascading down a rocky hillside. Bixby was in the pond and under the waterfall, using it like a shower. His bathrobe and a towel were draped over a nearby boulder.

But the idyllic pond wasn't the real attention-grabber. It was the massive old oak tree with an enormous tree house, seemingly built with pieces salvaged from a shipwreck, like the one in *Swiss Family Robinson*, entwined in its big, sturdy branches.

As I got closer, though, it appeared to be more of a contraption than a shelter, the tree's height harnessing gravity, and waterwheel providing mechanical power, for an as-yet-unseen ball, or several of them, to roll along an intricate, interweaving series of bamboo sluices and tracks, leading to wooden gears, pendulums, seesaws, levers, and vine-operated pulleys that ultimately did something deep inside the structure . . . or perhaps it was just an enormous piece of kinetic art. Could it be some kind of clock?

I walked around the base and saw several chutes, each leading to individual tree stumps positioned under them, and, farther along, I saw a box shaped like an electronic console, with six wooden levers resembling tillers on a boat sticking out of the top. A bunch of ropes, resembling vines—or perhaps they actually *were* braided vines, I don't know—dangled from the tree and disappeared into the console, where I supposed they were yanked by the levers.

I was trying to figure it all out when Bixby said, "Good morning, Wally. Are you all settled in now?"

"Yes, I am, thank you." I turned to face him as he stepped out from under the waterfall, naked from the waist up. I couldn't help noticing that he was in terrific shape. Not muscle-bound, like someone training to play a Marvel superhero, but fit and strong, not one molecule of excess body fat. Everything was in just the right proportion, which made me jealous. You don't get a body like that sitting around the house eating Cheetos. He had to be doing some kind of exercise, unless he had extraordinary genes. "I ran into Detective McGregor."

"We sleep together occasionally when she isn't in a relationship and even sometimes when she is. She's a lot less uptight in bed than she is on the job, or maybe I'm just gifted in the erotic arts."

Uh-huh. I wasn't sure if that frank disclosure was due to his neurological disorder or was simply a personality flaw. But I worried about what would happen to me if McGregor found out about it.

"I didn't ask you to tell me any of that," I said. "And whatever you do, don't suggest to her that I did. This conversation never happened."

"Did she bite your face off?"

"Nearly."

"She's so grumpy in the morning," Bixby said. "Would you like some breakfast?"

"Sure, that would be nice. I haven't had a chance to go grocery shopping yet."

"Go to the tree, pull the first lever for fresh-ground coffee, the second lever for toast and fried eggs."

I went to the console-box thing and pulled the first two levers. A slot opened at the top of the tree and a series of marbles started rolling down various bamboo tracks. One ball hit a lever that swung a sluice in front for the waterwheel, siphoning off some water that ran down a carved path, setting a wooden gear in motion. I could hear things clacking, thunking, dripping, grinding, and hissing in the tree, and even a few bells going off.

"Will this call a butler or something?"

"*You* are my butler."

I ignored that and gestured to the elaborate contraption entwined with the tree. "Then what is all this?"

"My parents created and built their own *Swiss Family Robinson* tree house, but with a *Gilligan's Island* sense of comedy, just for fun. Mom designed the house, Dad created the outrageously intricate mechanism that runs through it, which does simple things in ridiculously complicated ways, like making a cup of coffee, frying eggs, and toasting bread."

"They did all this for you?"

"For all of us," Bixby said, almost wistfully. "We'd have a morning swim and afterwards the Castaway Contraption, as Dad called it, would serve us breakfast."

"What do the other levers do?"

"The third one makes pancakes, the fourth makes orange juice, and the fifth activates the orchestra."

"The *orchestra*?"

"Player piano, drums, harp, and various wind instruments," Bixby said. "I guess it's more of a band than an orchestra."

"And the sixth lever?"

"It activates all the booby traps on the property."

"Like what?" I asked.

Bixby shrugged. "The usual. Poison darts. Swinging spike balls. Punji pits. Giant rolling boulders. Et cetera."

"You're joking."

"It's more effective, and a lot cheaper, than an alarm system or cameras."

The pulley system deposited a mug on a tree stump. A moment later, a tiny bucket came down on a rope and poured hot coffee into the mug. A moment after that, a basket lowered a plate with two pieces of toast and two perfectly fried eggs on it.

I was amazed. Walt Disney couldn't have topped that. Or Willy Wonka.

"You'll find utensils in the basket," Bixby said.

"You had a charmed childhood." I got the utensils out of the basket, picked up the plate and mug, then went over to a boulder by the pond to eat my meal. "Who wouldn't want to live in their own private Disneyland?"

"It wasn't all Zip-a-Dee-Doo-Dah."

Before I could delve into that, Melissa Priddle emerged from the trees, carrying a slim Louis Vuitton messenger bag.

"I see you've discovered Bixby's magic tree house," she said to me. "Are you going skinny-dipping, too?"

I didn't realize that Bixby was naked. I'd only seen him from the waist up. I looked at the pond and saw him swimming toward the shore, his naked butt visible now in the water.

"No, not today," I said, turning back to her. "Are you?"

Bixby said, "Wishful thinking, Wally."

I felt my face blushing. How could I have asked that? Being around Bixby seemed to make everyone behave like they'd been shot in the head. "I didn't mean it that way."

Her pleasant expression hadn't changed. Perhaps she was frozen in dismay?

"That you'd like to see her naked?" Bixby said. "Yes, you did, and so would I." He stood half-naked in the water and beckoned her into the pond with a big smile. "Come on in, Melissa, the water is great."

How could he say that to his employer? It was sexual harassment, blatant sexism, and just plain rude.

I said, "He didn't mean to say that. It's his condition." I tapped my head. "I know he has enormous respect for you."

"Enormous," Bixby said. "More so now since I started imagining you naked."

Oh. My. God.

"You'll have to forgive him," I said, stammering now, seeing my job slipping away and myself living in my car. "It's his traumatic brain injury. He's got even less control over it early in the morning."

I had no idea if that was true, since I'd never seen him early in the morning before, but it was all I could come up with. I was sweating everywhere.

"Relax, Wally." Melissa smiled and sat down on a boulder next to me. "I'm used to it, but I'm glad you're trying to mitigate the damage. I came by because I have a new case for Bixby and I love watching his kinetic sculpture in action."

Bixby said, "Do you mean me or the tree?"

I said, "He didn't mean that, either."

She set her briefcase down, went over to the tree, and pulled the third and fourth levers. Pancakes and orange juice.

"What's the case?" Bixby called out from the pond.

Melissa scaled a small winding staircase into the tree, presumably to watch the domino effect as the balls activated things—pendulums, pulleys, and gears. One ball triggered a small wooden lever that released an orange from a bamboo chute into a cradle, where a second ball released a spring-loaded cleaver that split the fruit and sprang back into place.

I went back to work eating my eggs, which a chef couldn't have prepared better than that tree, and the coffee was as good as anything served at Starbucks.

"A woman fell down a staircase last Saturday at the Woodland Hills Mall and was killed." She watched the cradle tip the orange halves onto two sharp stones, while a wooden arm, powered by a pulley connected to the waterwheel, pressed the fruit, extracting the juice into another bamboo sluice, which poured it into a woven reed mesh to remove the pulp and seeds. "Her shocking death generated a ton of publicity, the kind that can suddenly and permanently turn a booming mall into a vacant teardown within months. You didn't hear about it?"

"I don't read the papers."

Melissa peered into the tree, fascinated by whatever was going on in there to make her juice and pancakes. "Nobody reads newspapers. There's this new thing called The Internet."

Bixby strode naked out of the pond, not the least bit self-conscious or bashful. If I had that body, I probably wouldn't be, either. "Which side do we insure?"

Melissa glanced back at him as he was toweling off, but she was relaxed about it, as if he was someone she'd seen naked before. I was the only one who seemed uncomfortable with the situation. It made me wonder if they, too, had an intimate relationship.

"The mall owner, who is under enormous pressure from the stores to quickly settle with the woman's family and make this nightmare go away." She came down the stairs and stopped in front of one of the stumps as a cup dropped from a chute and then was filled with fresh-squeezed orange juice pouring from a bamboo sluice. "But before we cut what will probably be a low eight-figure check, I want you to make sure the mall was truly at fault."

Bixby slipped on his bathrobe and tied it shut. "You called her death shocking and a nightmare. Why?"

"It happened at a newly built, but not yet in service, staircase that doubles as an architectural sculpture. It spirals down from the second floor and will lead people to the big food court that's still under construction." Melissa sipped her orange juice and waited for her pancakes to appear. "She tripped on a step, lost her balance, tumbled down, and got impaled on four pieces of rebar sticking up from the foundation of an uncompleted 'Mall Directory' display at the bottom of the staircase."

I asked, "Was something wrong with the step?"

"It was much narrower than the other steps," she said. "In fact, a construction worker stumbled on the same step on Friday and reported the problem to his supervisor."

"There's a science to the height of each step and the amount of flat surface on top," Bixby explained to me. "Most steps have a height of about seven inches and a surface of less than a foot, with a clearly visible edge so you know where it ends and the next one begins. Once you've walked down a step or two, your mind notes those measurements, and you unconsciously assume that the rest of them will be exactly the same. So you stop paying attention. But if a step *isn't* the same as the rest, and if you aren't holding the handrail, you could have a very nasty fall, particularly if the staircase is very steep and there isn't a landing for every eight feet of rise. And I suspect that this one did not and, on top of that, had curves not ordinarily found in a traditional staircase."

"That's true," Melissa said. "It has a real wow factor."

"More like an *aaaaaaaaah* factor," Bixby said, screaming like a person falling to his death.

I couldn't tell if his brain injury was to blame for that remark or if he was just making a joke in very bad taste. So I simply said, "Given the danger, I'm surprised the mall didn't fix the step right away."

We heard the whoosh of Melissa's plate of pancakes sliding out of a chute onto a stump. She went to get it.

"It was scheduled for repair on Monday." She picked up her plate, got some utensils, and joined me at my boulder. "In the meantime, there were two stanchions with a retractable tape line between them in front of the staircase to indicate that the steps were closed, but someone unlatched the tape."

Of course that happened. I've seen kids do that at the post office and in movie theater lines. For some reason, they find retractable tape barriers fascinating. But after this fatal accident, I expected the mall to overreact and maybe use concrete K-rails, perhaps even topped with razor wire, to keep people off staircases or escalators that weren't ready to be used.

Bixby asked, "Was she drunk, drugged, or otherwise impaired?"

"Nope. The ME ruled that out." She took a bite of her pancakes and smiled like a child with a slice of birthday cake. "How is it that a tree makes the best pancakes in Los Angeles?"

"Did she have some kind of medical episode?"

"Not until she got impaled," Melissa said while she ate. "The evidence screams that gross negligence, bad design, and faulty construction caused her death."

"Do you have her death on video?"

"Of course," she said.

Once Melissa finished her breakfast, we placed our plates in a wicker basket that was whisked into the tree for cleaning by pulling the console's sixth lever. (Yes, Bixby was joking about the security system.) After that, Bixby led us down a cobblestone path to his screening room.

But it wasn't a room in his home. It was a separate building, an adorably small-scale replica of a 1930s, art deco–style movie theater complete with a stand-alone ticket booth, a marquee, and movie posters for *Goldfinger*, *The Wizard of Oz*, and *Planet of the Apes* framed outside. In the small lobby were a popcorn machine, a soft-drink dispenser, and an array of candies in display cases.

We went through the lobby and down into the intimate theater, which had three staggered rows, stadium-style, of four plush reclining seats that faced a big screen. In the back of the room, I saw a control console with a computer keyboard, an embedded screen, and various cable inputs that I assumed operated the curtain, the lights, the projector, and other equipment.

Melissa knew exactly where to plug in her iPad and how to activate the system, which told me that she'd been here many times before. The curtains opened, revealing the screen, and then we saw several security camera images of a young woman in a shopping mall, walking toward the curving staircase, which spiraled down from the second floor, where there were many stores and customers, to the first, which was dark, vacant, and clearly still under construction. The woman on-screen was slightly chubby and wore a loose-fitting, floral-patterned minidress with spaghetti straps.

"Her name is Caroline Crowley. She was thirty-five years old and single," Melissa said. "She worked as public relations specialist at a crisis-management company."

"The mall could have used her expertise now," Bixby said.

On-screen, Crowley walked toward the staircase with intent, as if she knew where she was going. She started down the stairs and then, at the point where it sharply curved, she glanced up and to her left and her eyes widened in shock. She immediately stumbled and toppled down the stairs like a rag doll, leading to her gruesome death, which I won't describe out of respect to her, her family, and your sensibilities. There's no sense being gory. But I will say it was ugly.

Bixby went over to the iPad and swiped the video back to the beginning, freezing the image of Crowley when she was only a few steps from the stairs. "Look at her. She didn't go down those stairs out of idle curiosity. She's heading there for a reason. What was it? Where was she going?"

I'd noticed the same thing, as you know, and I felt proud of myself for it. I didn't say anything at the time because I didn't think my observation was relevant. And because I was the assistant, not the detective, but then I knew to trust my incredible eye for detail, at least as it applied to character. I mean, aren't we all just characters in someone's story and the hero of our own?

Melissa said, "There's nothing open down there yet. Maybe she just wanted to check out the progress of the new food court."

Bixby shook his head. "She looks too determined for that. She's not carrying any shopping bags, either. What was she doing at the mall?"

Melissa shrugged. "Sometimes women just like to shop."

Bixby pinched his fingers on the iPad, zooming in on Crowley's feet on the big screen. Her feet now filled the theater. "She's wearing flip-flops."

Her toes were nice and manicured, the nails bright red and glossy.

"You're saying that's why she tripped?" Melissa said. "I don't think that's a winning argument for the mall or for Triax."

"Look at her toes. Her nails are bright red."

I'd noticed that, too, remember? It was only two paragraphs back. But it would have been hard not to miss those details because they filled our field of vision. What I didn't get was why it mattered.

He zoomed in on her hands. Her fingernails were bright red, too. "So are her fingernails. She came to the mall for a manicure and pedicure."

I asked, "How do you know?"

Melissa answered before Bixby could. "She's wearing flip-flops because she just had her toenails done and is letting them dry."

Bixby shook his head at me. "You really don't know anything about women, do you."

No, I didn't.

You need to live around women to pick up details like that, or around women who have manicures and pedicures, and neither my mom, nor any of my girlfriends in Owensboro, ever did. It was a luxury they couldn't afford.

Melissa put her hand on my shoulder. It felt nice. *Very* nice. "He didn't mean that, Wally. It's his condition."

Bixby said, "Women won't get near him because of the excessive farting."

She removed her hand from my shoulder. I spoke up quickly in my defense.

"It wasn't me," I said to her, though it sounded more like imploring. "It was a character I played in a drug commercial. I assure you I have a terrific colon."

A terrific colon?

What the hell was I thinking saying that?

Melissa offered me a weak smile, probably out of pity. "Good to know."

Bixby unfroze the video and let it play until Crowley paused to glance up and to her left. He froze the frame again. Crowley looked startled, but there was more going on in that expression, and I say that as an actor. I was impressed by what I saw. There were many emotions at work on her face. Longing. Sadness. Shock. I could spend hours in front of a mirror trying to replicate that same richness of expression.

"What did she just glance at?" Bixby said. It was a rhetorical question, of course, but he looked at Melissa for an answer. "Are there other camera angles on the second floor so we can see what she saw?"

"There must be," she said. "They've got cameras all over the mall. But I don't have that footage. When you get to the mall, ask Paul Wetzel to show you the videos. He's their head of security."

Bixby scowled. "He couldn't detect his own foot."

"Try not to tell him that," she said.

"I'm curious," I said to Bixby. "Do you know him or do you just assume that all mall cops are stupid?"

"Of course they are or they wouldn't be mall cops. They'd be real cops."

Melissa shook her head. "Good luck today, Wally."

She unplugged her iPad from the console, killing the image on the big screen, and stuck the slim device in her Vuitton bag. Then she pulled out a file and handed it to me. "I hope for your sake that the mall cops are unarmed."

I watched her go. She had a nice ass.

"Nice ass," Bixby said.

For a moment, I feared that I'd spoken my thought out loud. I was relieved it was him and not me. "That's crude and inappropriate."

"You were thinking it, too."

Yes, I was, and I'm sure the look on my face betrayed me. So I didn't try to deny it. I embraced my guilt. "It's one thing to think it, and another thing to say it."

"It doesn't make you any less crude and inappropriate."

"But nobody will know that I am because I haven't announced it."

"That makes you a fraud," Bixby said. "I pride myself on being authentic."

"I don't think being an authentic boor is something to be proud of."

"I'm going to get dressed and then we'll go to the Woodland Hills Mall." Bixby headed for the door and I followed him.

"That's a relief."

"What is?"

"That you're actually getting dressed. I was worried you'd go like that."

We went outside but along a different path this time, one that led to the house instead of the pond.

"The time code on the video indicates that Caroline Crowley fell at 11:27 a.m. While I'm getting dressed, call the mall cop. Tell him we're coming. Ask him to look at the security video and backtrack Crowley's movements to the moment she arrived at the mall. I want to get there at the same time that she did. Find out where she parked, too."

"Why? Isn't the staircase what you need to look at?"

"That's irrelevant."

"I thought Miss Priddle asked you to determine whether the mall is at fault for Crowley's death."

"I never answer the question I'm supposed to answer."

"Because you like to irritate people?"

"Because it's never the right question," he said.

"What's the right one in this case?"

He stopped and faced me. "What was Caroline Crowley doing at the mall?"

"Does it matter?"

"You're an actor," he said. "What do you ask yourself before you begin every scene?"

"Why am I here? What does my character want?"

"There you go." Bixby started walking again.

"But the answers won't change the fact that if the step wasn't too narrow, Crowley wouldn't have fallen."

"Of course they will. Because if she wasn't at the mall, she wouldn't have slipped on that step."

We crossed the arched bridge over the creek. "So it's her fault that she was killed because she was there?"

"Well, she certainly wouldn't have died if she wasn't, at least not there, at that moment, impaled on the unfinished base for a directory of stores," Bixby said, then turned to me as we reached the back door to his storybook house. "So why was she?"

"To get a mani-pedi."

"Why did she need one last Saturday morning?"

"What does that have to do with slipping on a step on a staircase to nowhere?"

"That's right. That's the key question. I'm impressed. You catch on quick." Bixby opened the door and went into the house, pleased that we'd reached an understanding.

But I didn't understand anything.

CHAPTER SEVEN

I walked around the house to the motor court, took out my iPhone, and made the call to Paul Wetzel while I waited for Bixby to show up.

Wetzel seemed friendly enough and told me he'd been instructed to cooperate with us in every way. I asked him for all the security camera video that Bixby wanted, especially the alternative angles on the floating staircase. He said he'd send me a link so we could look at the video archives, from any camera anywhere in the mall, for that day as we pleased. But he told me that Crowley parked near the southwest entrance and arrived at the nail salon at 10 a.m. and left at about 11:10.

I thanked him, and then warned him about Bixby's neurological condition, that it was like Tourette's, and that he might say offensive things that he didn't really mean. Wetzel appreciated the heads-up.

"I heard from Triax that he's a genius," Wetzel said.

"And if you hadn't heard," I said, "he'd be the first one to tell you."

"Because of his condition?"

"Because he's a genius who knows that he is. He's also rich and handsome."

"I may shoot him on sight," Wetzel said.

"That's what I'm trying to prevent by telling you all this."

"You should have left out the rich-and-handsome part. I'm neither of those things and resent people who are."

"Don't we all," I said, though truthfully I had the handsome part covered. I disconnected the call just as Bixby stepped out of the house.

He wore an impeccably tailored dark-blue Tom Ford suit and tie with a Rolex watch and shoes shined to a sparkle. Bixby was more than handsome. He was movie star, supermodel, professionally styled, AI-airbrushed to perfection, impossibly handsome.

"Why are you all dressed up?" I asked.

"I want to look like a cop."

"To rub Wetzel's nose in the fact that he's not one?"

"I'm too rich to be petty. I'm doing it to induce people to talk to me who might otherwise be reluctant to do so."

"Are you carrying a gun?"

He opened his jacket to show that yes, he was, in a holster on his belt. "It adds authenticity."

"Isn't it a crime to impersonate a police officer?"

"I'm not," he said. "But I have no control over what people assume based on how they interpret what they see."

Well, I would soon learn that was an outright lie. He knew exactly how visual cues could be used to influence people into making the assumptions you want them to make and so much more.

But he'd made a mistake. *Nobody* would assume a guy in a Tom Ford suit was a cop. And certainly not a guy as good-looking as him. I didn't say that yet. Instead, I told him what I'd learned from Wetzel, specifically about when Caroline Crowley arrived.

"Great. You still have time to put on a shirt, jacket, and tie, too," he said. "You do have those, right?"

I did, but I'd rolled them into a ball and stuffed them into a trash bag when I'd moved. "They're off-the-rack and all wrinkled. They need to be ironed."

He waved away my concern. "Don't worry. Most detectives don't know how to use an iron, especially those who live only for the job."

Oh, I liked that.

"I can use it for my character. You might try the same thing."

Bixby looked down at his suit. "What's wrong with this one?"

"Nothing, if you're trying to convince people you're a British spy with a license to kill."

He thought about that for a second, then said, "Go change. I'll meet you back here."

I hurried back to the guesthouse and thought about my character, about his long years on the LAPD, his struggles with alcoholism, his history of failed marriages, and his current addiction to hardcore pornography.

I got dressed in the wrinkled suit and realized that Bixby was absolutely right. It completely fit this character. I was firmly in the character's world-weary, emotionally scarred mindset, though I wished I had a gun, too, to truly inhabit the role.

I rushed back to the motor court to find Bixby leaning against an old Ford Crown Victoria base-model sedan that might as well have been a black-and-white patrol car with LAPD logos slapped all over it. The Crown Vic screamed "police."

Bixby had changed clothes, too. He'd ditched the Tom Ford suit, the Rolex, and the shiny shoes. Now he wore an old, wrinkled sport coat, a tie that was twenty years out of date, a white shirt, a pair of jeans, and an old Timex on his wrist.

"Where did you get that coat?" I asked.

"It belonged to my father. He wore it when he pitched his inventions to potential investors, except he wore a bow tie and sometimes a brown wool trilby hat with it."

I assumed the watch belonged to his father, too. "I'm surprised you have an old Crown Vic in your car collection."

"It's not just any Crown Vic." Bixby stroked the hood. "It's the plain-wrap I drove when I was an LAPD homicide detective. It's got nearly half a million miles on the odometer. I bought the car at auction when the department retired it."

"So you have it for sentimental reasons." The same could be said for him still having his father's clothing and living in his childhood home.

"And for situations like this," he said.

"When you want people to mistake you for a cop."

"Once a cop, always a cop. But it doesn't hurt to have a few props."

"I agree," I said. "Do you have an extra gun I could borrow?"

"No, I don't."

"It doesn't have to be loaded."

"I am licensed to carry a concealed weapon," he said. "You're not."

And with that, we got into the Crown Vic and headed for the Woodland Hills Mall, only a few miles north on Topanga, in the flats of the San Fernando Valley.

He told me that the Woodland Hills Mall was built in the mid-1960s and had been remodeled and expanded multiple times, reinventing itself with each new owner and facelift. The latest owner, Southfield Properties, was in the midst of gutting the old, dreary food court and creating a "food hall." That simply meant scrapping food-court mainstays like Hot Dog on a Stick, Sbarro, Cinnabon, and Mrs. Fields and replacing them with local chef-branded concession stands for a "food trucks in a parking lot" feel, but with an upscale vibe. And without the trucks.

"But that won't save this place or most of the others like it around the country," Bixby said. "The enclosed shopping mall was a flawed retail concept from the start because they weren't ever designed for shoppers."

"Who were they designed for?"

"The developers, who are in the business of renting property, not selling goods and services. It's their tenants, the stores, who care about shoppers. But the tenants are stuck trying to work within their little cubbies."

"I never thought of a mall that way."

"That's why most malls are so ugly outside. What matters to the developers or owners are how many tenants they can cram inside, an environment that they completely control. And if you don't have a car, you aren't welcome to visit."

"What makes you say that?"

"I don't. The building does. It's visually unappealing. You can tell just by looking at it that it will be hard and unpleasant to walk in off the street. To get in that enormous box, you've either got to cross a huge parking lot from the farthest possible point or go through a big, dark, unappealing parking structure, filled with moving cars and exhaust fumes, just to find an entrance. Who walks to a mall? Nobody. That's no accident. It rules out a certain class of people."

He said that just as we arrived at the mall. And he was right. It was a concrete island in a vast sea of asphalt. I'd never thought of that before because I always drove to malls and had never walked to one.

Bixby asked, "Where did Caroline Crowley park her car?"

I checked the file. "On the west side, outside the fourth entrance, near the Cheesecake Factory."

It was roughly in the middle of the mall.

My phone dinged. It was a text from Paul Wetzel, the mall security guy, with the link to the security video.

Bixby found a parking spot outside the Cheesecake Factory. We still had a few minutes before the time Caroline Crowley arrived.

"We've got the link to the security camera footage," I told Bixby as I clicked the link on my phone and went to the page.

"Let's see Crowley arrive," Bixby said.

What I got on-screen were a bunch of thumbnails screenshots from dozens of different cameras, all keyed to the same start time. Wetzel had made it easy for me.

I picked the camera that was mounted directly across the mall from the nail salon, on the other side of an opening down to the first floor, which was actually subterranean. That made the second floor technically the ground floor, although it wasn't listed that way in the mall directory, which was confusing.

The nail salon was on the west side of the mall, south of Neiman Marcus, the northern anchor store for the property. On camera, the nail salon was in the center of the screen, so the Neiman Marcus was stage right.

I leaned close to Bixby, sharing my phone screen with him, and tapped the thumbnail, setting the video in motion. Within a second,

Crowley arrived at the nail salon from stage left, or from the south if you were looking at the mall from a bird's-eye view instead of on my screen.

"Pause it," Bixby said. I did. "The nail salon is two doors down from the Neiman Marcus department store. But Crowley is coming from way down here, from the south, when there are at least two entrances that are much closer to her destination."

"Does that mean something?"

"She didn't know where the nail salon was or she would have parked closer to it. She picked the middle to play the odds. That means she'd never been here before."

"No, it doesn't," I said. "I've been to this mall a hundred times, but I can't tell you where the nail salon is. I didn't even know there was one here until today."

"That's because you aren't a woman or a gay man."

I gave him an exaggerated look of dismay, an expression that would have earned a big laugh from the studio audience if we were on a sitcom. "You think only gay men have manicures?"

"I think very few straight men do."

"And you believe all gay men have their nails done?"

"A higher percentage of them are more likely to than straight men."

"Why? Because they are effeminate, is that what you're saying?"

"Because they take more pride in their grooming," Bixby said.

"That's an offensive stereotype."

"It's a fact," he said. "Eighteen percent of heterosexual men regularly have manicures compared to seventy-five percent of gay men."

"You made that up," I said.

"Yes, I did. The point is, why did Crowley come to a mall she was unfamiliar with to have her nails done? Or did she come here for a different reason and have a mani-pedi on a whim?"

"What does any of that have to do with her falling down a staircase?"

"Exactly. Until we know that, we know nothing. Let's see more of that video." He gestured to me to keep playing, so I did. Crowley walked into the nail salon. "Okay. Now swipe to her coming out."

I did. She came out, seemed to look right at the camera, then walked to her left, or rather stage right from our point of view, toward the Neiman Marcus, and offstage, at least from that camera angle.

"She didn't go back to her car," Bixby said. "Why not?"

"Maybe she decided to do some window-shopping or was looking for a bathroom." Yes, that was it. I thought about poor Casey with his colitis and the metaphorical toilet that followed him everywhere. "That could be why she was going downstairs with such urgency."

Bixby shook his head, dismissing my explanation. "There are bathrooms in the department store and they are always much nicer than any in the mall. All women know that."

"They do?"

"Women know where all the best bathrooms are."

"How can you say that like it's a fact?"

"Because I have spent a lot of time with women," Bixby said. "You should try it, but first you'll have to be more selective about the roles you accept. Avoid the ones involving erectile dysfunction, explosive acne, chronic bad breath, excessive sweating, and rampaging toenail fungus."

I took whatever roles came along because I needed the money, and I enjoyed the challenge of playing complex characters, but he wouldn't understand that. He made things happen for himself and he wouldn't ever have to worry about paying his bills.

"Do you want to look at the opposite camera angle?" I asked, referring to the camera above the nail salon, facing the other side of the mall, where the camera we were watching from before was mounted.

"We don't have time," he said. "We'll watch it as we go along."

We got out, strode across the parking lot to the mall entrance, went inside the air-conditioned box, turned left, and then walked along the west-side concourse toward the Neiman Marcus and nail salon.

The interior of the mall was essentially a two-story square donut. To our right, across the wide open space beside us, was the eastern concourse, which could be reached by either doing a circuit of the mall or cutting across a few strategically placed bridges. At either end of the mall, and at those bridges, were escalators or staircases to the stores below.

From where we walked, we could see below to the first floor. There were more stores down there, but as we neared the northern end, a temporary wall sealed off that section from shoppers and announced that a new food hall was coming soon.

The food hall, called Eatville, was nearly completed, and almost ready to be occupied, which was why it was now opened up to view from the second floor. For months, while the old food court was gutted and remodeled, this portion of the first floor had been hidden by plywood and plastic sheeting. I used to be a regular customer of the food court when I'd lived, until twenty-four hours earlier, in nearby Canoga Park.

"You're being manipulated," Bixby said. "Can you feel it?"

"Nope."

"The floors are flawless. There's no broken glass, uneven pavement, or dog shit to watch out for. The lighting is perfect. There are no shadowy corners or dark alleys. You'll never encounter a mugger, beggar, drug addict, or whore. There is nobody here but people just like you, doing the same thing you are. Everything is designed keep your full attention where the tenants want it: on their storefronts."

"You say it like I have no free will."

"You do, but only when it comes to deciding which store to enter and if you're going to buy something," he said. "Up until then, you are at the mercy of the design."

"I don't go anywhere in here that I don't want to."

"It makes you want to."

"What does?"

"The design. The products you see, the air temperature you feel, the music you hear, the fragrances you smell that are coming from each store are scientifically, psychologically, and emotionally designed to draw you in. And once you are inside, the height of the shelves, the materials on the floors, the width and shape of the aisles, the colors on the walls, and the way the products are displayed all work together to lead you where the store wants you to go. And to buy what they are most eager to sell. Nothing in this place is random or an accident."

"Except what happened to Caroline Crowley," I said.

"We don't know that yet."

"We saw it."

"We don't know what we saw," Bixby said.

A portly man in a suit almost as wrinkled as mine stood outside the nail salon. He had an earpiece, the kind Secret Service agents wear, a cord dangling from his ear and down under his coat.

"You must be Edison Bixby." The man offered Bixby his hand.

Bixby shook it. "You must be the mall cop."

"Paul Wetzel. Like the pretzel place." He patted his gut. "God, I love 'em. Thank God there isn't one in this mall anymore or I'd be finished."

"Because you're already really fat."

I spoke up quickly. "He meant to say 'stout and hearty.'"

Wetzel waved off the slight. "It's okay, I know I'm chubby."

Bixby said, "Can I call you Pretzel?"

"Not if you like your nose." Wetzel offered his hand to me. I was glad I'd prepared him for Bixby. "You must be Wally Nash. You can call me Paul."

"Thank you for all your help, Paul."

"Pretzel is better," Bixby said.

I ignored him and pressed on. "We both appreciate how quickly you organized the security camera videos for us."

"My pleasure. The owner of the nail salon is Mai Vu. Would you like me to introduce you?"

"No," Bixby said. "We can take it from here, but stick around. I'm going to have questions for you."

I quickly added: "If you don't mind, Paul."

"Not at all." Wetzel shot a glance at Bixby. "I look forward to watching the genius at work."

"Good idea. You might want to take notes, too."

"I have a steel-trap mind."

CHAPTER EIGHT

We followed Bixby into the nail salon, which had a tiny waiting area on one side, with couches and a coffee table, and the front desk on the other. The coffee table was covered with copies of a magazine about chocolate confections. The magazines looked good enough to eat. There were also various issues of *People* and *House Beautiful* nearly buried underneath them.

Bixby approached the proprietress, who sat on a stool behind the counter, but before he could speak, Wetzel said: "Morning, Mai."

She smiled at him. She was a thin Vietnamese woman, perhaps in her forties. "Don't tell me you're finally coming in to have your disgusting nails done."

"What's wrong with mine?" Wetzel looked at his nails. It looked like he trimmed them with his teeth.

"They are gross."

"They certainly are," Bixby said in a clipped, official tone that suggested both authority and bureaucracy. Or, if you're familiar with ancient TV shows, Jack Webb as Sgt. Joe Friday on *Dragnet*. Or, if you're familiar with old movies, Dan Aykroyd mimicking Jack Webb as Sgt. Joe Friday in *Dragnet*. "I'm Edison Bixby, this is Wally Nash. We're investigating the death that occurred here on Saturday."

"Such a sad story. But at least she died with beautiful nails. Her family will appreciate that if it's an open coffin."

"So you remember her?"

"Someone gave her a deluxe mani-pedi treatment as a gift and set up the appointment."

"Do you know who it was?"

She shook her head. "It was done online. She didn't know who it was, either. She said it was an unsigned gift from an appreciative client for her excellent work."

Bixby looked at me. "Someone wanted Caroline Crowley to be here, in this mall, at a specific time." He looked past me to Wetzel, who was thumbing through the chocolate magazine. "Are you paying attention?"

Wetzel didn't bother lifting his eyes from the chocolate cake centerfold. "She had a free nail job waiting for her. That's really exciting. Let me know when something involving mall security comes up."

Bixby turned back to Mai. "Is the manicurist who worked with Crowley here today?"

"I was one of them. I did her hands, Lori worked on her feet." She gestured to another Vietnamese woman working on a client. I'd never been in a nail salon, so the plush recliners the female clients sat in, with their feet in some kind of mini Jacuzzi, while a manicurist filed or painted their fingernails, were all new to me. It looked relaxing.

"You'll do," Bixby said to Mai. "What can you tell me about Caroline Crowley?"

Mai took a deep breath, then said, "She was single, was dumped by the love of her life, and she dealt with it by gorging on pizza, ice cream, and anything else she could stuff in her mouth, gaining thirty pounds in just a few months, which made it very hard to get a date, which made her eat even more. So she went on the keto diet and had lost ten pounds by giving up carbs."

Bixby seemed astonished. "She told you all that about herself?"

"She didn't even notice us. She told the blond woman in the next chair, who was having a pedicure and reading that magazine." Mai gestured to the chocolate magazine Wetzel was skimming and practically drooling on. I think if he was given a choice between taking home that magazine or *Playboy*, the chocolate would win over the cheesecake.

"Did the two women know each other?" Bixby asked.

"They were strangers. The blond woman was here first."

"How did the conversation start?"

"Crowley told the other woman that she wanted to eat her magazine."

Bixby looked back at the magazines on the table for a moment, then shifted his gaze back to Mai. "Why do you have so many copies of that magazine in your shop?"

"It was free. Someone left a stack outside our door on Friday with a note saying 'Courtesy of Chocolate Mania.' So I brought them in. Women like to read something while they wait for a chair. The magazines we had are six months old."

"Do you have the name of the woman who was reading the magazine?"

Mai shook her head. "She was a walk-in and paid cash, like most of our clients."

"Did she leave before or after Crowley?"

"Before."

I couldn't figure out why he was so interested in the magazine or the other client. Crowley fell down the steps, she wasn't pushed.

Bixby nodded and went to the doorway to the concourse and stood there, looking across the open chasm to the floor below. I stepped up beside him.

Directly across from us was a vacant storefront, the windows obscured with some kind of white paint. I looked above it and saw the security camera that took one of the videos we'd watched in the parking lot.

To our left, directly in front of the Neiman Marcus, was a set of dead escalators that went down to the first floor, where the food hall was in the final stages of construction. Access to the escalator was blocked with caution tape. To our right, about twenty yards away, was a bridge across the open expanse above the food hall and the free-floating staircase that Crowley fell down.

"The store across from us is directly at eye level from here and unoccupied," Bixby said. "It would be hard to not look at it if there was something interesting to see. But there isn't. Why did she stop here and look at it so intently?"

"Maybe she wasn't looking at the store but somebody who was in front of it."

"Let's see the video and find out."

I called it up on my phone and showed it to Bixby. Nobody was in front of the store. But there was a poster affixed to the inside of the store window advertising 1 CARB KETO TREATS YOU CAN'T RESIST with a photo of a chocolate brownie drenched in thick frosting.

Bixby glanced at Wetzel and the cover of the magazine in his hand. The brownie on the cover was almost identical to the one on the poster.

"No wonder she was interested," I said.

Bixby took my phone and brought it over to Wetzel. "When was this sign put up and when was it taken down?"

Wetzel glanced at the screen. "I don't know. I've never noticed it." Bixby nodded, as if that confirmed something for him. "But if the answer is important to you, I'll have my guys go through the security video to find out."

"I already know the answer," Bixby said.

"You do?" I said.

"Now we know why she turned to the left and walked around to the other side of the mall, rather than turning right and going straight back to her car. It was for a closer look at that poster."

Bixby, Wetzel, and I walked the same path she did, and at the same time, too. It was kind of creepy, matching our progress to hers on my phone, step-by-step. As we neared the window on the opposite side of the mall, the frosted-glass hiding the empty store inside, I zoomed in on the same window in my video and the poster taped to it. Below the headline, the poster read DELECTABLE, DECADENT, DELICIOUS GUILT-FREE KETO TREATS FOR $1. POP-UP KIOSK TODAY ONLY ON THE FIRST FLOOR.

She must have thought it was her lucky day. I showed the screen to Wetzel.

"What the hell?" he said. "There were no pop-up kiosks downstairs on Saturday or any other day, anywhere else in the mall. We don't do pop-ups."

At that moment, we smelled the mouthwatering aroma of fresh-baked cookies. Wetzel broke into a smile. "Good news. You got here right when the fresh-baked cookies come out. If we hurry, we can beat the mob."

Bixby said, "Does this happen every day at this time?"

"Yeah, every two hours or so. I can't resist the smell."

"Nobody can," I said, my mouth watering, too.

"Plus they always slip me one for free." He patted his belly. "I had six-pack abs when I started this job." Wetzel got moving.

"I suppose he didn't have a fat ass, either," Bixby said.

Luckily, Wetzel was too far away to hear the unfiltered remark. The cookie shop was several storefronts away, and a line was already forming at the counter.

"Keep your voice down," I said. "Body-shaming is unacceptable."

"I wasn't shaming," he said. "I was observing."

"You don't have to share every observation."

Bixby and I followed Wetzel to the cookie shop. I looked down at the phone. A few days ago, Crowley followed the same path to the cookie shop where we were. I showed the screen to Bixby.

"The aroma of hot cookies," Bixby said. "That's what drove her to the stairs. She couldn't have these cookies, but she could have the keto ones."

Wetzel lined up for his cookie. But Bixby kept going, heading to the stairs, which came at the midpoint of a bridge across the chasm.

The opening to the stairs, which curled down to the first floor, was now crisscrossed with yellow caution tape and two stanchions, with a retractable tape line between them, blocking the way.

The base on the first floor for the unfinished mall directory, on which Crowley had been impaled, was now completely covered with a tarp.

Bixby looked to his left, the same direction that Crowley glanced when she was midway down the stairs, at the curve. "Show me the camera view on that spot. I want to see what she saw."

It took me a moment, and while I searched, Wetzel came up eating a cookie in one hand and holding a paper bag in the other. "I don't know how you could walk away from fresh, hot cookies. But don't worry, I got you both one."

Bixby said, "That's all I could think about."

His sarcasm was wasted on Wetzel. I found the camera angle Bixby wanted. It was from a camera mounted on the west concourse and aimed straight across to the east concourse. I tapped on the thumbnail to get the video moving. "Here it is."

Bixby looked over my shoulder.

What Crowley saw was a redheaded woman in a red summer dress, her face hidden by a sun hat and large sunglasses, walking on the second-floor concourse.

The woman in red looked down at the staircase, and it sounded like she said something, though I couldn't make it out. An instant later, there was a scream from the staircase. And then there were screams everywhere as people rushed to the railing and saw Crowley's body impaled on the rebar. Screams echoed up and down the mall. But the woman in red simply turned and headed down a nearby corridor.

I replayed the sequence again without being asked. And as I watched, lots of questions came to mind.

Who was that woman? What did she say to Crowley that startled her? And why was the woman in red so calm after seeing Crowley's gruesome death?

Bixby turned to Wetzel and pointed to the corridor. "What's down that hall?"

"The restrooms and the back doors to all the stores along the northeast half of the mall."

"Do you have cameras in there?"

"Of course." Wetzel licked chocolate off his fingers. "Do you think we're fools?"

"Yes," Bixby said.

I winced. It would be impossible to make an excuse for that remark.

Wetzel stared at him. "Screw your cookie. I'm keeping it." He offered the bag to me. "You can have yours, though. I like you."

"Thanks." I reached into the bag and took out a cookie.

Bixby was still looking at Wetzel. "Here is what you will see on the hallway cameras. The woman in red will enter the back of the vacant store, then emerge a few moments later with the keto pop-up sign. Then you will see her leave the mall, but your cameras will lose her in the parking structure before she gets to her car."

"How do you know?" Wetzel asked.

"Because I can see all the clues you missed in your investigation."

"I didn't investigate anything."

"That's abundantly clear," Bixby said, brutally honest, as always. But I wasn't sure if this remark was a slip.

Wetzel's face turned red, not with shame, but anger. "How was I supposed to know that somebody got into the vacant store and put up a poster? And who cares, anyway? No harm was done."

"Caroline Crowley is dead."

"What's that got to do with some stupid keto poster?"

"Everything," Bixby said. "Not seeing that is why you're a mall cop and not a real one."

"Really? Are you going tell that to LAPD Detective McGregor, too? If you are, I really want to be there to see it."

I did, too.

Bixby was clearly startled by the remark, and it was nice to see, since he always seemed to be so far ahead of everybody else. "She handled this case?"

"Yeah." Wetzel was also enjoying Bixby's discomfort. "Not that there was anything for her to do. It's obviously an accident."

Bixby grimaced. I don't know whether it was the use of the word "obviously" or that McGregor was involved in this case.

I asked, "Who do you think the woman in red was?"

"Probably the same woman who was talking to Crowley in the nail salon, only then she wasn't a redhead and certainly wasn't wearing a red dress," Bixby said. "She left the salon before Crowley did to put up the poster inside the vacant store, change her clothes, put on a red wig, and wait for precisely the right moment."

"To do what?" Wetzel asked.

"Kill her."

Bixby said it like it was the most obvious—forgive me for using that word—thing in the world.

Wetzel and I stared at Bixby, both of us dumbfounded. Now that's an adjective I've never used before, but it's the perfect word for what we were. We'd both just found out we were dumb. And if we hadn't known it, the expression on Bixby's face would've told us.

"Have you two been sleeping for the last fifteen minutes?"

Wetzel spoke in a patronizing tone. "Look at the video again, Bixby. The woman in red couldn't have pushed Crowley down the stairs *because she wasn't on the staircase.* She was standing a floor above Crowley."

Bixby sighed wearily. "The woman distracted Crowley to instigate the fall."

I didn't get it, either. "How could the woman have known that Crowley would twist around to look at her at the same instant her foot landed on a step that was way too narrow?"

"Because that woman, or whoever is actually behind all this, sabotaged that step in the hope that she would fall."

Wetzel said, "Nobody made Crowley walk down those stairs."

"You're wrong," Bixby said. "Someone clearly teamed up with the mall to make her do it."

"Now you're accusing the mall owners of being involved?"

"Of course not," Bixby said. "I'm accusing the building itself."

Wetzel regarded Bixby in slack-jawed disbelief. "You're not brilliant. You're crazy."

"The building where a crime occurs isn't just the place where it happened, it's an active accomplice," Bixby said. "Because its design made the crime not only imaginable, but possible."

"What crime?" Wetzel said.

"Murder."

Wetzel reached into the bag and held out a cookie to Bixby. "Eat your cookie. You need it. You have dangerously low blood sugar."

"I feel fine."

"You aren't thinking straight. If it's not low blood sugar, it's something worse, like a stroke or whatever happened to your head."

"I was shot."

I said, "Take the cookie, Bixby, before he changes his mind. It's great."

Bixby did and started eating it.

Wetzel turned to me. "Should I call an ambulance?"

Bixby answered his question while he ate his cookie. "Call your crack security team instead. Have them find any video of the construction crew working on this staircase last week and track those individuals down. I want their names. Also get me the video of the arrival at the salon of the mystery woman who was getting a pedicure beside Crowley. I want to see her departure, too, though we know exactly where she went. And, finally, I want the video of whomever dropped off the magazines outside the salon on Friday."

"What's that going to tell you?" Wetzel asked.

"Probably nothing I don't already know, but we need to be thorough when investigating a homicide."

"Nobody got murdered here, and certainly not by the building," Wetzel said. "It's impossible."

"Humor me."

Wetzel shook his head and walked away.

Bixby looked at me. "Do you see how it's possible?"

I did.

Someone subliminally manipulated Crowley, using her keto diet and hunger for sweets, to that staircase, which that mystery person sabotaged so that a distraction, at just the right moment, would make her lose her balance, tumble down the steps, and get impaled on the exposed rebar below.

It was a murder disguised as an accident.

And best of all, the victim murdered herself.

"I do see," I told him, "but I'm not sure I believe that's what happened. It seems too far-fetched."

"That's because you're an actor and you don't know the killer's motivation."

I noticed that he wasn't calling me a "failed actor" anymore. That was encouraging. "You don't know it, either, but you still believe that she was murdered."

"It's not a question of belief, Wally. I'm simply looking at the facts. It's no different than finding the body of a woman who was strangled to death. Murder is murder."

"I don't think there has ever been a murder like this."

"All murders are like this," Bixby said. "Homicide is achieved through design."

"Okay, fine. Who was that woman in the salon? Why did she change into a red wig? And why did Crowley seeing her, or hearing whatever she said, startle her so much that she fell?"

"I don't know," Bixby said. "Is Crowley's address in that file?"

I opened the file and looked at the cover page. "Yes, it is. It's a house in Sherman Oaks."

"Good," he said. "Crowley can't give us the answers, but her house will. Before we go, though, there's something vital that we need to do."

"Get all that video from Wetzel?"

He shook his head. "Get more of those cookies while they are still warm."

CHAPTER NINE

Bixby gave me a history lesson as he drove us east across the valley on Vanowen Street toward Sherman Oaks. Before 2009, the northwest corner of Sherman Oaks that we were heading to was once the southeast corner of Van Nuys, which didn't have nearly the same prestige or the higher property values associated with its southern neighbor.

So the homeowners in that corner of Van Nuys, desperate to jack up their property values, lobbied the Los Angeles City Council to let them be part of Sherman Oaks instead. The campaign worked and their property values soared, while prices tumbled in Van Nuys, which was viewed as more run-down, crime-ridden, and ethnically diverse (which is a politically correct way of saying Hispanics were becoming a greater majority of the residents, making the whites feel increasingly uncomfortable).

And yet the houses and streets in the tiny cluster of blocks that seceded were still exactly the same—all that had changed was their collective name and, with it, the entire perception of the place.

"That's why Archibald Leach, Frances Gumm, Issur Demsky, Roy Scherer, and Thomas Mapother changed their names to Cary Grant, Judy Garland, Kirk Douglas, Rock Hudson, and Tom Cruise," I said. "So they would be more sellable as actors. Perception is everything, especially when you are trying to create an image."

"What are you going to change your name to?"

"What's wrong with Wally Nash?"

Bixby shrugged. "It sounds like a character-actor name to me."

"It didn't hurt Tom Hanks or Gene Hackman to keep their names."

"Maybe they would have become superstars faster if they hadn't. You might get more roles if your name was Derek Gunn or Clint Steele."

"Yes, but they'd all be in porn movies."

Bixby slowed as we neared Crowley's modest one-story 1950s-era tract home, which looked like all the others on the street. A car was parked in the driveway and an old couple was coming out of the house, each of them holding some women's clothing. The old woman was crying.

"Oh crap, this isn't good," Bixby said. "Those are her parents."

"How can you tell?"

"Because they are carrying out some of her clothes and crying. My guess is that they're getting something to dress Crowley's corpse in for the open coffin at the funeral. They'll never let me in the house."

That was true. They wouldn't want to talk with an investigator for the mall's insurance company. They'd see him as trying to shift the blame for what happened to their dead daughter.

"They'll let me in," I said, and put on my sunglasses. "Pull hard and fast to the curb and then don't say a word when we get out. I'll do all the talking. Follow my lead. Just make sure they see that holster on your hip."

Bixby pulled up to the curb with a screech, like a cop rushing to make an arrest. The parents turned in surprise to look at the car, and what they saw were two cops, I was sure of it. So that's what I became.

I got out with a grimace on my face, one I'd been carrying ever since I took a knife in the gut from a drug-crazed rapist that I'd still managed to arrest and put away for life. But I still felt that blade every time I hit the street.

I approached the couple. Their eyes were puffy and red from crying. "Are you Caroline Crowley's parents?"

The man spoke. "Yes, we are. Mark and Deborah Crowley."

"I'm Frank Hellinger, and this is my partner, Earl Butz." I tipped my head to Bixby. "We're deeply sorry for your loss."

They glanced from me to Bixby, who had his hands on his hips, parting his jacket just enough to show his holstered gun.

"Why are you here, Detectives?"

Detectives. The props and attitude had worked. But mostly it was due to my indelible performance. I said, "We're investigating the mall for criminal negligence and involuntary manslaughter in the killing of your daughter."

"I don't know what we can do to help," Mark said. "We weren't there."

"You can let us inside her house for a few minutes."

That immediately raised suspicion with Deborah Crowley. "Why? She was killed in the mall, not in there."

I was ready for that.

"I've never met your daughter, Mrs. Crowley, but I've known hundreds of others like her, people whose lives were brutally cut short by horrible violence." I took off my sunglasses, slipped them into my pocket, and rubbed my eyes—that way they were a bit raw and teary as I met Deborah's gaze. She still had fresh tear streaks on her cheek. It wouldn't take much for me to reach her.

"I want to be relentless in my pursuit of justice for Caroline. But first, I need to get a sense of her as a person, to feel her in my heart, so she's not just a name on a file, she's an open wound in my soul that I need to heal."

Tears were running down her cheeks again by the time I was done. But I still had to make the sale.

"To do that, I need to be inside her house," I said. "Where she lived, where she loved, and where she dreamed. You felt her in there today, didn't you?"

Deborah nodded vigorously and shared a look with her husband, who was teary-eyed, too. "It's so painful to go inside now."

"I want to feel the same pain," I said. "And make it my own."

Mark Crowley, a bit overcome with emotion himself, cleared his throat. "Take all the time you need, Detective."

I nodded, grimaced again, slipped on my sunglasses, and went inside, Bixby silently following me.

Once we were inside, he closed the front door and confronted me. "Earl Butz?"

"That's what you took away from that performance? Your character's name? I got us in the house," I said. "I did my thing, now you do yours."

"Why couldn't I have a gritty name like Frank Hellinger?"

"Because I wanted them focused on me, not you. Hellinger sounds like a tough, dogged cop. Butz does not."

We were in the living room, which was very feminine. Lots of blue, pink, and red. Lots of pillows and an afghan on an overstuffed floral-upholstered couch. There was a collage of framed photos on the wall of a thin Caroline Crowley with another woman, about her same age and build. In some photos they're arm in arm, in others hugging or kissing. Clearly this was someone Crowley loved, probably the woman she'd told the stranger in the nail salon that she'd recently broken up with.

"When I get dumped," I said, "I don't keep pictures of the woman on my wall."

"You might if she was the love of your life."

"It would just make me hurt more."

"But it's such sweet pain," Bixby said.

I regarded him with interest. "Are you speaking from experience?"

"I'm speaking from hers." He gestured to a bookcase. The shelves were filled with romance novels and DVDs of Hallmark movies. "She was a hopeless romantic. Romance movies wallow in heartbreak. She probably thought her ex would come back to her someday, preferably at Christmas."

We drifted into the small galley-style kitchen. It was neat and clean, probably because she didn't do much cooking. There were boxes of assorted keto chocolate bars and a loaf of keto bread on the counter.

I opened the pantry, and it was filled with more keto stuff. Low-carb tortillas, low-carb chocolate cereal, low-carb chocolate brownie mix, low-carb chocolate cookies, low-carb chocolate chips, low-carb chocolate shakes, and sugar-free chocolate-covered almonds. I didn't have to open the freezer to know I'd find low-carb chocolate ice cream in there.

"She sure loved chocolate," I said.

"That's why the chocolate triggers at the mall were so effective on her," Bixby said. "But especially the smell of those cookies. Whoever wanted Crowley dead knew her and the science."

"You don't have to meet Crowley or be a scientist to know that. Most people love chocolate."

"That's because chocolate is a proven aphrodisiac," Bixby said as we moved out of the kitchen and, coincidentally, into the bedroom, which had an even stronger feminine vibe. "It contains phenylethylamine, which sparks euphoria that mimics postcoital pleasure, and theobromine, which surges blood to the genitals."

"Also, it tastes great," I said.

"But unless you were closely acquainted with Crowley, or broke into her house, you wouldn't know that she was particularly susceptible to the smell of chocolate."

"Why?"

Bixby went to one of the two matching nightstands. It was cluttered with two romance novels, an assortment of hand creams, some lip balm, a box of Kleenex. He opened the drawer, revealing three different vibrators and a jar of lubricant. "She was heartbroken, dieting, sexually frustrated, and, most importantly, hooked on romance novels."

"What do romance novels have to do with it?"

"That's where the science comes in. Studies have shown that when the aroma of chocolate is subtly introduced into a bookstore, sales of romance novels increase by as much as 40 percent."

"But she wasn't rushing down the stairs because she was desperate to find a bookstore," I said. "It was to get one-carb chocolates."

"It was much more than that. The smell of hot, melty chocolate jacked up her hunger, her sexual desire, and her heartache, priming her for the crucial moment in this scheme."

"Which was?"

"I'll show you," he said.

We left the bedroom and went across the hall to her office. This space wasn't feminine at all. It was totally business: A desktop computer. Printer. Scanner. File cabinets. Office supplies.

But what instantly struck me was the screensaver on her computer. It was a photo of Caroline Crowley and her lover at the beach.

Her *redheaded* lover . . .

. . . who was wearing *the same red dress* as the mystery woman at the mall!

"It was seeing her," Bixby said. "It hit Crowley like a bullet and was just as lethal."

Of course Crowley would whirl around to look at her, particularly if the woman called her name. "Why would her ex go to such elaborate lengths to kill her?"

"She wouldn't." Bixby took out his phone and snapped a photo of the screensaver. "It was someone playing the part, dressing to re-create an image that would have an instant, staggering impact on Crowley. There was no guarantee that she would fall, or that the tumble would cause her death rather than a serious injury. But I believe whoever designed this incident would have been pleased with *any* violent outcome."

"That someone must have hated Crowley a lot."

"Or the people Crowley worked for."

Bixby picked up some stationery from the desk and held it up for me. It was from Bernheim, Sutton & Associates, the crisis-management company she worked for. I didn't get the significance.

"Do they have a lot of enemies?"

"They're a public relations firm that makes excuses for corporations and individuals who've done really awful things."

"And something really awful was done to Caroline Crowley."

It sounded like something Hellinger would say, if he were a character on a TV show. It was the perfect zinger for a *Law & Order* act break. I was very happy with myself.

But then Bixby said, "And there's no excuse for it."

He stepped right on my line! How could he do that to me?

Bixby looked around, then at me. "Do you see a camera in the room?"

"No, why? Is there one?"

"You seem to think so." And then he mimicked me, looking into a nonexistent camera somewhere to his right: *"And something really awful was done to Caroline Crowley."*

"I *knew* it. You purposely stepped on my line."

"I don't know what you're talking about."

I turned to the same imaginary camera and repeated what he'd said: *"And there's no excuse for it."* Then I shifted my gaze back at him. "My line was so much better, but you had to have the last word at the end of the scene."

"That's nuts. There's no camera. There's no audience. This isn't *Law & Order*."

"You're right. It's closer to *Monk*."

"I'm not obsessive-compulsive or socially awkward," Bixby said. "Besides, your line didn't work without mine. It was only half the thought. My line completed the thought and gave it profound impact."

"*Profound?* You are so full of yourself."

He peeked into an adjoining bathroom. "Oh my God. Would you look at that?"

I rushed up to the doorway. "Is it a dead body?"

"Of course not. The parents were just in here. I think they would have noticed a corpse."

"So why did you make it sound like it was?"

"A corpse wouldn't shock me. This did."

I followed his gaze. All I saw was the bathtub-shower combo. "It's a shower. We earthlings use it to cleanse our bodies."

"Can you tell by looking at it how it's operated?"

"Of course I can."

I went over to the shower. There was the fixed showerhead, a handheld showerhead, and the bathtub faucet. But there was just one round, black knob, which looked like a hockey puck glued to the tile, that controlled them all.

It was very stylish, but I had no idea how it worked.

"Go ahead," Bixby said. "Turn on the cold water on the handheld showerhead."

I leaned into the shower and turned the dial. Nothing happened. I pushed it. Nothing happened. Then I pulled it and scalding hot water blasted out of the fixed showerhead, soaking my hair. I yelped and jumped back, nearly stumbling over the toilet.

Bixby handed me a towel.

I took it and dried my hair. "Is that a clue?"

"It's a crime. Showers are simple devices. You need to control two functions: the water flow and temperature. Then you pick whether the water comes out of the showerhead, the handheld, or the tub faucet. How to do those things should be evident on sight. But this shower was designed for style, not usability."

He examined it for a moment. Now that the puck had been pulled out, I saw that it was only half of the knob. There were two other concentric circles remaining. He turned one, and water came out of the handheld instead of the fixed showerhead. He turned the next one below it and put his hand in the water stream to test the temperature. He pushed it all back in to turn it off.

I said, "How do you get the water to come out of the bathtub faucet?"

Bixby ran his hand around the faucet. "There's a button underneath."

He pressed it, then pulled the black puck out again. The water came out of the faucet. It was the first shower I'd ever seen that needed an instruction manual.

"That's very interesting," I said, "but what does it have to do with Caroline Crowley?"

Bixby pushed the puck back in to turn off the water and stood up. "It's probably why she got dumped."

"Because her lover scalded herself in the shower?"

"I'd dump somebody who values design over usability."

"You drive a 1959 Cadillac," I said. "What do those enormous tail fins have to do with usability?"

"Stability in flight. They're aerodynamic."

"Cars don't fly." I put the towel back on the rack.

"And they never will without fins," Bixby said. "We have to go. We've been in here too long and Crowley's parents will get suspicious."

"Okay, just give me a minute to get back into character."

I went to the kitchen, found some hot sauce in the cupboard, dabbed some of it on my finger, and then licked it. The sauce was so hot, I was surprised it didn't eat away the flesh on my finger. My eyes immediately teared up and my nose started to run. It made me look very emotional. I resisted the urge to drink some water so that I could use the discomfort in my performance.

I was ready.

We went outside. As Frank Hellinger, I thought about my daughter, who was a heroin addict, and my wife who left me for my partner, and how all I had left in my life were my badge and all the dead people that I fought for.

I approached Crowley's grieving parents, who stood side by side at their car, facing the front door as we came out.

"Thank you," I said. "I know her now. I feel the pain." I touched my fist to my chest. "I will get her justice."

Deborah Crowley sniffled. "That's all we want."

"And $20 million," Mark Crowley said. Deborah looked at her husband in shock.

He held up his hands defensively. "No amount of money will bring our daughter back, Deb. I want to get the mall owner where it hurts them the most. Money is the only thing that has meaning to them. We'll create a charity in her name."

That seemed to mollify her. She nodded in agreement. "She would have wanted that."

I doubted that having a charity created in her name had ever crossed her mind, but it was a nice sentiment anyway.

Bixby said, "You should use some of the money to remodel her shower."

Mark was clearly perplexed by the remark. "What?"

To distract the man, and to stop Bixby from replying, I took Mark Crowley by the shoulders, turned him to face me, and looked him in the eyes.

"You have my word, Mr. Crowley. I will *never* rest until this is done. Everybody counts or nobody counts."

Mark nodded. So did his wife. So did I.

Bixby and I got in the car and we sped off, peeling rubber, in true *T.J. Hooker* fashion.

When we were a block or so away, Bixby asked, "Everybody counts or nobody counts? What does *that* mean?"

"I don't know. I heard it in a cop show. But I had to say something after your remark. I told you not to say anything."

"I wish it was that easy," he said.

"Sorry, I forgot about your brain injury."

Bixby waved it off. "It's okay. It doesn't matter what the phrase means. I believed it was something Frank Hellinger would say."

It was a tremendous compliment, the highest an actor could receive, particularly if you're improvising your lines. I was touched.

"You did?"

"You totally inhabited the character. You were Hellinger. I even sensed a certain *soupçon de tristesse* behind his words."

It was there. Bixby wasn't imagining it.

"I was thinking about everything that Hellinger's devotion to the badge has cost him. His wife left him and his daughter is a heroin addict living on the streets. The badge and the dead, the Caroline Crowleys of this city, are all he has."

"That's it," Bixby said. "His daughter turning tricks for her next fix. That's what I sensed."

He said it straight-faced, but I sensed a certain *soupçon de bullshit* behind his words.

"You're ridiculing me."

"Not at all. That was great work, Wally. You're a big improvement over the ventriloquist as my assistant."

"What about the dummy?"

"You're getting there," Bixby said. "But it's only our second day together. I have hope."

I left it at that. We were heading west on Burbank Boulevard, and I could see the 405 freeway on-ramps at the next intersection. "Where are we going now?"

"To Santa Monica to see Melissa," Bixby said. "I have to stop her from writing that check to the Crowleys."

Forty-five minutes later, we were in Melissa Priddle's office at Triax and Bixby explained everything to her, his presentation illustrated with the videos from the mall and, finally, the photo of Crowley's screensaver of her ex-girlfriend.

Melissa patiently and quietly listened to all of it, revealing nothing on her face about what she was thinking. She waited until Bixby was finished and sat down in the guest chair beside me before she finally spoke.

"That's a very compelling and frightening story, but it doesn't change any of the facts."

"It changes everything," he said to her. "Weren't you listening?"

I tapped my forehead, which was becoming my symbol for Bixby's neurological inability to always think before he spoke. "What he means is that he doesn't understand why you aren't convinced by his compelling argument."

"No, Wally, he's genuinely pissed off," she said, then looked at him. "The undisputed facts are that Caroline Crowley visited the mall, went down an unusually twisty staircase, tripped on a faulty step, and tumbled to her death, impaled on four bars of exposed steel."

Bixby shook his head. "No, she was lured to the mall and subliminally led to that staircase, where she was intentionally distracted so she'd slip on a sabotaged step and fall to her death."

"A dangerous step that was reported to the mall operator on Friday, a day before the accident, and nothing was done to repair it."

"Because the construction crew doesn't work on the weekends. The killer knew that."

"Even so," Melissa said, "there were no barriers to prevent people from using a staircase that the mall operator knew was dangerous."

"Because the killer removed the stanchion tape."

"Which only illustrates that the mall's safety measures were woefully insufficient. Not only that, it was negligent to have exposed rebar spikes so close to the base of the stairs."

"It was a mistake that the killer exploited," Bixby said.

"It was a lethal hazard," she countered, "one that wouldn't have been exploited if it wasn't there."

I turned to Bixby. "She sounds like you now."

Melissa leaned forward on her desk and faced Bixby. "I understand everything you're saying. But I asked you to determine if the mall was responsible for Crowley's death and everything you've just told me confirms that they were."

I thought about what Bixby himself told me about a building's role in a crime. By his own definition, Melissa was right.

"The mall is an accomplice, but not the killer," Bixby said, as if reading my thoughts. "That person or group is still out there."

"Group?" I said. "I thought it was just the mystery woman in red."

"There's also whoever sabotaged that step, who I assume was disguised as a construction worker. There could be two, three, or even more people involved in the plot. Or it could be just one person who hired several innocent people to perform individual tasks but they had no idea that the final result would be murder."

Melissa leaned back into her seat again. "Your entire theory is a string of assumptions."

"Someone gave Crowley the mani-pedi. Someone left the chocolate magazines at the nail salon. Someone made the keto pop-up poster. Someone put up that poster in the vacant storefront. And someone dressed up exactly like Crowley's ex-lover startled her. Those aren't assumptions. Those are provable facts."

"It sounds to me like a cruel but innocent prank that went unexpectedly and tragically wrong because of the mall's bad design and negligent safety measures."

"This was not a prank." Bixby was adamant. "This was a murder, conceived and executed by someone with considerable financial resources and a deep understanding of how design can be used to manipulate people."

He might as well have been describing himself.

"We're done," Melissa said. "I'm settling with the Crowleys. They'll sign an NDA. The media will drop the story. Business will continue at the mall. Everybody will be happy."

"Except your accountants," Bixby said. "You're throwing away tens of millions of dollars."

"We are a global insurance company with $150 billion in loss reserves to pay settlements. Twenty million dollars is a blip, a rounding error for us."

That argument struck me as a contradiction. So I said, without thinking, "Then why did you hire Bixby to save you money on claims if you don't give a shit?"

I regretted my words the instant I said them.

She fixed me with a cold glare. "The question I'm asking myself now is why we hired you."

But I hoped that didn't mean she couldn't still fall madly in love with me.

Bixby spoke up. "You didn't, Melissa. I did. And Wally is right."

She now regarded him with genuine surprise. "You've never said that about an assistant before."

"What if the police say it's a homicide? Would that make you hold off on writing the check?"

"The police aren't saying that," she said.

"Because they don't know it's one yet," he said. "I'll tell them and they'll listen. My case-closure rate is legendary. Give me another day."

"Even if it's a murder, that doesn't absolve the mall operators of their liability in Crowley's death."

I spoke up, but this time I'd thought about what I'd say. "The mall could argue that it does and sue you for prematurely settling a claim that irrevocably damaged their reputation and drove away shoppers."

Bixby regarded me with curiosity, but she glared at me coldly again. I felt the odds were rising against Melissa and I having an epic romance.

She said, "When did you become a lawyer?"

"In an episode of *Matlock*, the reboot with Kathy Bates and not the original with Andy Griffith, that briefly dealt with a similar claim."

"I didn't see that credit on your IMDb page."

"It was a nonspeaking part," I said. "The defendant was an insurance company. I was one of their lawyers at the defense table, silently analyzing the testimony and offering my tactical wisdom in notes that I passed to the lead attorney. Matlock destroyed us. The same could happen to you."

The attorney might have won the case if he'd read my notes, and if we weren't shackled by a script that led to a predetermined verdict. That old hag Matlock had to win every time.

But I saw the expression on Melissa's face soften, and felt our chances of finding true love together had marginally improved. She shifted her gaze to Bixby.

"Okay, you have one day. If the LAPD doesn't launch a homicide investigation tomorrow, this case is closed."

We left her office, taking the temporary reprieve. Once we were far out of earshot, Bixby said, "Was that *Matlock* story true or were you lying?"

"You mean was I acting? I'm flattered that you can't tell."

"Don't be," he said. "I couldn't tell when the dummy was lying, either."

"Now that I've bought you another day, where are we going?"

"To find the motive for Caroline Crowley's murder," he said.

CHAPTER TEN

The offices of Bernheim, Sutton & Associates were on the second floor of an office tower on Wilshire Boulevard along the so-called Miracle Mile, not far from the La Brea Tar Pits, which was still coughing up the bones of the dead dinosaurs that had been stuck in it, hoping for a miracle that never came.

That's not how that stretch of Wilshire got its name, of course. I think it had something to do with a developer, just like the famous Hollywood Sign did, and so many other things Los Angeles is known for. The Hollywood Sign originally read HOLLYWOODLAND and was essentially a billboard advertising new homes being constructed in the hills. Over the decades that followed, the letters that made up "land" eventually collapsed, and what remained of the sign became an icon known all over the world.

As for Miracle Mile? I had no idea.

We took the elevator to the second floor instead of the stairs, which I soon regretted. Bixby took one look at the elevator's control panel and scowled.

"Would you look at that?"

I did. The "Door Open," "Alarm," and "Door Close" buttons were in a row at the top.

The buttons for the floors were in three columns directly below them, descending from 5 to 1 in the first column, 10 to 6 in the second, and 15 to 11 in the third, like so:

All the buttons were the same size and color.

"What's the problem?" I asked, and hit the button for the second floor.

"I could think of a dozen better, more intuitive mappings for these buttons."

"What's wrong with this one?"

"Nothing, if you enjoy having the fire alarm go off several times a week or being stuck in an elevator for hours."

That was one of my fears. I never stepped into an elevator if I thought I might have to use the bathroom in the next few hours.

Bixby went on. "If you hit 'Door Open' but then want to hit 'Door Close,' you would naturally hit immediately next to it, which is 'Alarm,' not 'Door Close.' Why place another button between the two? It invites error. And, because the floor buttons are arranged from the bottom up, you are more likely to hit the 'Alarm' button when you want to go to the eleventh floor, rather than looking at the bottom of the panel for that button. It would make more sense to have the 'Door Open,' 'Alarm,' and 'Door Close' buttons at the bottom, with the two door-related buttons directly next to each other."

"Nobody expects elevator controls to make sense," I said. "They are all different."

"That's a major problem," he said. "They should all be the same. There is a near conformity, across countries and cultures, on scores of other things, like traffic signals, telephone and calculator keypads, blenders and food processors, and the driver's portion of automobile dashboards."

"I can see why you are so upset," I said. I was convincing, because I am a professional actor, but I was being insincere.

We arrived at our floor and stepped out into a lobby furnished with several unoccupied couches and a sleek glass-and-steel reception desk, the words Bernheim, Sutton & Associates written in gold letters on the wood-paneled wall behind the attractive pink-haired young woman who greeted us.

"Welcome to Bernheim, Sutton & Associates," she said. Her smile seemed genuine even if her hair did not.

Bixby approached the desk. "I'm Edison Bixby, an investigator for Triax Global Insurance." He handed her his card, then tipped his head toward me. "And this is Wally Nash, my personal trainer."

She handed the card back to him. "You bring your trainer with you to work?"

"He makes sure I eat right and get in all of my steps."

"You could have taken the stairs instead of the elevator," she said.

"I'm in a hurry."

"We're on the second floor," she said.

"You look like a clown," he said.

"What?" she said, clearly offended.

"It's your hair," he said. "And your makeup. Do you do children's birthdays?"

I spoke up fast. "Ignore him. He hates being called out on his laziness. You want to know the truth? He's wearing SPANX to hold in his flab. When he takes it off, it's like opening up a canister of Poppin' Fresh dough."

I made a popping noise.

She grinned. "I'd be irritable, too, if I was wearing one of those."

Bixby wasn't amused, nor did he seem to appreciate that I'd gamely tried to cover for his blurt of traumatic corpo-whatsit. "I'm investigating the tragic death of Caroline Crowley and I don't want to waste a second."

Her smile evaporated and she started to cry. The change in mood was instantaneous and, as an actor, I envied her ability to summon tears so quickly, though she had both genuine grief and personal offense to draw upon. I went around the counter, picked up the box of tissues on her desk, and offered it to her.

"It's okay. Relax."

She took a tissue, wiped the tears from her eyes, and tried to gather herself. "I'm sorry. It's just that Caroline was such a sweet person and I'm still trying to process the shock."

"We understand," I said. "We're shocked by it, too."

Bixby took a slim bag out of his jacket pocket and offered it to her over the counter.

"Have a chocolate chip cookie, you'll feel better."

She slipped a cookie out of the bag and glanced sideways at me. "You let him carry around cookies?"

"This is why I can't leave him alone for one second. In six months, firefighters would need the Jaws of Life and a crane again to get him out of the house."

"Again?" she said to me, then looked at Bixby with wide eyes.

He said, "I need to talk with Caroline's boss right away."

She picked up the phone receiver, typed an extension on the keypad, and told whoever it was on the other end who Bixby was and why he was there. She listened for a bit, set the receiver down, and smiled at Bixby. "Mr. Stamper will see you now. He's in the corner office at the end of the hall."

"Thank you," I said, and I headed down the hall with Bixby, walking past rows of secretaries sitting at desks in front of office doors. When we were out of earshot of the receptionist, I whispered, "Personal trainer?"

"Acting improv," he said. "I don't want you to lose your edge while you work for me."

"Have you already forgotten Frank Hellinger?"

Stamper stepped out of his office into the hallway to greet us with a grim, serious expression on his face that looked more like he was having digestive problems rather than struggling with difficult emotions. Perhaps he needed Tremvoya.

"I'm Jeff Stamper, senior vice president. I was Caroline's supervisor." He offered his hand to each of us and we shook it, then he waved us into his office. "Please come in. We're all horrified and grief-stricken by her death. She was so talented and had such a bright future." He cleared his throat, grimaced, then closed the door behind him. "Pardon me, the emotions are still pretty raw. Who does Triax insure in this tragedy?"

He gestured to his guest chairs and took a seat behind his desk.

"The mall." Bixby sat down. I did, too.

"I'm confused," Stamper said. "What can we possibly do to help you determine the scope of the mall's negligence?"

"You're confused because your expertise is helping your clients minimize, excuse, or deny responsibility for their negligence and that's all you know how to do."

If Stamper wasn't confused before, he certainly was now. "Are you here to hire us for the mall?"

"I'm here to find out who murdered her. I believe it has something to do with her work. I need to know what crises Crowley was spinning for you."

"I don't like the way you're characterizing the important service we provide."

I could see that things were going terribly wrong for Bixby, so I stepped in to save the situation. "But you liked Caroline, Mr. Stamper. This is about her and making sure whoever was responsible for her death is punished. We think somebody was so offended by one of your spin campaigns that they killed Crowley to get back at this company or one of your clients."

"And it might only be the beginning," Bixby said. "You could be next."

Stamper went pale. "Shit."

He stood up and started sorting through the files on his desk, searching for something. While Stamper was distracted, Bixby whispered to me, "Never underestimate the power of self-interest."

Stamper said, "She wasn't the spokesperson on any of the incidents that I'm about to share with you, but she was a part of the team involved in creating and disseminating the messaging." He found one of the files he was looking for and held it up. "Soar Airlines. An emergency door on a plane blew open in flight and a woman was sucked out. She wasn't wearing a seat belt."

"Definitely her fault," Bixby said.

"Agreed. That was our take." Stamper set it aside and picked up another file. "The Tiki Wiki Hotel in Honolulu. A guest was having a party in his thirteenth-floor room. Twenty people were dancing on the deck when it collapsed. They all plunged to their deaths."

"They should have known the thirteenth floor was unlucky," Bixby said.

"They should have known not to cram onto a tiny deck and start stomping." Stamper picked up another file. "Big Sombrero Restaurants. Sixty people in twenty-two states were poisoned by fecal matter in their guacamole."

"That's what happens when restaurant workers don't wash their hands after using the bathroom," Bixby said.

"No," Stamper said, sitting down again, "that's what happens when the FDA doesn't regularly inspect avocado farms."

"Right," Bixby said. "My mistake."

I could see how those cases, and the crisis-management company's defenses for their clients' negligence, could really piss off the victims and their families and make them want revenge. But how would Bixby narrow down the number of suspects?

Someone barged through the office door behind us and angrily shouted, "Edison Bixby!"

We turned in our chairs to see a stately gray-haired man with a scowl on his flushed, jowly face. He clearly wasn't glad to see Bixby. "When I heard you were here, I thought it was a sick joke."

Bixby wasn't flustered at all and responded casually. "Do you think Caroline Crowley's death is funny, Gordon?"

Stamper looked at the older man, who needed suspenders to keep his pants on over the lower half of his stomach. "You two know each other?"

Gordon slammed the door shut. "I haven't seen Edison Bixby since he was seventeen years old."

"Back when your flabby chest wasn't resting on your big belly," Bixby said. "Have you looked into getting a bra in your old age?"

I didn't bother making excuses this time for Bixby's rudeness, uncensored or not. These two obviously had history and maybe Gordon deserved the insults.

"Did you work here?" Stamper asked Bixby.

"Hell no," Gordon said. "The little prick sued us."

I hadn't heard about *that* lawsuit. I turned to Bixby. "Did you win?"

"I settled for five million dollars," he said. I whistled. "I should have demanded more."

Gordon came around the chairs to face us and pointed a gold-ringed finger in Bixby's face. "You signed an NDA."

"Relax, so did he." Bixby gestured to me.

I smiled at Gordon. "I'm his personal trainer. Keeping him buff."

Bixby gestured to Stamper. "And I'm sure he's signed one, too, with all the secrets you have to keep around here."

Stamper met Bixby's gaze. "Why did you sue us?"

"Monarch Motors hired Bernheim, Sutton & Associates to absolve them of responsibility for the car crash that killed my parents. So you spread the false story that my father was a drunk driver and it was his fault. I proved it was the design of the car that caused their deaths."

Gordon said, "I argued against the settlement, but I wasn't in charge here then. I am now. We aren't settling a goddamn thing."

Bixby looked up at him. "I didn't come here to get money out of you, Gordon. I'm here for Caroline Crowley."

"She doesn't get any, either. She didn't fall down our stairs."

"No, she didn't. She fell at the Woodland Hills Mall . . ." He paused for a moment, considering something, and then smiled. "Which is owned by Southfield Properties."

He looked at Gordon and Stamper expectantly, waiting for their reaction. Gordon and Stamper shared a wary look. Bixby nodded to himself and went on: "The same company that owns the Tiki Wiki Hotel and hired you to blame the deadly deck collapse on someone else. That's why she was killed."

"Wow," I said, stunned not only by the connection he'd deduced between Bernheim, Sutton & Associates and Southfield Properties, but also by the surprising connection between Bixby and the crisis-management company.

Bixby said, "Are you pointing the finger at anyone besides the victims?"

Stamper replied, "Archibald Twain, the architect who designed it."

Gordon glowered reproachfully at Stamper for answering, then shifted his gaze to Bixby and his expression morphed into a smirk. "Isn't that what you'd do? Blame the designer?"

Bixby nodded. "The building is always an accomplice."

"I'm glad we have your stamp of approval. I'll sleep soundly tonight. Now get the fuck out of my office."

Bixby rose, and so did I.

As we passed Gordon on our way to the door, Bixby said to him, "You need to change your diaper. I can smell it."

Once we were in the hallway, heading to their lobby, I said, "How did you know the mall is owned by the same company that owns the Honolulu hotel?"

"It was an educated guess."

We crossed the lobby to the elevator and I hit the call button. "Well, it was amazing. Just like everything you saw at the mall."

"None of it was hidden. It was all out in the open for anybody to see."

"But somehow only you saw it. You exposed a murder that nobody else would have known about, and even uncovered the motive behind it, and the day isn't even over yet."

"I've been faster, but I'm not the man I used to be," Bixby said. "That's what happens when you're shot in the face."

The elevator arrived and we stepped in. I pressed the button for the ground floor. "Who do you think killed Crowley? Is it a family member of one of the victims?"

"It's probably Archibald Twain, the disgraced architect," Bixby said. "He has the motive and design expertise to pull it off."

"What's next?"

"Getting the evidence and making the arrest. But, despite my ride and the gun on my hip, I'm not a cop anymore. Luckily, I know someone who is."

We reached the building lobby. As we stepped out, Bixby pressed the "Alarm" button. The bell rang loudly.

"Oops," Bixby said and continued walking.

CHAPTER ELEVEN

When we got back to Bixby's house, he told me to follow up with "fat-ass Paul Wetzel," get whatever video the mall cop had gathered, and then meet him in his movie theater at 6 p.m. with all the surveillance footage. That's when he was going to present his case to Detective McGregor.

It had been an exciting day, unlike any I'd ever experienced before, and I was still jacked up when I got back to the guesthouse.

What Bixby figured out at Lawrence Keefer's home was impressive, but what he'd discovered at the mall was astounding.

Caroline Crowley didn't fall down a staircase, she was pushed. It may not have been by an actual pair of hands against her back, but it might as well have been.

It was both frightening and amazing to see how easily and fatally she'd been manipulated. And I only saw it because Bixby revealed it to me. It was as if he'd deconstructed a brilliant magic trick, only this was one that nobody even realized they'd seen. He truly had a superpower. But what frightened me was that someone else had it, too.

The killer.

And, if I believed Bixby, so could anybody who designed things. They had the power to manipulate us. To make us want things. Go places. Feel certain emotions. And behave in certain prescribed ways.

And, apparently, to kill ourselves.

If not to throw ourselves down a flight of stairs, then maybe to smoke a pack of cigarettes we know could give us cancer, or drink too much to seem sophisticated or cool, or take unnecessary drugs, injecting ourselves with poisons or fillers, or risk deadly and radical surgery to appeal to some unachievable, unnatural ideal of beauty that only exists in airbrushed or digitally enhanced images.

There were a lot of people with that power over us and, as far as I knew, only one man able to clearly see it.

Edison Bixby.

And now I was his assistant, a temp job that I was treating as a new role, like any other I might be cast to play.

But it was becoming clear to me that I could accomplish more in this role than any other I'd ever acted in before. It was an opportunity to do something important. To save lives and get justice for those who couldn't be saved.

I thought that it could be the most important part I'd ever have, even if it couldn't possibly win me a Tony, Emmy, or Oscar.

I'd just have to find another role for that.

I'd missed two calls from my agent while we were out, but I ignored them and called Paul Wetzel instead. He not only sent me the links to the additional videos but shared with me what little he'd learned about the delivery of the chocolate magazines and the construction worker who'd sabotaged the step.

I downloaded the new videos, along with all the other important footage we'd already seen, onto my laptop and spent the next few hours editing them all together into a chronological narrative that matched Bixby's theory of the crime. I wanted him to be able to convince McGregor that he was right.

By the time I was done, it was nearly 6 p.m. and I realized I'd powered through the day on just two fried eggs, some toast, and a couple of chocolate chip cookies and that I was ravenous. But my guesthouse refrigerator and cupboards were empty, so I hoped I could talk Bixby into letting me raid his refrigerator before McGregor showed up. I wouldn't want to pass out during the presentation.

I grabbed my laptop and hurried over to Bixby's little movie theater. The marquee had changed. It now read:

The Puppet on the Staircase

I crossed the small lobby and went into the screening room, where Bixby, dressed in his Tom Ford suit, was putting two bottles of champagne in a bucket of ice on a long table overflowing with food.

There was a shrimp tower, a bowl of salad, a basket of rolls, a tiny bowl of caviar with blinis and crème fraîche, and an array of sterling silver platters of sliced prime rib, roasted chicken, fruit, vegetables, and gourmet pastries. At the end of the table was a stack of plates, a dozen assorted pieces of silverware, cloth napkins, and three champagne flutes.

"Wow," I said. "Is this just for the two of you or can—"

He interrupted me. "Help yourself. Just leave some for us."

"I'm not an animal."

"You're practically foaming at the mouth."

I set my laptop on the control console, grabbed a plate, and started piling food on it, my stomach growling like Godzilla rampaging across Tokyo.

Bixby watched me load up. "McGregor will be here any minute now. Do you have all the video ready?"

"I do. I also have an update. United Parcel Service delivered the chocolate magazines to the nail salon from a UPS Store in Tarzana. Maybe McGregor can get a warrant to see who dropped the magazines off at UPS for delivery."

"She might have a hard time convincing a judge there's probable cause. Sending confection magazines to a nail salon for free isn't a crime."

By the time I was done with the shrimp tower, it was more of a shrimp stump. But I made up for it by leaving the caviar untouched. I wasn't a fan of fish eggs. They were too salty and fishy for me.

“There’s video of a construction worker sabotaging the step on Friday morning,” I said, “but he was wearing a hard hat that completely obscured his face. He was there for about two hours. There’s no video of him arriving or leaving.”

“What about the blond woman who talked with Crowley in the salon?”

I ignored the salad and rolls, stocking up on prime rib and chicken, grabbed some silverware, and brought my bounty over to the console. I’d go back for dessert.

“The cameras never got a clear shot of her when she entered or left the salon, but you were right—she went from the salon to the back corridor. And a few minutes later, the woman in red came out. The rest went just like you predicted. The cameras tracked her when she returned to the empty store, took down the poster, and headed for the parking garage, but lost her after that.”

“Let me see the blond woman that Crowley spoke to in the salon.”

My mouth was full of shrimp, but I powered up my laptop and played the video of the blond woman leaving the nail salon.

She wore a big yellow sun hat with a wide brim that made it easy to pick her out of a crowd but also impossible to see her face. She walked past the Neiman Marcus toward the other side of the mall, where the empty storefront and cookie place were. I swallowed my food and froze the frame on her.

“She knew where every camera was,” I said, “and exactly what they could see, just like a trained actor would.”

Bixby plugged a USB cable into my computer and hit a few buttons on the console. An instant later, the image on my laptop appeared on the big screen.

“An actor would have made sure we saw her face and from the best possible angle,” he said. “But she’s definitely not hiding herself.”

“She does stand out in a crowd,” I said, cutting into my prime rib. “That may be the brightest yellow I’ve ever seen.”

“It’s like she’s giving us the finger.”

"It's your imagination." I switched off the video. "She's part of the perfect murder, staged in a way that nobody would ever question was an accident. So there was no reason for the killer to think anyone would ever look at this video."

"We are."

"Only because they didn't expect Sherlock Holmes and Watson to get the case."

Bixby laughed. "Is that how you see the two of us?"

"Absolutely, only without the homoerotic subtext."

That's when McGregor came in. "Homoerotic? Is there something you want to tell me, Bixby?"

He turned to look at her. "Great rack."

"Is that your way of saying that getting shot in the head didn't alter your sexuality?"

"I believe I've demonstrated that to you on multiple occasions, and that's just in the last twenty-four hours."

"I'll accept that." McGregor snatched a shrimp from what remained of the tower. "You said you had something important to show me."

"I do." He gestured to the rest of the spread on the table. "But first, can I interest you in some Dom Pérignon? Or perhaps some caviar?"

"Both," she said.

Bixby began by taking a bottle of Dom out of the ice and popping the cork.

She watched him pour three glasses. "Are you celebrating something?"

"You closed a big case today." He handed her a glass.

"That's news to me," she said.

"The day isn't over yet." He brought a glass over to me, then picked up one for himself and took a sip.

She sipped her champagne, too, but regarded him suspiciously over the rim. "Are you trying to butter me up?"

"I'm trying to get you drunk," Bixby said, preparing a plate of caviar. "Not fall-down drunk. Or vomit-in-the-street drunk. More like, happily sloshed."

I spoke up quickly. "What he means is that he knows you need to relax after a long, difficult day on the streets."

McGregor turned, as if noticing me for the first time, though I knew it was an act, and a bad one. "You think I walk the streets, Fartman? What do you think I am, a hooker?"

"I think you're out there fighting crime, kicking down doors, rousting perps, and making collars."

"I'm a detective," she said. "Not a beat cop in 1975."

Bixby offered her some caviar and toast on a plate. "Beluga caviar, straight from the Caspian Sea. The very best."

The caviar seemed to mollify her, much to my relief. She took the plate and her champagne and sat down carefully in one of the theater seats so she wouldn't spill anything on herself. "Okay, let's get this over with. What do you want me in a drunken stupor to see?"

Bixby nodded to me, and I cued up the videos as he went to the front of the theater and stood to one side of the big screen, which was black for now.

"Last Saturday, a woman was killed at the Woodland Hills Mall. Since it was not a natural death, you were sent to check it out."

McGregor visibly tensed up. I could see it just watching her from behind. She didn't like where this was going. "Yes, I was. A woman tripped, fell down a staircase, and got impaled on a bunch of rebar. It was a gruesome accident."

"It was murder."

"Oh, for fuck's sake." McGregor turned in her seat and snapped her fingers at me. "Fartman, bring me that bottle of champagne."

I did. She took the bottle from me, filled up her glass, then set the bottle on the chair next to her. "There is no way that was murder, Bixby. She was alone on the staircase. I've seen the video."

"So have I. In fact, I've got it right here."

He gestured to me. I played the video. And all the others, including the newest ones, as Bixby methodically explained how Caroline Crowley was lured to her death at the mall. He was about to tell her what he found at Crowley's house when McGregor abruptly stood and grabbed the now-empty champagne bottle by the neck. She was going to leave.

"Wait," Bixby said. "I'm not done yet."

"I am." She threw the bottle at him, narrowly missing his head. The bottle shattered against the screen. "With this. With you. With everything. You are one deeply fucked-up individual."

McGregor snatched her empty plate and headed for the aisle. I shrank down in my seat at the console and hoped that she wasn't coming for me next.

Bixby spoke quickly, but calmly. "The killer knows how to use design to influence behavior. I'm the only detective who could have seen that this was murder. You can't blame yourself for missing it."

She pivoted and frisbeed the plate at him. He ducked. The plate smashed into the wall and broke into pieces.

"I don't," she yelled at him. "Because it never happened. It's a figment of your psychosis."

"But you just saw the evidence."

"What I saw is that you are so desperate to make me look stupid that you're trolling my cases, searching for mistakes and an opportunity to wow everyone with your awesome brilliance. It's pathetic. I thought you cared about me."

"I want to save you from your mistake so that you, not me, can solve the case."

"How generous, you sick son of a bitch."

Bixby took a step toward her. "Crowley worked for Bernheim, Sutton & Associates."

That seemed to hit a nerve with her. She said, "The crisis-management company."

"One of their clients is Southfield Properties, the owners of the Woodland Hills Mall."

"Monarch Motors was also one of their clients." McGregor was putting pieces together.

"Yes, they were." Bixby had her full attention again now. "Crowley was killed because Bernheim Sutton is trying to blame Archibald Twain, an innocent architect, for Southfield's negligence in the death of several people in the collapse of a hotel deck. But he's not innocent anymore. Now he's a murderer."

She nodded, and when she spoke again, her voice was soft, the anger gone. "This isn't about me."

He stood in front of her, face-to-face. "That's right. Now you understand."

She nodded. "It's all about you. You're still fighting for your parents, even after all these years."

His expression changed. She'd made the wrong connections. "That's not it at all."

"You were triggered as soon as you learned that Caroline Crowley worked for Bernheim Sutton. Then her accident absolutely had to be a murder. You saw what you wanted to see."

"I saw what was there," he said. "What nobody else could see."

"Of course you did, Bixby. Because nobody else is carrying your heartbreak. It's so obvious," she said tenderly. "And so sad."

McGregor made a convincing argument. The logic was sound. But I saw what Bixby did, too.

Or did I simply *want* to see it?

Had I been sucked into Bixby's psychosis?

"I'm sorry." She stepped forward and drew Bixby into a hug. "I should have known."

Bixby sighed, giving up, and looked forlornly at me over her shoulder.

I took my laptop, and the tray of pastries, and quietly slipped out of the theater, leaving the two of them alone.

CHAPTER TWELVE

I peeked out my window an hour or so later and saw that McGregor's car was still parked in the motor court, so I went to the theater and crept inside. The food was all there, as I suspected it would be, forgotten in the heat of their passion. I took as much as I could carry back to the guesthouse and stocked my refrigerator with meat, fruit, and vegetables. There was no sense letting the food spoil while Bixby and McGregor had makeup sex.

Early the next morning, I found Bixby swimming in the pond.

"How did it go last night?" I went to the tree and pulled the levers for coffee and pancakes like it was a common thing to do. *Doesn't everybody have a breakfast-making tree?*

"I'm confident that she doesn't have any doubts about my sexuality."

I sat down on a boulder. "I was referring to the case."

"She still thinks it's all about me dealing with the trauma of being abandoned by my parents when they were killed."

"Are you?"

"Every day," Bixby said. "Why do you think I still live in my childhood home and do what I do the way I do?"

"So McGregor was right."

"She wasn't entirely wrong."

My coffee was delivered. I went over to get my mug. "Are you saying that now you think Caroline Crowley's death was a prank gone wrong, that it had nothing to do with Bernheim, Sutton & Associates?"

"Of course not," Bixby said. "I'm psychologically and neurologically damaged, but I'm not insane."

Melissa Priddle stomped out of the trees and declared, "Are you insane?"

Bixby said, "Wally and I were just discussing that."

I looked at him. "You really need a trip wire across the path that's attached to a cowbell to announce when someone is coming."

"That's not a bad idea."

Melissa marched up to the edge of the pond and for a moment I thought she might continue right into the water to confront him.

"Bernheim Sutton just announced that Edison Bixby, the renowned LAPD homicide detective, has proved that their beloved employee, Caroline Crowley, was murdered, absolving Southfield Properties, a respected company that they know and trust, of any responsibility for her death. Where would they get that idea?"

"From me," Bixby said.

"You told them that?" When she was angry, somehow her British accent got even more British. I thought it was incredibly sexy.

"Not in those words."

"What were you thinking?"

"I was trying to convince them to help me uncover the motive for the murder of their beloved employee, and I did."

Bixby told her how he managed that while I listened and ate my pancakes.

When he was done, Melissa sat down on a tree stump and groaned. "After all that, it didn't occur to you that Bernheim Sutton might rush to sign up Southfield and offer to handle this crisis for them, too?"

"How could they? It was their employee who was killed at Southfield's mall. It's a conflict of interest."

"Their only interest is making money," she said. "And you gave them a perfect opportunity, and to do so off of your reputation, the one you earned after shaming one of their biggest clients into a historic legal settlement when you were just a pimply-faced teenager. They will never get over that humiliation."

"I didn't have pimples," Bixby said. "I've always had perfect skin."

"Of course you have," I said.

Bixby ignored me and said to her, "What are you going to do now?"

"Wait and see what the LAPD does."

Bixby looked past her and said, "I think we are about to find out."

I followed his gaze and saw McGregor staggering out of the trees, her hair askew, and wearing only Bixby's smoking jacket over her naked body. "My captain just called to tell me that Bernheim, Sutton & Associates held a press conference to declare that the great Edison Bixby, with his perfect fucking case-closure record, says Crowley was murdered, so now I've got to investigate her accident as a homicide."

"Congratulations," Bixby said.

"It wasn't a murder!" McGregor shouted.

Melissa faced Bixby and crossed her arms over her chest. "You're sleeping with a homicide detective?"

"We don't get much sleep."

McGregor reacted to Melissa as if she'd just blinked into existence like Elizabeth Montgomery on that old sitcom *Bewitched.* "Who the hell are you?"

"Melissa Priddle, Triax Global Insurance."

"This is all your fault," McGregor said.

"How do you figure that, Detective?"

"You hired him," she said.

"I didn't know it would lead to this."

"Have you met the man? What did you think would happen? He's using this case, and all the others you give him, to exorcise old demons and get back into the spotlight again."

I'd had enough of all the complaining.

"Can I interest anyone in breakfast?" Bixby, Melissa, and McGregor all stared at me. "You'll all feel better after you eat and you'll realize that you have nothing to be angry about."

McGregor directed her anger at me. "Who asked for your opinion, Fartman? You aren't part of this."

"Which is why I can see this little drama objectively." I looked at Melissa. "All that's happened is that you don't have to pay any insurance claims, at least for the moment." I shifted my gaze to McGregor. "And you have to investigate a homicide, which is what you do every day. Big deal."

McGregor said, "There. Is. No. Homicide."

"Then that's what you'll find," I said. "Back to status quo. No loss."

Melissa said, "We'll have to write the Crowleys a very big check."

"Which you were going to do anyway. In fact, you said it would be hardly more than a rounding error for Triax. So, it's business as usual," I said. "However, if McGregor proves that Crowley's death was the accident you both believe it was, it will humiliate Bixby and destroy his reputation. That's a win for both of you. Imagine how much better your lives will be if Bixby is humbled."

Melissa and McGregor shared a smile at the thought.

Bixby said, "But that's not going to happen, because I'm right."

I turned to him. "And if you are, you will be celebrated again as a brilliant detective."

"I'm already celebrated."

"And if Bixby is right, and it is murder, you both win." I looked at McGregor. "You'll have the glory of arresting a diabolical killer." Then I looked at Melissa. "You'll have the glory of saving Triax a $20 million payout. And Bixby gets the satisfaction of getting Caroline Crowley the justice that she deserves. So what is there for any of you to be pissed off about?"

McGregor nodded. "You have a point."

Melissa also nodded. "Yes, he does."

Bixby faced the two women. "So we're all good?"

The women said *no* in unison and left the pond without saying another word to us.

Bixby looked at me. "Women are so irrational."

"I'm glad they were gone before you said that."

"The case isn't closed yet." Bixby got out of the pond and put on his bathrobe. "We still have more work to do."

"Weren't you paying attention? McGregor is on the case. You got what you wanted last night."

"McGregor is a good detective, but she's not qualified to go up against this kind of high-level adversary." Bixby put on his slippers but didn't seem in a hurry to get back to the house. I figured that he was giving McGregor time to leave so he could avoid another confrontation.

"What adversary?"

"Archibald Twain, the architect who designed the Tiki Wiki Hotel in Honolulu and Caroline Crowley's murder."

"I don't understand," I said. "Didn't you present the case to McGregor because you need the authority of her badge to continue the investigation?"

"She'll have to find the mysterious construction worker, the mystery woman, the physical evidence, and the money trail that ties Twain to the plot."

"So what's left for you to do?"

"Meet Twain face-to-face," he said.

"What's that going to accomplish?"

"It might put a scare into him."

We heard the sound of tires peeling out. That had to be McGregor leaving in a fury, even though I'd proven to her there was nothing to be angry about. Maybe she just liked the sound because it primed her for action.

"Won't alerting Twain that you know that the accident was murder, and that he's the prime suspect, motivate him to start covering his tracks?"

"I hope so," Bixby said, heading for the house now that McGregor was gone. "Because the cover-up always makes things worse. The smart ones don't do a thing."

"I think he's proven that he's very smart," I said.

"Not smarter than me."

Archibald Twain's architectural firm was based in San Francisco, but he lived in the East Bay, on a vast estate in the rolling hills of Danville. So that's where we were headed. A black Suburban limo picked us up at Bixby's place and took us to Van Nuys Airport, where a private jet was waiting. The limo drove us directly to the plane. We didn't have to walk through a terminal or go through a TSA security check. I was already wowed and I wasn't even in the plane yet.

We stepped inside the jet. The interior was paneled in mahogany with brushed metal accents and the big, overstuffed seats were upholstered in beige leather. The windows were larger than those in commercial aircraft, letting in a lot of natural light. I took a seat across the aisle from Bixby. The leather was incredibly soft and smooth.

The captain came out of the cockpit, reminded us that the galley had alcohol, soft drinks, and an array of sandwiches for us, and told us to enjoy our forty-five-minute flight to the airfield in Concord, California. I was shocked by how fast the flight would be.

To put the travel time in perspective, it would take us less time to fly to Northern California than it would to drive from Bixby's house in Topanga Canyon to downtown Los Angeles in light traffic.

We were in the air a few minutes later, and as soon as we hit cruising altitude, Bixby pulled a laptop out of a side panel near his seat, opened it up, and started typing on the keyboard.

He studied his screen. I started exploring the various cubbies around my seat to discover what treasures they contained. One had a laptop identical to Bixby's inside, one was stuffed with candy bars, another was full of bags of peanuts and crackers, another was a slim refrigerator stuffed with goodies, including beer. I took the beer and popped it open, even though it was only 10 a.m., just because it was there, then extended my footrest and prepared to enjoy the ride.

Bixby gave me a sideways glance. "Comfortable?"

"I could live in here."

"I'll take that as a yes."

I gestured with my beer at his computer. "What are you doing?"

"Researching Twain some more. His firm specializes in hotels, shopping centers, and office buildings. He also wrote a book called *Persuasive Spaces* that's taught in cognitive science, design, and architecture courses. He's an expert at using space to influence human behavior."

"That doesn't mean he used that knowledge to manipulate Caroline Crowley into tumbling down those stairs."

"You sound like McGregor. Do you think she's right about me?"

"I believe a person is innocent until proven guilty. Shouldn't you?"

"In this case, it's a matter of probability," he said. "The likely number of people on earth who have both the specialized skill set to murder Caroline Crowley this way and a strong motive to do so is, at most, one."

"You haven't looked very hard."

"Not every mystery is a whodunit with a body, three suspects, and Christoph Waltz did it."

There was no point in arguing with him. His mind was made up and he hadn't even talked to Twain yet. That actually bolstered McGregor's argument and it worried me.

Another chauffeured Suburban, almost identical to the one that took us to Van Nuys, met our plane on the tarmac at Buchanan Field in Concord. Once again, we didn't even have to step into a terminal. This was how to travel. I knew I'd have a hard time flying commercial ever again, not that I could afford even that.

We drove about twenty minutes south on the 680 freeway to Danville, then headed east into the grassy foothills of the Diablo Range. We approached a big, wrought iron gate and speaker box. The chauffeur rolled down the window and hit the buzzer. A man's voice replied from the speaker with "Yes," but it was posed as a question. Bixby answered from the back seat.

"My name is Edison Bixby. I'm an investigator with Triax Global Insurance. I'd like to talk with Mr. Twain."

The gate opened and the chauffeur drove up the driveway to one of the most unusual homes I'd ever seen. It looked like an enormous sea snail shell with windows that was embedded upright into the side of a grassy hill. I'd never seen anything like it.

I said to Bixby, "Your parents would have loved this."

I didn't know them, of course, but based on their house and property, it felt like a safe assumption.

"You're right," he said. "But I'm not surprised by Twain's creativity. The best murderers are imaginative."

"What qualifies as 'best'?"

"The ones who have the skills to actually get away with it."

We got out and were greeted at the door by a bald, well-built man in his fifties who looked like he was auditioning to be the new CEO of SPECTRE. He wore a black mandarin-collared blazer over a white T-shirt and jeans. All that was missing to make the picture complete was a scar on his face and a white cat in his arms. I almost turned to Bixby and said "He's *definitely* the bad guy."

"Welcome, Mr. Bixby," he said with a vaguely European voice. "What an unexpected surprise."

"You know me?"

"I have followed your career with great interest." He looked at me. "And you are?"

Bixby answered before I could. "Wally Nash, my caddy."

"So let me get this straight," Twain said. "You were on your way to the Blackhawk Country Club and since you were in the neighborhood, you thought you'd stop by to meet me?"

"I'm puttering around on a case you might be able to help me with and couldn't pass up the opportunity. It involves a fatal accident at a Southern California mall owned by Southfield Properties."

"It wasn't an accident. It was incompetence."

"I haven't told you anything about it yet."

"You don't have to. I know Southfield. Come inside."

We stepped inside. The interior of the house felt organic, like he'd actually moved into and remodeled an enormous dinosaur snail shell that he'd excavated from the earth. He was a human hermit crab with a gift for interior design. The furniture also had an organic, rounded-fossil feel to it and it integrated perfectly with the house. It had to be one-of-a-kind stuff.

"Please sit down." He gestured us to take a seat in his living room, which had a towering ceiling that tapered into a glass point at the top.

Bixby and I sat down in two of the unusual chairs. The furniture was not only great to look at, but also surprisingly comfortable.

Twain read the expression on my face.

"I'm a big believer in human-centered design, Mr. Nash." He sat in a big wingback chair that could have been picked from the evil villain furniture catalog, and yet it also appeared as plantlike or biologically derived as the other pieces. "If a chair is attractive but uncomfortable, then it's a failure."

"Did you design the house and the furniture?"

"I design everything in my life that I possibly can."

Bixby said, "You want to be in complete control of your environment."

Twain swiveled the chair around to face him, effectively cutting me out of the conversation, which was fine with me. "Everybody wants that, but I'm one of the lucky few who can come close to achieving it."

"You also try to do the same for your clients in the buildings you design for them."

"That is the nature of architecture, Mr. Bixby. Winston Churchill famously observed that we shape buildings, but after that, they shape us. I make sure I design exactly how the buildings will do that."

"How did that work out in Hawaii?"

I winced when Bixby said that. But Twain seemed to take the blunt, insensitive swipe in stride.

"The cause of that tragedy was not my design. It was the construction, which I had nothing to do with. Southfield used substandard materials to save money, exacerbated by nonexistent oversight, to meet an unrealistic opening date."

"And yet nobody wants to work with you anymore, not even your own firm," Bixby said. "All of your pending construction projects were scrapped, your publisher recalled your book, and the Hawaii attorney general is considering filing criminal charges against you."

"I welcome the scrutiny because that is what will clear my name," Twain said. "But you're right, I have been found guilty by the court of public opinion. But you know how cruel that can be. Or was your father actually a drunk driver?"

If Bixby was stung by the smoothly delivered rebuke, which he thoroughly deserved, it didn't show. "You must be furious. I was."

"What you did was extraordinary, but I don't have your ingenuity or your audacity."

"You don't? You live in a giant snail shell with windows."

(Okay, so I stole Bixby's description of the place. I never claimed to be a great writer.)

Twain said, "You were also a child at the time. I'm older and wiser than you were. I have the patience and experience that you did not."

"That's why I'm here."

"Finally," Twain said, then he actually swiveled his chair to look at me. "I was wondering when he'd get to that. How about you?"

Bixby said, "A woman named Caroline Crowley fell down a staircase in a Southfield mall and was impaled on the exposed rebar of an uncompleted directory display."

Twain swiveled back to Bixby. "What caused her fall?"

"Negligence. The incomplete staircase wasn't properly blocked off. And she lost her balance on a step that was too narrow, most likely sabotaged. Southfield is obviously to blame."

I noted his use of "obviously" and didn't believe it was an accident. He meant it facetiously.

"If the liability for her death is clear," Twain said, "you wouldn't be here."

"I believe that she was lured to the building and that it conspired to kill her."

Twain was intrigued. He steepled his fingers and regarded Bixby with keen interest.

"The building did it?"

"It was certainly an accomplice. As you wrote in your book, 'A task can't be completed that the space doesn't allow or suggest.'"

"You can't blame the architecture for human acts of malice or malfeasance."

"Yes, I can. You also wrote: 'Creatures adapt an environment to achieve their needs, but only if the environment makes it possible.' The design of the staircase allowed for the sabotaged step to be fatal."

"A person can be pushed down *any* staircase and die."

"She pushed herself. That's the beauty of this murder. And every murder is a design."

Bixby briefly explained how he thought Crowley was manipulated into being on that sabotaged step at the precise moment she was distracted by the woman in red, and how the structural curve at that point in the staircase made her fall, if not her death, inevitable. A sabotaged step anywhere else on the staircase wouldn't have had the same potentially fatal impact. The killer took advantage of a flaw in the design.

Twain said, "What a fascinating theory. So what do you want from me?"

"I'm having a hard time convincing Triax that's what happened and that Southfield is only partially liable for Crowley's death."

Twain chuckled. "You want me to defend Southfield? If so, you've got the wrong person."

"You wrote a book on how design, combined with sensory cues like lighting, images, and smells, can be used to influence human behavior and outcomes, especially in stores. I want to know if you think the murder that I've described is possible."

"It's improbable but entirely possible," Twain said. "The question is who would have the ability to conceive of such a complex scheme and also the resources to stage it?"

Bixby smiled. "Someone with a deep background in human-centered design who is both patient and experienced."

Twain smiled back at him. "Or a layman with extensive design knowledge who also possesses audacity and ingenuity. In either case, Mr. Bixby, it would take a powerful motive. I understand wanting to cause Southfield serious trouble, but why kill this particular woman?"

"Crowley was one of the employees at Bernheim, Sutton & Associates, the crisis-management company hired by Southfield, tasked with blaming you and your incompetence for the hotel deck failure."

Twain's smile faded away. "Are you accusing me of killing her?"

"Yes."

Well, that was blunt, but I didn't bother jumping in to smooth out that remark. I wanted to see if it landed. But Twain's expression hadn't changed.

"If I did do it, you would have a very hard time proving it."

Bixby shrugged. "Every human action leaves a trail. You wrote that, too."

"I suppose I should be offended by your accusation, but I'm not," Twain said. "As a designer and educator, I'm intrigued by this entire scenario and I'm delighted that you shared it with me. However, has it occurred to you that someone might be framing me to distract you from discovering the true killer?"

"No."

"Why not?"

"Because it's ridiculous," Bixby said.

"More ridiculous than going to unprecedented and outrageous lengths to lure someone to a shopping mall to possibly trip down a staircase and perhaps die just to get back at two companies?"

"Yes."

Twain offered him a thin smile. "Not if it's you."

I was startled by the unexpected and clever way that Twain deftly turned the conversation and the accusation against his accuser.

Bixby laughed, then said, "And I came here to let you know what I've done?"

"It would be truly diabolical," Twain said. "Or perhaps you just wanted to ease your guilt by indulging in a little confession, which I hear is good for the soul."

"The problem is," Bixby said, "I don't have a motive for shaming Southfield, killing Crowley, or destroying you."

"That we know of. But everyone leaves a trail, or so I am told." Twain rose from his seat, a signal for us that this discussion was over. We got up, too. He led us to the door. "This has been very interesting and a thrill to actually witness you at work. I can't wait to see how this mystery turns out."

"You'll be the first to know," Bixby said.

"In the meantime, enjoy your game." Twain opened the door for us. Bixby walked out and, as I followed, Twain asked me: "How is he as a golfer, Mr. Nash?"

"He takes big swings, but today he scored a hole in one."

I was very proud of that line. I wasn't sure if I truly believed it, but my delivery was exceptional.

We walked out, climbed into the back seat of the Suburban, and Bixby told the driver to take us back to Buchanan Field. Off we went.

I said, "Did you enjoy that little cat-and-mouse game?"

"Immensely. And you?"

"It was quite a performance from both of you, but I am not sure what it accomplished."

"I got the measure of the man. Didn't you?"

Archibald Twain seemed like the perfect, tailor-made adversary for Edison Bixby, equally matched against him in every way. I couldn't have imagined a better one. But what I said was: "I kept waiting for him to show us his piranha pool or for some tall guy with steel teeth to walk in and serve us canapés. What happens now?"

In a Bond film, it would be an attempt on our lives as we drove to the airport, perhaps by men with machine guns shooting at us from a car, or by an assassin on a motorcycle equipped with flamethrowers, or by a swam of kamikaze bomber drones.

I kept my eye on the rearview mirror and hoped the Suburban was equipped with antiaircraft weapons.

"I've done as much as I can without a badge," Bixby said. "Now we go back to Los Angeles and hope Twain starts trying to wipe away his trail so McGregor can catch him in the act."

"Are you sure she can?"

"Twain is a master of design but he's an amateur at crime. McGregor is very good at what she does."

"But not as good as you," I said.

"That goes without saying."

"And yet you keep saying that about yourself."

He tapped his head. "Must be that pesky bullet."

"Have you ever told McGregor that you think she's a very good detective?"

"That also goes without saying."

"I wouldn't be so sure," I said.

CHAPTER THIRTEEN

The announcement from Bernheim, Sutton & Associates that Bixby believed that Caroline Crowley was murdered naturally generated a lot of press interest. But Bixby declined every interview request, saying the case was in the capable hands of LAPD homicide detective Bridget McGregor. I don't know if she appreciated the plug, or that Bixby was staying out of the case, because she was a no-show at the house that night.

The next morning at 8 a.m., I got a text from Bixby, telling me that I'd be reprising my role as Frank Hellinger and to meet him at the motor court in an hour, dressed for the part. I did as I was told and found him waiting for me, dressed again in his father's suit, beside his Crown Vic. I was sure he was carrying his gun, too, and wished I also had one, just to add that extra frisson of authenticity to my part.

"Good morning, Frank," Bixby said cheerfully.

"Do we have a new case from Miss Priddle?"

"Nope, we're still on the Crowley case."

It was as if the last two days had never happened. "I thought the plan was to let the cops be the cops."

"McGregor is not moving fast enough."

"Have you heard from her?"

"No," he said.

"Then how do you know if she's working fast or not?"

"Because she didn't contact Twain before we did."

I didn't have a lot of sympathy for McGregor, Bixby's former friend-on-the-force with benefits, but he'd set unrealistic expectations for her. "Maybe she's waiting until she actually has some evidence to hit him with."

"She won't ever get it at the rate she's going."

"Not everyone solves cases in a couple of hours," I said. "Or less."

"Then it's a good thing that I do."

He got in the car and so did I. The Crown Vic was both a prop and another piece of wardrobe for us to wear. It really helped me become Frank Hellinger. Bixby started up the engine and it growled. Not a Bugatti growl, but one that was more feral, perhaps even rabid.

"Where are we going?" I asked.

"Back to the Woodland Hills Mall to chase down the construction worker who sabotaged the step." He sped down the driveway and fishtailed out onto the road. It was exciting. I could almost hear the action music cue in my head. What we really needed was our own theme tune.

"The security footage doesn't reveal who he is or where he went."

"Watching the video and stopping there is what mall cops do," Bixby said. "Getting off your ass and investigating is what real cops do." He gave me a look. "What kind of cop is Frank Hellinger?"

I felt every minute of Frank's years on the backstreets and dark alleys of Los Angeles, slogging through the sewage of crime and corruption up to his ankles, and the anger for justice that drove him onward, ever onward.

"If I'm not kicking open doors or kicking ass, I must be dead."

"That's the spirit," Bixby said.

We got to the mall in ten minutes. It wasn't open for business for another hour, but the construction workers renovating the food court were already on the job and probably had been for a few hours.

A chunk of parking lot in front of one of the southeast entrances to the mall had been cordoned off with cyclone fencing that enclosed a construction office trailer, portable restrooms, piles of various building materials, stacks of scaffolding, and other job-related supplies. The gate was open, and a big sign on the fence announced that only authorized personnel were allowed entry, and that all workers, suppliers, subcontractors, and other visitors were required to check in with the guard or the front office.

Bixby parked amid a bunch of pickup trucks and we got out, falling into step behind a line of workers wearing hard hats and yellow vests who were heading to the gate. Each person stopped and presented themselves to the linebacker-size, uniformed African American security guard, who aimed a gun-shaped scanner over their photo ID cards, which dangled from lanyards around their necks. When the guard got a chime from his scanner, he nodded and let the person pass.

When we got to the gate, the guard gave us the once-over and grunted in recognition. He didn't know us. But he knew we were The Man.

The guard said, "What can I do for you, Detectives?"

Bixby said, "I'm Killinger, this is Hellinger. We're investigating Caroline Crowley's death."

"Who is that?"

I stepped up close to the guard. "The woman who fell to her death last weekend in there." I pointed at the mall behind him. "From your sabotaged staircase." I reached out and flipped his ID tag, which had his name and photo. "*Gerald.* That sticky feeling you've got on your hands that you can't wash off, not even with a sandblaster, is her dried blood."

Gerald wasn't rattled. "I don't do any construction. I don't have sticky fingers. All I do is this."

Bixby said, "Spell it out, Gerald. What's the procedure?"

Gerald hiked up his utility belt, which had more crap on it than Batman's. Flashlight. A walkie-talkie. A fat ring of keys. Handcuffs. Baton. Gloves. Zip ties. Purell. Cell phone. A roll of Mentos. A holstered Taser. An empty scanner holster.

"I scan each badge as people go in and out," he said. "If I hear a bell and see a green light on the device, the person is good to go."

"Do you compare their faces with the face that comes up on your screen?"

"Of course I do. That's the job."

He demonstrated it for us with a worker who squeezed past us to check in. We heard the bell from the scanner, then saw the green light and the worker's face show up in black and white on the screen, matching the ID he wore. Gerald made an exaggerated show of checking the face to his screen, but I'd bet he mostly counted on the sound of the bell and rarely compared faces.

"I'm surprised you haven't been replaced by a machine yet," Bixby said. "But you will be."

"What's that supposed to mean?" Gerald said.

I jumped in before Bixby compounded the insult of his uncensored remark. "If your scanner doesn't ding, Gerald, what happens?"

"I send them to the front office for screening. Sometimes it's just a bad chip or something in the badge. But if the light is red, and I get a buzz instead of a ding, it means they were fired or are banned from the property, and I order them to leave."

I said, "Do they listen to you, Gerald?"

"If they don't, I've got this." He patted his Taser with affection.

I gestured to it with a nod. "You ever had to use it?"

"Once or twice," Gerald said, puffing up his chest. He was proud of it. "You ever had to use yours?"

He gestured to my jacket. I didn't have a gun peeking out, but he assumed from the glimpse he'd gotten of Bixby's that I had one, too. The power of suggestion is strong.

"Mine is a .357 Magnum, and yeah, too many times. Same goes for Killinger. On the street, they call us Kill and Hell. Because that's what we do and that's where they go."

Gerald's gaze drifted over to Bixby's face, lingering on that ugly scar, and he knew what I'd said was true, that hell was filled with men who'd crossed us.

"It's rude to stare at my grotesque scar," Bixby said.

"Sorry," Gerald said.

"No, you're not, and now you can't take your eyes off of it, which makes it worse," Bixby said. "Are the workers scanned again on the way out at the end of the day?"

"They are," Gerald said, forcing himself to look anywhere but at Bixby's scar. "It's how they prove they did a day's work."

"What happens if someone goes in but doesn't come out at the end of the day?"

Gerald tapped his radio, obviously grateful to have something else to look at. "I get an alert from the office and we go look for the guy."

"Who is 'we'?" I asked.

"We have four other private security guards on-site."

Bixby asked, "Has that alert ever happened?"

"Once. Turned out the guy fell off some scaffolding and was unconscious. He's still in the hospital."

"Where was he working?"

"Doing some electrical work over by the grand staircase."

I heard a bell, but it wasn't from his little scanner. It was entirely in my head.

"When did that happen?" I asked.

"Last Thursday," Gerald said.

"It was a bad week at the mall."

Bixby gestured to the construction trailer. "Is the boss in?"

"Yeah. His name is Ruiz."

Bixby and I walked past the guard, who never checked our IDs to confirm our identities, but he did make sure we went to the trailer and not into the mall. I banged on the door. A gruff voice inside told us to come in.

We did. A barrel-chested man sat behind a desk covered with blueprints and teetering piles of bulging folders and loose paper, everything stained with coffee-mug rings as if it were his official stamp. The offending coffee mug was gripped in one of his huge hands.

"What can I do for you?" he asked without rising from his creaky seat.

"You could have this office fumigated," Bixby said.

"What did you say?" The man set his mug down hard, stamping another file with a coffee ring.

Bixby stepped up to the desk. "I'm Edison Bixby, with Triax Global Insurance. This is Frank Hellinger. We are investigating Caroline Crowley's death."

Ruiz nodded. "It was a terrible tragedy. It set our work back two days."

I said, "Yikes, that is a tragedy."

That slipped out before I could stop it, and I didn't have Bixby's excuse.

Bixby said, "We need to know if there were any regular workers or subs who were on-site last Friday but haven't been back. Same for Monday or Tuesday. You can call Pretzel Wetzel to check us out."

"You call him Pretzel?"

"Everybody does. He loves it."

"It's all cool. I was told you might be coming." Ruiz turned to his computer, which was on a side table. The keyboard was missing letters and the back of his dusty monitor was covered with fingerprints. He typed on some keys and squinted at the screen. "Five people. Three are subs, two are regulars."

"Can you give us a printout with their names, photos, and contact information?"

"Our printer sucks. If you give me your phone number, I can shoot it all to you now."

Bixby did. Ruiz typed some more, then clicked a mouse that was even dirtier than the keyboard. The pictures, dates of entry and exit, and their personal contact details came in as text messages.

Bixby showed them to me.

Two of the subs were African American, which ruled them out as suspects, since the construction worker on the video appeared to be Caucasian, even though we didn't see his whole face. That left the two regulars, Derek Swale and Mort Dinkins. Either one could be our guy.

Bixby scrolled through the information on Swale and Dinkins, then said, "Swale hasn't been back since Friday, Dinkins since Tuesday. Do you know why?"

Ruiz took a pull from whatever was in his mug. It looked like crude oil. "Swale got food poisoning, and Dinkins bailed for a better-paying gig. He's radioactive to me now."

"Were either of them working on the staircase?"

"Nope. The stairs were done. We just needed to buff and shine 'em before the Eatville opening."

I said, "A crew of crime scene cleaners did it for you instead."

"Yeah, and they were amazing," he said. "I may have them do my family room. Four kids and a dog with an irritable bowel are hell on shag carpet."

"Give the dog Tremvoya," I said.

Ruiz picked up a pen and made a note of it on a blueprint. "Will it cork her up?"

Bixby gestured to me. "It worked for him. Thanks for your help."

"Likewise," Ruiz said, looking at me.

We left the trailer, walked past Gerald, and were nearly at the Crown Vic when I said, "I never took Tremvoya. My character did."

"My mistake," Bixby said. "It's just that you make your characters so real, it's hard to tell you apart from them."

"I wasn't in the commercial. I got replaced the day before you hired me. And it hasn't aired yet."

Bixby shrugged. "Since it's a drug for explosive bowels, and you recommended it, I naturally assumed that you played a character who needed it. Speaking of characters, they call us Kill and Hell?"

I repeated the next line, just as I'd performed it before: "Because that's what we do and that's where they go." Then I slipped out of character again to say: "I thought it added a little nuance to our characters. What did you think?"

"It might have been too subtle."

We got into the car.

"I believe I know what you got out of all that," I said. "You believe that either Swale or Dinkins knocked that guy off the ladder near the stairs so he wouldn't be a witness to the sabotage on Friday and possibly able to ID him after Crowley's fall."

Bixby nodded and started the car. "You're getting the hang of this. Or is it Hellinger who is?"

"I *am* Hellinger."

Bixby backed out of the parking spot. "But you aren't all the guys who need powerful drugs with terrible side effects to control their disgusting afflictions?"

"To a lesser degree. Which one do we see first? Swale or Dinkins?"

Bixby steered us across the parking lot toward Topanga Canyon Boulevard. "The one who got a better gig."

"Dinkins. Why him?"

Bixby pulled into traffic and headed south, toward the freeway.

"Because being a no-show since Friday would be too obvious and I think he was being a smart-ass with his excuse."

I said, "And we both know how much you hate a smart-ass."

Mort Dinkins lived in Reseda, a few blocks north of the Ventura Freeway. Reseda was mostly farmland until the 1950s, when all of the orange groves and lettuce fields were mowed down to make cheap tract homes for returning GIs.

Dinkins owned one of those old, small homes, built by the hundreds. Most of those homes that were still standing showed their age and their cheap construction or had been defaced with awkward second-story additions and ugly garage-into-room conversions that made them look worse. Those remodeled houses were like famous actors ruining their faces with bad plastic surgery in a desperate attempt to pretend they aren't aging, which can't be done.

But Dinkins had put some work into keeping the house looking good, probably on his own. His neighbors on either side had demolished the original homes and put up bloated two-story monstrosities that were crammed onto their small lots. His home reminded me of a guy in the economy section of Spirit Airlines, squished into the middle seat between two morbidly obese people. Because that guy was usually me.

The big houses bulged against his fences and cast shadows over his place. But that wasn't all that was casting a shadow over Dinkins. (That's some foreshadowing, in case you missed it, and since I haven't done it since chapter 1, I think I can get away with doing it now. But I won't keep you in suspense long.)

Parked beside the Ford F-150 pickup in the driveway was a plain-wrap Dodge Charger that screamed "police" just as loudly as Bixby's old Crown Vic.

"It's Five-O," I said as we drove up to the house. "Is that good news or bad news?"

"We won't know until we go to the door." He pulled up to the curb and shut off the engine. He studied the house for a long moment, then said, "You can come along but Hellinger stays in the car."

I gestured to the gun I could see peeking out from under his open jacket. "What about your iron?"

"You mean my gun?"

"Isn't that what I just said?"

"This isn't 1880. I'll leave it and my holster in the gun safe in the trunk."

"You don't want to get into trouble with Johnny Law."

"That's right," he said. "I've got to get you a new slang dictionary."

We got out of the car, he popped the trunk and put his gat inside the safe, and we strode up to the house. Bixby knocked on the door. It was a knock that somehow conveyed both confidence and authority. I'd have to learn how to do that. It was a nice character trait for a cop.

The door was opened by a Hispanic man in his forties, dressed very much like us, who had an LAPD badge clipped to his belt. He immediately recognized Bixby and broke out in a big grin.

"Bix! How are you, man?" He pulled Bixby into a warm hug and clapped him on the back.

"Brilliant, wealthy, and gorgeous."

They parted and the man took a good look at him. "You haven't changed. Except for that nick on your face. Did you cut yourself shaving?"

"Tweezing my eyebrows."

The man let go of Bixby and gave me an amiable smile. "And you are?"

"Not as smart, nearly broke, but handsome in a way that doesn't make you want to strangle me. Wally Nash." I offered him my hand and we shook.

"That makes two of us, man. Abel Calero, LAPD Homicide."

Uh-oh, that wasn't good news.

Abel shifted his attention to Bixby. "Does your insurance company think Dinkins' death was suicide?"

"There's no doubt that it was murder," Bixby said, even though we didn't even know before now that Dinkins had died.

"Glad to hear it," Abel said, "because I'd have a hard time believing a guy could chop his own head off with an axe, unless you told me he did, Bix. Who is his beneficiary? It might help us figure out who did it."

That's when McGregor came up behind Abel and my testicles went into hiding so deep in my body they were stuffing my nose.

"Oh, for fuck's sake," she said when she saw Bixby. "I ought to arrest you for stalking, you psycho."

"Is the body still here?" Bixby started to step into the house, but McGregor gave him a hard shove that nearly knocked him off his feet.

"No, it's not. It was moved hours ago. But this is still a crime scene and you are a civilian. You are not welcome here."

Abel cleared his throat. "Can someone please tell me what's going on?"

She gave Bixby another shove, so now the three of us were standing outside the house, while Abel remained in the doorway.

McGregor said, "This lunatic is following every case I'm on, desperately looking for a way to prove me wrong."

I spoke up in his defense. "It's a coincidence we're here."

Her head whipped around, the full force of her fury aimed at me. It was like opening a hot oven. "Who asked you to speak? And why are you two dressed like cheap accountants?"

Abel said, "Hey, I'm wearing the same coat that he is."

He gestured to me, but McGregor's back was to him and, frankly, she probably didn't even hear him. Her attention was on Bixby again.

He said, not the slightest intimidated: "We were chasing down Mort Dinkins. How did you find him before we did?"

"His girlfriend came over last night and discovered that his head and body were no longer connected. She thought it was a bit suspicious and called the police. She'd last spoken to him yesterday afternoon, when his head was presumably still part of his body. Why are you here? Did you learn about his murder from the news? Or do you have a snitch in Homicide who tells you when I'm assigned to a case?"

She looked back accusingly at Abel, who held up his hands in an expression of innocence and said, "It wasn't me."

Bixby said, "Mort Dinkins was the construction worker who sabotaged the stairs at the Woodland Hills Mall."

She groaned. "Do you have any evidence?"

"He didn't show up for work . . . and he's headless."

Abel said, "Sounds like a good reason to miss work to me."

Bixby went on: "Yesterday Archibald Twain discovered that I know he orchestrated Caroline Crowley's murder. A few hours later, Dinkins lost his head. It clearly means that Twain is spooked and is now desperately covering his tracks."

"Let's assume for one second that I buy that," she said. "How did this criminal mastermind discover that you know?"

"I told him."

McGregor ran her hands through her hair and sighed, a self-calming activity that was having no effect. "So, if what you say is true, Dinkins is dead because of you."

"He's dead because he was part of the plot to kill Crowley."

It was more than she could take. For a moment, I thought she might slug him. "Get out of here, Bixby."

He didn't move. "You have to find the other participants in this plot before Twain has them killed and then has the killer taken out, too."

It sounded to me like the beginning of a vicious circle. Twain could end up hiring killers to kill the killers that he'd hired for the rest of his life. I guess that's one of the problems with not murdering people yourself. Someone else always has leverage against you.

She gave Bixby another hard shove, pushing him farther away from the house. "You're delusional. If you meddle in any of my cases again, I will arrest you for obstruction of justice and 5150 you. Are we clear?"

"Twain is—"

She shoved him again, interrupting him. "Are. We. Clear?"

McGregor was daring him to say another word.

So, he said, "Are you as aroused as I am?"

She slapped him so hard across the face that he nearly suffered the same fate as Dinkins.

"I'll take that as a yes." Bixby held up his hands in surrender before she could strike him again and backed away toward his car.

I did, too.

She stood on the front walk, hands planted on her hips, watching us and shaking with rage, until we drove away.

Bixby smiled at me, his eyes watering and his left cheek red from the slap. "That went well."

I looked at him incredulously. I say that because I quite consciously summoned my best version of that facial expression. "It *did*?"

His smile didn't waver. "Absolutely. It's a big win."

"But Dinkins is dead. He can't tell us anything."

"He's already told us plenty," Bixby said.

"How? We couldn't talk with him. *Because he's headless.*"

"That's as good as a confession, for himself and for Twain. It's in McGregor's hands now."

"I thought it already was. Isn't that what happened when her captain told her to reopen the investigation into Crowley's fall?"

"Yes, but this lights a fire under her and points her at Twain," he said. "He didn't kill Crowley himself. He hired people to carry out specific steps in his plan. It's all about following the money now and you need search warrants for that, which I can't get anymore."

"So you're really going to stay out of it?"

"Twain is panicking. He's not thinking clearly. He's self-destructing. Now she'll be able to take him down. My work is done."

I was glad to hear it, for our sake. I had the feeling that he'd finally pushed McGregor too far. But something she'd said in her fury didn't make sense to me.

"What did she mean when she said that she'd 5150 you?"

"It's a reference to the section of the California Welfare and Institutions Code that allows a person experiencing a severe mental health crisis to be detained and sent to a psychiatric facility against their will."

"Uh-huh," I said. "And you still think this was a win?"

Bixby waved off my concern. "Relax. She threatens to 5150 everybody she's angry with who's been shot in the head."

CHAPTER FOURTEEN

Bixby didn't hear anything from McGregor for the next two days and he didn't reach out to her, either. We had no idea if she was making any progress at all on tying Archibald Twain to the murder plot.

Making things worse, we didn't get a new case from Melissa Priddle to occupy his time or brighten his mood. Either there were no cases at Triax worthy of his attention or she was still mad at him for opening his big mouth at Bernheim, Sutton & Associates.

I was worried that she was mad at me, too, for not stopping Bixby from telling them his theory, or at least smoothing out the damage he'd done. But I didn't believe anybody could have done that, including the ventriloquist and her dummy.

Without any news on the Crowley case, or a new investigation to work on, Bixby retreated into the house. I didn't even see him either morning at his pond or at his amazing breakfast tree.

I had no idea what he was up to and I began to worry that if some work didn't come his way soon, I'd be let go and would have to move into my Hyundai. That was too depressing to even contemplate, especially after enjoying Bixby's guesthouse and his private jet.

So I left a few messages with my agent, pestering him for some auditions, even though I'd ignored his earlier calls. While I waited to hear back, I decided to pop into my acting class in Santa Monica to sharpen my instrument. I surprised myself by chatting up actress LaPorsche Jackson, an African American goddess, and invited her to be my scene partner that night, something I'd never had the guts to do before. She astounded me by agreeing. I realized that my short stint working with Bixby had made me feel like a different man. Or perhaps I was just emulating his self-confidence.

The teacher was an old character actor whose name I won't mention but whose face you'd recognize because he made his living guest-starring on *Vega$*, *Matt Houston*, *T.J. Hooker*, and every other Aaron Spelling production in the 1980s and '90s.

He gave me and LaPorsche the following improv situation to run with: We were two strangers standing in a subway train who were physically jostled together by a sudden lurch. She was a woman thinking of leaving the city because it had crushed her hopes and I was a man who'd just arrived to chase his dreams.

And . . . *action!*

We mimed the train lurching. From the instant our bodies touched, I felt an electric charge. As we engaged in our improvised conversation, our chemistry was off the charts, and that connection didn't end when the scene was over. That's how authentic our performances were. We *became* those strangers on the train.

We left the class almost immediately and I casually suggested that she come home with me, as if her agreement was a given. It turned out that it was. LaPorsche said yes.

The only thing that threatened to break the sensual spell was my Hyundai, which didn't reflect the personality of the confident, bold new man at the wheel. Just as I felt the sensual charge dimming between us, it heated up again when she saw Bixby's unusual house.

LaPorsche was awestruck. We got out of the car and I briefly explained my living situation, emphasizing my decisive role in Bixby's investigations, as I led her through the property to the storybook guesthouse.

She compared me to private eye Thomas Magnum, who lived on author Robin Masters' Hawaii estate and drove a red Ferrari while solving crimes. I liked the comparison. I was a lot like a young Tom Selleck, but I quickly realized that she was thinking of Jay Hernandez, the guy in the *Magnum P.I.* reboot, who didn't have one-tenth of Selleck's charisma or mine. I didn't hold that against her. We enjoyed a night of wild passion, but to go into more detail would be crude and ungentlemanly. Let's just say that we ignited the sheets and were lucky we didn't set off any fire alarms.

Our creative and energetic erotic exertions left us so exhausted that we didn't get up until late morning. We put on bathrobes (yes, the guesthouse had robes, towels, and even slippers for two, like a first-class hotel—now you can see why I hated to leave) and I led her to Bixby's idyllic pond for brunch and a skinny-dip. We were still swimming when I heard:

"Oh, here you are, Wally."

I looked up and saw Bixby standing at the edge of the pond. He was dressed in a vintage bowling shirt, faded jeans, and running shoes and had a happy smile on his face. We definitely had to get a cowbell on the path, I thought, even if I had to string it up myself.

"I'm sorry," I said. "You're usually an early riser. I thought you already had your swim."

"That's not why I'm here," Bixby said, then he did an exaggerated double take, like something out of a bad sitcom. Think Darrin Stephens in *Bewitched*, after Samatha wiggles her nose and turns his favorite easy chair into a walrus. "Wait, is that a woman I see?"

"You don't have to act so surprised."

"She must not be familiar with your oeuvre."

LaPorsche spoke up. "I got familiar with his oeuvre for the first time last night."

"I'm referring to his body of work," Bixby said.

"That's what I was talking about," she said. "And it worked just fine."

I gave her a look. I was glad she rose to my defense, but I thought it had been pretty spectacular. "Just fine?"

She rose from the water, stark naked and totally unabashed, and stood in front of him, practically striking a pose. "I'm LaPorsche."

"That's funny," Bixby said, looking at her up and down and up again. "I have three LaPorsches. And they're all black, too."

Oh shit, I thought. What a racist, horrible thing to say. How would I smooth over *that*? I scampered naked out of the water, grabbed my bathrobe, and brought LaPorsche hers as I said, "Bixby means he likes the color black, especially on German sports cars, and was not implying, even in jest, that he owns women, or believes that any human being can ever be owned. It was a compliment."

But LaPorsche wasn't listening. She took the bathrobe from me and only covered herself loosely with it, leaving it gaping open. "You like black Porsches?"

Was she flirting with him?

"The color doesn't matter," he said. "It's what's under the hood. I enjoy racing them hard and fast around the track."

Was he flirting back with her?

"Speed is fine, as long as there are lots of twists and turns before the finish line . . ." She gave him a mischievous smile.

They were *definitely* flirting. And I knew if I didn't do something about it, they'd be on the ground in sixty seconds. I cinched my bathrobe tight around me and stepped between them.

"NASCAR is my jam, too. Big fan," I said. "I idolized Dale Earnhardt when I was a kid. I painted a big #3 on my Corolla. Is there anything else, Bixby?"

They both stared at me.

He said, "Yes, we have a case and it's urgent. I'll meet you in front of the house in fifteen minutes." Bixby turned to her. "Nice to LaMeet you, LaPorsche."

"Likewise," she said.

Bixby left. She watched him go. Only then did she draw her bathrobe closed and tie it shut. She seemed oddly pleased with herself.

I shook my head sadly. "Poor man. He'd be lost on a case without my wise counsel."

I hurried us back to the guesthouse, where I quickly got dressed while she remained in the living room.

"I'm terribly sorry for the rushed goodbye and not being able to drive you back to the theater," I said, once I was fully dressed and ready to go to work. "It's not my style at all. But duty calls. Do you mind calling an Uber?"

"No worries, Wally. We're good."

"Maybe we could do this again sometime?"

She took a pen off the kitchen table, scribbled something on a napkin, and handed it to me. Her name and phone number were on it.

Yes!

"Here's my number. Give it to Bixby," she said. "Tell him to call me next time he's in the mood to race a LaPorsche."

WTF? How could she say that to me after our epic erotic encounter?

I said, "I'm pretty sure he was talking strictly about his cars."

LaPorsche gave me a chaste kiss on the cheek. "You're sweet, Wally, and last night was nice. But after just *talking* to that man, I'm gonna need a cold shower. See you around."

She dropped the bathrobe into a clump on the floor and padded naked into the bathroom. I watched her go, realizing it would be the last time I'd have that view again, then I went outside to meet Bixby, who was waiting for me beside his '59 Caddy.

"Let me guess, she's an actress."

"We're in the same acting class, where we hone our skills. She was my scene partner last night." It already seemed like a distant memory. I got into the car and slammed the door. He got in and we drove out.

"Were the scenes from *Basic Instinct*?"

"Very funny. It was an improv exercise. We were two strangers on a subway train. We had an immediate spark that couldn't be denied."

"So why was she flirting with me?"

"Why were you flirting with her?" I snapped at him.

"Because I can't help myself," he said. "Bullet wound."

"You can't use that excuse for all your rude behavior."

"You're right," Bixby said. "You're supposed to excuse it for me."

"She was only briefly attracted to you because you're a zillionaire with a big house. I can't compete with that."

He steered us north on Topanga, toward the San Fernando Valley. "Then she's not worthy of you."

I gave him a look to see if he was serious or not. It was hard to tell. "You really think so?"

"She's an opportunist. You want someone who appreciates you for who you are, and isn't simply attracted to someone who is rich, gorgeous, and brilliant."

"You say that as if I am not any of those things."

"You aren't," he said.

Did that slip out before he could stop himself? I didn't see any cringe of embarrassment or regret on his face. But then again, I never had when any of his other slips had happened.

Whether his remark was intentional or not, I didn't need to be reminded of any more of my shortcomings. I'd been humiliated enough for one day, so I changed the subject. "What's the case? And why is it so urgent?"

He had a big smile on his face. I suddenly realized that this was the happiest I'd seen him in days, and not because he'd nearly stolen a woman away from me.

"It's from McGregor. Another murder landed in her lap yesterday and she needs my help."

"She couldn't solve it?"

"On the contrary, it's open and shut and the killer is in custody."

I was confused. "Then what does she need you for?"

"To prove that the man that she arrested is innocent."

That only confused me more.

As we headed east on the freeway toward downtown, he explained that a lawyer named Alan Rook was murdered in his firm's office, in broad daylight, and that the killer was retired LAPD Detective Art Malcolm, who'd been a mentor to both him and McGregor.

When I asked for more details, he told me he didn't have any and that we'd learn them together in a meeting with Malcolm at Men's Central Jail, which was where we were heading.

The Men's Central Jail was located in downtown Los Angeles and was built in 1963 to hold up to 3,300 inmates awaiting trial. Over a decade later, an addition to the jail expanded the hold capacity to almost twice as many men. But by 2025, it was a crumbling, overcrowded hellhole that held 19,000 men, three times as many as it was designed for. Men slept on the floors because there weren't enough beds. Viruses raged within its walls. Sewage backed up in its aging pipes. It was ranked as one of the worst jails in the nation and had been slated for closure for years. But it still stood, and work had yet to begin on a new facility to take its place. As a result, little or no money was being spent on upkeep. It made a Soviet gulag seem like a resort property by comparison.

I was not looking forward to our visit.

At the jail, we presented our ID to the officials, then went through a security scan that was just like going to LAX for a flight to anywhere, except we were both patted down. At least we weren't strip-searched and nobody explored our body cavities for cell phones or drugs, which somehow were frequently smuggled into the cells.

After being cleared, we had to be buzzed through several more gated checkpoints by deputies as we moved into progressively more restricted areas of the jail. I couldn't see the prisoners in their cells, but I could hear the muffled rumbling of their voices from where they were crammed tightly together, deep inside somewhere. And despite all of the cleansers on the floors, and fans and air filters in the place, I could smell them, too. The odor was thick, coming out of the vents like sludge, and reeked of sweat, shit, and despair.

The walls were gray, the harsh fluorescent lights making them appear a sickly green or beige, a paint color that could be called institutional vomit. The floors were the standard scuffed linoleum, so standard that they might even have been delivered pre-scuffed. As an actor, I noticed the security cameras everywhere and was hyperaware that we had an audience watching us. If I picked my nose, the security staff of the entire jail would know about it, and probably search my nostril for contraband.

We finally ended up in a corridor where McGregor stood waiting for us, an iPad under one arm, on the other side of the gate. It was clear from her body language, and her simmering glare, that she had conflicting emotions about seeing Bixby again.

As an actor, adept at understanding character, I knew that she resented herself for needing his help but also resented him for casting doubt on her investigation of Crowley's fatal fall . . . and showing up at the Dinkins house. Those were complicated emotions to play at once, and I made a mental note of her posture to use myself in a role someday.

McGregor didn't greet us, or even acknowledge that I was there. She simply launched into what she had to say to Bixby. "They put Malcolm in solitary lockup for his own protection. He made a lot of enemies in his day and some of them could be repeat offenders who are in here now."

"I'll bail him out," Bixby said. "When's the arraignment?"

"This afternoon," she said, "but considering the brazen and brutal nature of the crime, and that Malcolm is an ex-cop, the bail will be astronomical."

"I'm astronomically rich."

"He's astronomically guilty."

"If that's true," Bixby said, "then why did you call me for help?"

"Because I can't believe he did it, even though the evidence is overwhelming."

"You aren't worried about me making you look bad?"

That was blunt. I wasn't sure if the coarse remark was the result of his brain injury, or if he was needling her, or if he just wanted to know what he was getting himself into.

"I need to be able to live with myself if I put Art Malcolm away," she said, surprising me with her candor. "If you can't prove him innocent, then I won't have any doubts and neither will anybody else."

There was a compliment for Bixby buried in there, an acknowledgment that he was more skilled than her, and it couldn't have been easy for her to admit that to him or to herself. Perhaps she was self-conscious about being so nakedly honest with her answer, because now she seemed to notice I was there and didn't like it.

"This isn't an insurance case," she said to Bixby. "Why is Nash here?"

That was a good question and I didn't know the answer, either. But at least she'd called me by my name. That was progress.

"For an objective point of view on this case," Bixby said. "He's the only one of us who will have one."

"He's also the only one of us who has never worn a badge."

As she walked ahead, leading us down the corridor to the meeting room, I said to Bixby, "That's not entirely true. I was LAPD Detective Frank Hellinger on *Bosch*."

"Ah, so that's where you got his name."

"It's the name that I gave him. I felt that being identified in the script only as 'Detective #2' didn't really capture his essence, or his experience on the mean streets that I silently conveyed in the background of each squad room scene I was in."

McGregor paused outside the door and looked at me. "Be silent in the background this time, too."

She opened the door and we went into a windowless room, where a pale, balding, middle-aged man in an orange jumpsuit slouched in a metal seat, his uncuffed hands clasped on his round belly, which belied how thin he was everywhere else. Former detective Art Malcolm had the sagging skin of someone who'd lost a lot of weight very fast. My guess was he was on Ozempic and that his belly was all the body fat he still had left after a few months of injecting himself. I wondered how obese he'd been before. His demeanor brightened as soon as he saw Bixby and he straightened up in his hard seat, which was bolted to the floor.

"Thank God you came, Bixby. If anybody can get me out of this, it's you." Malcolm looked past Bixby to me. "Who is he?"

"Wally Nash. My apologist."

"Your *what*?"

"Ever since I got shot in the face, I say offensive things."

"Isn't that how you got shot in the face?"

Bixby sat down across the metal table from Malcolm and so did I. McGregor stood behind us in a corner, her arms crossed judgmentally under her breasts.

Bixby said, "You've aged a lot since I last saw you, Art."

I quickly added, "He means you seem so much wiser."

"If Art was wiser," Bixby said, "he wouldn't be in here."

I looked sympathetically at Malcolm. "That's Bixby's way of saying that he feels terrible that you're in jail and that he will do whatever he can to get you out. But first, he needs to know your story."

Actually, I was the one eager to know it and to fulfill my responsibility as the one objective observer in the room. I could feel McGregor's furious gaze on my back, as if she were shooting laser beams from her eyes.

Malcolm directed his answer to Bixby. "Do you remember what happened to my wife?"

"Sally took a bus to Las Vegas with her friends. The bus went off the road and rolled over a few times, flattening it, killing the driver, and leaving Sally severely injured." He recounted the facts dispassionately, like he was reading about a stranger in the newspaper and not talking about the beloved wife of somebody close to him.

"That's right." Malcolm didn't seem put off by the coldness of Bixby's answer. Maybe he appreciated his former apprentice setting a "just the facts" tone to their discussion to keep emotions in check. "We later learned the driver had been working twenty hours straight without sleep and proper maintenance hadn't been done on the bus. So all of the injured passengers got together, hired a lawyer, and sued the bus company, which settled with us the day before trial. We each got $500,000 after the attorney's cut."

"Seems low," Bixby said.

"It did to me, too. But our attorney, Alan Rook, told us that's because the bus company is small and underinsured, so we were lucky to get what we got. Except when we first received our check, it bounced. I raised hell with Rook. He gave me some complicated excuse that went over my head, apologized up and down, and issued a new check, which cleared."

"That story doesn't make sense," Bixby said. "Law firms are obligated to place settlement funds in a client trust account. The only disbursements are to clients. The account can't be overdrawn."

"That bothered me, too, even though my wife got all of her money and so did the others. I couldn't let it go. Once a cop, always a cop."

"I know the feeling," Bixby said.

"Me too," I said.

They both gave me a look, but they didn't understand how deeply an actor gets into character. I carry them all with me, including Hellinger.

Malcolm shifted his gaze back to Bixby. "I dug into it and found out the settlement was actually higher than Rook told us. He ripped us off. I got the evidence, too, from a guilt-ridden guy at the bus company. So I marched into Rook's office yesterday at lunch to confront the asshole. I found him in their law library on the fifteenth floor and I gave it to him."

McGregor said, "You mean you stabbed him twice with a letter opener, left it in his back, and stormed out of the office."

Malcolm looked at her, anger and hurt on his face. I took a mental photo for future acting reference.

"Of course not," he said. "How stupid do you think I am, Bridget? Do you really believe I'd kill a guy in broad daylight inside his law firm?"

"You were in a blind rage," she said. "You weren't thinking at all."

"He was alive and still a smug asshole when I left him in that fancy room."

Bixby asked, "How far did you get before Rook's body was discovered?"

"The security guard was waiting for me in the lobby with his gun drawn when I stepped out of the elevator. He was shaking so much I was afraid he'd shoot me by accident."

"So about five minutes later, considering you were fifteen floors up," Bixby said. "Were there any witnesses who saw the stabbing?"

McGregor answered for him. "No, but two people saw Malcolm go into the library, heard the argument, and then saw him rush out in a rage. Nobody else could have possibly done it. He was the only one in the room with Rook."

Bixby considered this, then asked her: "Do you have the crime scene photos?"

McGregor stepped forward and placed her iPad on the table. The image on the screen showed a man face down on the floor, in a puddle of his own blood, with a letter opener sticking out of his back. He was lying in an entirely glass-walled room with freestanding bookcases and a table with a computer monitor on top of it. The room looked cool.

She said, "He was stabbed in the chest and back, where the letter opener got stuck in his spine."

Bixby used his fingers on the screen to zoom in on the dead man's back. "Where did the letter opener come from?"

"It's part of a matching desk set that's in every lawyer's office," she said. "Only one letter opener is missing. It's from the office of a lawyer who is on vacation in Barbados."

"What was Rook doing in the library?"

I said, "That doesn't look like any law library I've seen before. It's a glass cube."

"They call it 'the library,'" McGregor said, "but the lawbooks are only for show, since everything is digital now. It's primarily used as a conference room."

"You're wrong," Bixby said. "The library's primary use is as an architectural art piece to influence clients. A law library is a symbol that conveys wisdom, professionalism, and dedication, while the high-tech nature of the room, a glass cube, demonstrates the firm is on the cutting edge."

"Thank you for correcting me," McGregor said bitterly. "It's deeply appreciated."

Something didn't make sense to me. "The room is all glass. Why didn't anybody see the murder?"

McGregor looked at me like it was the dumbest question she'd ever heard. "It's smart glass. It becomes opaque with the touch of a button, which is what Rook did the instant Malcolm came in."

Malcolm nodded. "That's right."

Bixby said, "I need to see the law firm's offices."

I said, "Because the building is always an accomplice."

McGregor glared at me for that, then turned to Bixby. "That's not a problem. The library has been sealed and everybody who was in the office yesterday is waiting to see us."

Bixby got up. He was done there. So I got up, too.

Malcolm looked at him imploringly. "I know how bad this seems, Bixby. But I'm telling you, I didn't do it."

"I believe you," Bixby said.

"I want to," McGregor said.

"Me too," I added.

Malcolm met my eyes. "That's a great comfort."

He was being sarcastic, but I still think that deep down he appreciated my honesty and compassion. I was someone objective, like a juror might be. But the truth was, I sided with McGregor. From what I'd heard, I believed Art Malcolm was probably guilty.

We stepped outside into the corridor. McGregor closed the heavy steel door behind us and immediately turned to Bixby. "You'll be dealing with two open-and-shut murders if Fartman opens his mouth again in an interrogation."

"Is that what it was? An interrogation?" Bixby said. "I thought we were simply listening to Art's side of the story. Did the details change in his retelling?"

"No, but his story sounds even weaker now than the first time I heard it. He was practically caught red-handed."

I thought about that and channeled my inner Hellinger. "Were his prints on the letter opener?"

"He's an ex-cop," she said to me. "He's not that stupid."

"Even in a blind rage?"

"He obviously wiped it afterwards with his shirttail or sleeve in the instant of clarity after he realized what he'd done."

"If you're right, why bother?" I said, putting myself in his situation. "He was apprehended five minutes later."

"Because Art Malcolm is a lot smarter than you are. He knew the lack of fingerprints creates a scintilla of doubt. If Bixby and I didn't know him, we wouldn't be having this conversation. Nobody would. They'd just arrest Malcolm and rejoice in the certain conviction."

Bixby said, "Then he's lucky to have us, isn't he?"

I asked, "Was there a scintilla of blood on his hands or clothes?"

"No," she said.

"Then he was already lucky," I said, very proud of my line.

"Or he's innocent," Bixby said, and the three of us headed down the corridor to the first of many security gates on our way out of the jail.

I waited until we were on the street, and McGregor had gone to her car, before I confronted Bixby.

"You did it again."

"Did what?"

"You stepped on my line," I said. "It was the perfect act out and you had to take it."

Bixby started walking toward the municipal parking lot that was reserved for jail visitors. "Act out?"

I kept pace with him. "The last line of dialogue before the commercial break. The 'David Caruso takes off his glasses' moment. It was also the perfect out for leaving the jail. The 'or he's innocent' that you interjected was implied in what I said—that's what gave my line its punch. Or it did, until you ruined the moment. To put it another way, I'd already taken off my sunglasses. The scene was over. You taking off your glasses, too, made you look silly and, frankly, a bit pathetic."

"Do you go through life as if you're on camera?"

Yes, I did. I still do. But I couldn't say that, or I would have sounded crazy. "I was on camera in there. There were cameras all over the jail. You can bet all the deputies were watching and listening."

He looked at me incredulously. "You were performing for the deputies in the security office?"

"An audience is an audience," I said. "What happened to 'the world is a stage and everybody is an actor'?"

He considered that for a moment. "Well, when you put it like that, my line was better. You need to up your act-out game. Do you think Art Malcolm stabbed Alan Rook?"

"Yes, I do."

"Why?"

"I can't see any other explanation."

"That's a stupid reason," he said.

"I can't think of a better one."

"Because you're trying to think like a detective, not an actor. Put logic and evidence aside. Is he telling the truth?"

I thought about Malcolm's performance in the room and asked myself whether I'd sensed a single forced emotion or false reaction. I didn't. Only a professional actor could have given a performance that convincing.

On the other hand, I'd learned from watching *Criminal Minds* and a thousand *Law & Order* episodes that sociopathic killers are often exceptional actors who've never had any training in the craft.

But did I believe that Art Malcolm, who'd spent his career chasing criminals, had a sociopathic killer's innate acting chops?

"I believe him," I said. "But reason tells me I shouldn't."

"Reason is highly overrated," Bixby said.

CHAPTER FIFTEEN

The law offices of Ramsford, Wilson & DeAndrea were in Century City, once a part of the Twentieth Century Fox Studios back lot that had been sold off in the early 1960s and developed as a collection of office towers to make up for the staggering losses of *Hello Dolly*, *Cleopatra*, and a string of other bombs. In 1987, one of the buildings was famously featured in *Die Hard*, in essence turning the office park into a Hollywood back lot once again, only now one with tenants and shops.

To be fair, by then the entire city of Los Angeles was just a big studio back lot. Almost every major street had been in a TV show or movie, either as LA or dressed up to be somewhere else, from Paris to Afghanistan. That's one reason the city was heaven for actors. You were literally living the dream, just by being there, even if you were unknown and not making dream money.

The law firm was on the fifteenth floor of one of the few remaining original Century City towers from fifty or sixty years ago that hadn't been demolished yet to make way for a newer, sleeker, taller high-rise. But this building, which once had spectacular views of Santa Monica Bay, now faced reflections of itself in the shiny cladding of other towers.

Bixby and I entered the firm's waiting room, where a young redheaded receptionist acted as gatekeeper to the set of glass doors to her right that led to the lawyers' individual offices. Those offices were off a hallway that wrapped around the library cube like a horseshoe.

McGregor stood in front of the receptionist's desk. Once again, she didn't bother with the niceties of a greeting. "I asked everyone who was here at the time of the murder to be here again today and everyone who was gone then to stay away. This is the crime scene as it was when Malcolm was here." She gestured to the redhead at the desk. "This is Sharon, the receptionist. There's no need for you to introduce yourself, Bixby. Everybody here already knows who you are."

I said, "What about me?"

"Nobody here cares who you are."

Bixby smiled at Sharon. "Tell me what you saw."

"Art Malcolm stormed in with this big file stuffed with papers under his arm and demanded to see Alan Rook. I said I'd see if he was in, but Malcolm just marched right past me through the doors."

Bixby took a step toward the doorway and glanced at the library. The glass was clear. We could see a glass door, identified by the handles, on the left and right side of the cube, but none on either end. He turned back to Sharon. "Was the library's glass transparent at the time?"

"Yes. So Malcolm could see that Alan was alone in there working and went right for him."

"Which door did Malcolm use?"

"The one to the left," she said. "He nearly mowed down Brooke Halsey as she stepped out of her office. He pushed open the door to the library and Alan immediately fogged the room."

It must have made the library look like an enormous ice cube.

Bixby asked, "What happened after that?"

"I could hear loud screaming and yelling. I'm sure that everybody could. Charles buzzed me to ask what was going on and I told him."

"Who is Charles?"

"Charles Ramsford," she said. "He's one of the two senior partners."

"Where is his office?"

She got up from behind her desk, went to the doorway, and pointed to the right of the library. "Corner office on the right. You can't see it when the glass is fogged because it's behind the library. He was in a meeting there with Marcus Wilson, another partner."

"Okay, then what happened?"

Sharon remained standing. "I went back to work. About five minutes later, Malcolm rushed out of these doors, red-faced and crazy-looking, and almost ran to the elevator. I was curious what all the yelling was about, so once he got into the elevator and the doors closed, I went straight to the library to ask Alan what—"

"Hold on," Bixby interrupted. "Why did you wait until Malcolm stepped into the elevator to go into the library?"

"I didn't want Malcolm to know we could hear the argument or that any of us cared about his temper tantrum. I didn't know it was much worse than that . . ." She suddenly stopped, as if her throat had run dry. "I took one look at Alan, ran back to my desk, and called security."

"Not 911?"

"It was obvious he was dead," she said. "And I didn't want his killer to get away."

I said, "You didn't scream when you saw the body?"

She gave me a withering look. "Why would I do that? Just because all the dumb bimbos in the movies do it?"

Yes. But I didn't say that. I just shrugged.

She looked at McGregor. "How come we never see men scream in a movie when they see a dead body? Am I right?"

McGregor nodded in solidarity. "I hate it, especially since men are such wusses. We see so much more blood in our lives than they do. Imagine if one of them had to give birth . . ."

"Or have a period? *Then* you'd hear some screaming."

They both shook their heads. It was true. The idea of either one gave me the willies.

Bixby said, "I'm going to talk with Brooke Halsey. You two can keep chatting about your uteruses."

"Uteri," Sharon corrected him.

Bixby, McGregor, and I went through the doorway and walked to the first office to the left of the library. He knocked on the half-open door to the office, which we could see was orderly and neat. And so was Brooke Halsey, a woman in her forties who was as stiff and pressed as her suit. She slipped an N95 mask over her nose and mouth.

"Please forgive the mask," she said as she stepped around the desk to greet us. "I can't risk getting COVID or anything else. I have court dates."

"No need to apologize," Bixby said.

"I'm glad to help any way I can, but frankly, Mr. Bixby, I'm surprised your expertise is needed here. It's not a puzzling case."

Halsey gestured to her guest chairs, and we all sat down. She squirted some Purell on her hands from a dispenser on her desk, then offered it to Bixby. "*E. coli* is everywhere."

"So are the Black Death, Ebola, and gingivitis." He helped himself to a dollop, then set the dispenser down on a stack of torn envelopes on her desk. She appeared to be offended, so it was Wally Nash to the rescue.

"In other words, you can never be too safe, so we appreciate this." I picked up the Purell and had a squirt myself. But Halsey didn't appear to be mollified by my charm.

Bixby said, "Did you hear the argument?"

"Nothing I could make out, but I could feel the rage in the killer's voice," she said. "I'm feeling some of that rage now myself."

"Should I be worried?" Bixby gestured with a nod to the shiny letter opener on the far corner of her blotter.

"I'm not angry at you for ridiculing my good hygiene but at Alan, for what he did."

"Dying?"

"Stealing money from our clients," she said. "We didn't know anything about it until his gruesome murder."

Bixby cocked his head. "How is that possible? Aren't there rigorous safeguards in place to protect your client trust accounts?"

"Obviously not rigorous enough. We're deeply ashamed. We're hiring an outside accounting firm to dig deep into all of this."

Bixby put his hands on the armrests of his chair, as if he was about to get up. I stood up first.

"The digging has already started," I said. "On Alan Rook's grave."

I could almost hear the act-out music sting. I looked at Bixby, who remained seated. So did everybody else. That was one way to beat me. Point for him. After an awkward moment, I sat down.

Bixby looked at Brooke Halsey and continued. "How can you be sure that Alan Rook acted alone and that other people at the firm weren't involved?"

"Alan had his personal demons, a substance abuse problem, to be specific, that led to some bad decisions. He went into rehab for six months and was back here on a probationary basis. We thought he was a new man. Clearly, he wasn't."

"That doesn't answer my question," he said.

"I'm confident he acted alone."

"Or are you relieved that dead men can't talk?" Bixby got up after his great line. So did I and, thinking fast, I said to him:

"Time to dust off our Ouija board."

Bixby scowled. Point for me.

McGregor gave me a look and, once we were in the hall outside the library, she said to Bixby: "What the hell is wrong with you two?"

We looked at each other innocently, then back at her.

Bixby said, "What do you mean?"

"Whatever it is, just stop it. Both of you. It's not funny."

"Murder never is." Bixby looked at me, daring me to try to best his line. But with McGregor glaring at me, I couldn't think of a better act out and was afraid I might get shot. Point for Bixby.

McGregor turned to him. "What next?"

"I want to see the two partners."

"Ramsford and Wilson. They were together in Ramsford's office when the murder happened, so they are waiting there for us now."

We walked down the hall and around the left corner of the library to Ramsford's office, which was in the opposite corner of the floor and had a commanding view of the next building and nothing else.

As we approached the open door, we could see two gray-haired men in expensive tailored three-piece suits waiting inside. They were the very definition of wise old men, just the sort of fellows you'd want if you were looking for a lawyer. One was black and sat in a guest chair, and the other was white, had a thick gold pinkie ring that would break most pinkies, and sat behind a huge desk.

McGregor said to us: "Charles Ramsford is the man at the desk. Marcus Wilson is the one in the guest chair."

Wilson didn't bother to stand, but he said, "I need to alert you that we are recording this conversation."

Both men held up their phones, the recording apps visible on their screens, then set them down again.

Bixby addressed both men: "Are you worried about ending up in court?"

"On the contrary," Wilson said. "That's our happy place."

Ramsford picked up his letter opener and pointed it at Bixby. "And this is a great opportunity. You're a lawyer's dream."

"I think you mean a prosecutor's," Bixby said.

"In your brief return to the LAPD after you were shot, there were seven lawsuits filed against the department arising from your sexist, racist, biased, and slanderous comments and offensive conduct. The city had to pay millions in legal settlements."

Wilson added, "I'm stunned they were willing to accept the liability of having you back."

Bixby glanced between them both. "You're hoping I'll say or do something actionable today and make you some money?"

Ramsford leaned back in his desk chair. "The odds are highly in our favor."

"Speaking of favors," Bixby said, "Art Malcolm did you a big one."

"What are you suggesting?" Wilson asked, and held up his phone again. "And be sure to speak slowly and clearly for the recording."

"I can't believe that anybody, especially a guy already on probation with the firm, could steal from the client trust accounts without you two knowing about it. But now that Rook is dead, you can blame it all on him and claim ignorance."

Ramsford smiled and wagged his letter opener at Wilson. "Ka-ching!"

Wilson said to Bixby: "Are you accusing us of engaging in a conspiracy to embezzle from our clients?"

I spoke up sharply before Bixby could. "Don't answer that."

Wilson and Ramsford seemed to notice me for the first time, as if I'd just whipped off my invisibility cloak. I didn't want Bixby replying without thinking first, since it might get him sued.

Ramsford asked, "Who are you?"

"Wally Nash."

He set down his letter opener and picked up a pen. "Wally. Hmm. Is that short for Walter? Wallace? Wallaby? We'll need to know later for our subpoena."

Wallaby—that was cute.

Bixby said, "Where were you when the murder happened?"

Ramsford set down his pen. "We were in this office, discussing the status of various cases."

"Did you two hear the argument between Rook and Malcolm?"

Wilson answered for them: "Not the exact words, just the tenor of them . . . and it wasn't coming from Alan."

"How do you know?"

"He avoided conflict."

"And he was a lawyer?" Bixby asked, incredulous.

"He knew when to remain silent."

"So you never actually saw Malcolm enter or leave the library?"

Ramsford said, "We didn't learn what happened until after Sharon discovered the body."

"Did you go take a look?"

"Of course we did."

"Which door did you use to go into the library?"

"The one on our side," Wilson said. "It's the closest."

So it was the one on the right, as opposed to the one on the left, which was opposite Brooke Halsey's office.

Bixby said, "And Malcolm and Sharon used the one on the other side, which you can't see from here in the corner when the library's glass is fogged."

"I assume so, since that would be the closest to them," Wilson said, "but we wouldn't know, because our door was closed."

Bixby abruptly turned and went out the door without a word. McGregor and I hurried to follow. He went down the hall and stopped at the office that was across from the door on the right side of the library. He opened the office door without knocking. It was furnished but unoccupied.

"Who does this office belong to?"

"The vacationing lawyer," McGregor said. "It was empty the day Malcolm was here."

"Where do you think Malcolm got the letter opener he used to kill Rook?"

"From Rook," McGregor said.

"Why did Rook have it?"

"Rook must have borrowed it from this office because he didn't have his own," McGregor said. "He was using the library as his office until his probation was over."

I said, "It's over now."

They both looked at me. McGregor said, "Thank you for that stunning insight."

But it was a point for me. Another great TV line. And Bixby couldn't top it. Instead, he went into the library. It was like being in an alien planet's zoo display of human lawyers at work, except there weren't any in there anymore. We were surrounded by glass walls, a few freestanding bookcases with lawbooks on the shelves, and a big table with a couple of Herman Miller office chairs arrayed around it. Legal briefs, open lawbooks, yellow legal pads covered with handwriting, a bottle of water, and a laptop were on the table. There was also a remote control, which I assumed was for operating the lights and fogging the glass.

Oh, and there was a huge bloodstain on the floor.

McGregor watched as Bixby walked around the perimeter of the cube, regarded the two doors, and then nodded to himself.

"Art Malcolm is innocent."

McGregor put her hands on her hips. "How do you know?"

"Bring everyone in and I will explain."

"You always have to make a show out of it." She raised her head and shouted, "Can everyone please come in here."

"I could have done that," Bixby said.

A still-masked Brooke Halsey and Sharon the Receptionist came in from the door on the left while Charles Ramsford and Marcus Wilson came in from the door on the right. Bixby looked at the two men, who were still clutching their phones.

"Are you recording this?"

"Absolutely," Ramsford said.

"Good. It might save me from having to testify at the trial."

Wilson said, "What trial?"

"The murder trial, of course," Bixby said. "Spoiler alert: Art Malcolm didn't kill Alan Rook."

Halsey shook her head emphatically. "That's impossible."

"Determining who committed the murder is a spatial problem, defined by this library, the two entrances to it, the offices and corridor that surround it, and the one entrance to this whole suite of offices, which is the doorway to the right of the receptionist."

"I'm also a paralegal," Sharon said, "and a massage therapist."

Bixby ignored her comment and pressed on. "The space in here, and in the outer office, created limitations on what could be done. It also created an affordance problem."

Sharon said, "You think Malcolm was a hit man?"

"No. What gave you that idea?"

"You said someone had to be able to afford it."

"I was referring to the different things an object can potentially *do*, what actions it *affords*," Bixby said. "A letter opener affords opening envelopes. But it has other affordances. Like tightening a screw, cleaning your nails, stirring your coffee—"

"Hopefully after cleaning it first," Halsey interrupted, with a shudder.

"Or it can be used as a weapon," he continued. "Once I considered the issues of space and affordances, it then came down to one basic fact: We are all designers. How we organize our personal space reflects everything about us. The solution to the mystery was the letter opener lodged in Rook's spine. That explained everything."

McGregor said, "I wish you would already. Speed it up."

But he wasn't going to be rushed. He was enjoying this.

"It didn't make much sense that someone would stab Rook in the chest, and then stab him in the back. The man was already dead. And we know it couldn't have been the other way around, because the letter opener was stuck in a vertebra. That left only one logical conclusion: More than one person stabbed Alan Rook. And it's someone in this room. You all had motive. You all knew about Rook lying to clients about the true amount of settlements because you were in on it, too."

Ramsford glanced at Wilson. "Are you getting all this defamation?"

Wilson nodded. "Every litigious word."

"When Malcolm came in here, and loudly confronted Rook with his evidence, you all heard every word, just like you heard McGregor call you in here."

Wilson said, "Because she shouted."

"And our doors were open," Brooke Halsey added.

Bixby waved away their objections. "You knew Rook was toast. When Malcolm stormed out, that gave you a split-second opportunity to save yourselves and the firm from going down with him and you took it." He looked at Halsey. "You grabbed your letter opener, the only object on your desk that afforded murder, and you rushed in here. What you didn't know was that Ramsford had the same idea and the same lack of objects within immediate reach that could be used as a weapon."

He walked over to Charles Ramsford and spoke right into his phone: "You also grabbed your letter opener. You arrived in here at the same instant that Brooke did. There wasn't time for words, just a shared glance, a silent agreement. You both stabbed Rook."

Bixby turned back to Halsey. "You stabbed him in the chest and Ramsford stabbed him in the back. Then you practically dived back into your office across the hall."

He looked back at Ramsford. "But you couldn't get your letter opener out of Rook—it was stuck in his spine. So you left it and dashed out an instant before Sharon came in. You snatched the letter opener from the empty office across the hall and returned to your desk."

He looked back at Halsey. "You cleaned your letter opener with hand sanitizer, hid the bloody tissues somewhere, and placed the murder weapon on your blotter in plain view for the police to see when they arrived."

Halsey said, "You can't prove any of that wild story."

"Your desk confessed to it," Bixby said.

Her eyebrows shot up and nearly flew off her face. "My desk? Did it talk to you, Bixby? Precisely how long have you been you hearing voices from inanimate objects?"

"Since he was shot in the head," Marcus Wilson declared. "He's neurologically damaged—anybody looking at that hole in his face can see that. So will any judge or jury. Nothing he says is credible."

Bixby ignored their comments and kept his gaze fixed on Halsey. "All the envelopes on your desk today have been torn open. That's because even though your letter opener was thoroughly cleaned, you're so afraid of germs that you still can't bring yourself to touch it. But I'm sure it hasn't been cleaned thoroughly enough. Our forensics team is the best in the nation."

She suddenly looked very ill.

Ramsford saw it, too. "Even if that's true, which it's not, you have no evidence whatsoever that the letter opener in Alan's back was mine."

Bixby said, "I don't need any because I have an eyewitness."

Wilson declared, "I'll vouch that Charles was with me in his office the entire time."

"I wasn't talking about you. I was talking about her." He met Brooke Halsey's gaze. "She's not going to take the fall for the embezzlement and murder on her own. Are you, Brooke?"

It was clear from the look on her face that she wasn't.

Sharon gasped. "Holy shit. If I'd been a second faster getting into the library, I might've been killed, too."

It was the most remarkable little mystery play I'd ever seen, and Bixby's performance was riveting. Even McGregor seemed blown away by it.

She cleared her throat. "Brooke Halsey, Charles Ramsford, and Marcus Wilson, you are all under arrest. You have the right to remain silent . . ."

As she recited their rights, she tossed Bixby a pair of handcuffs. He placed them on Charles Ramsford, while she cuffed Brooke Halsey. When McGregor was done, she pointed at Marcus Wilson. "Sit down and keep your ass in that seat." Wilson did as he was told. Then she looked at Bixby. "Watch him while I get the crime scene techs and some uniformed officers back here."

"It will be my pleasure," Bixby said.

I leaned close to Bixby and whispered: "How did you know it was Ramsford and not Wilson who stabbed Rook?"

"I didn't," he said. "I figured I had a 50/50 chance of picking the right one. I chose Ramsford because he was within easy reach of the letter opener and Wilson wasn't."

I looked at the two handcuffed killers and one accomplice and said, "I hope y'all know some good lawyers."

I waited for Bixby to step on my line, but he gave me the act out. Or should I say chapter out?

CHAPTER SIXTEEN

Bixby waited until the three homicidal attorneys had been taken away by the uniformed officers before he approached McGregor, who stood in the hallway outside of Brooke Halsey's office, keeping a watchful eye on the CSU techs as they photographed and then bagged the lawyer's letter opener. I stood behind Bixby, so I only had a glimpse of what the techs were up to.

McGregor said, "This is the one time I'm glad you've proved me wrong."

"You should have been glad every time," Bixby said. "Otherwise several murderers would have gotten away with their crimes or you would have jailed some innocent people."

"You could have just accepted my thanks without insulting me."

I spoke up: "You didn't actually thank him."

She spun around to look at me. But at least she didn't also draw her gun and shoot. "Why are you talking?"

Bixby said, "If you really want to thank me, you could tell me what's happening with the Crowley case."

She turned back to him, any gratitude she might have had completely gone. "The investigation is ongoing."

"What does that mean?"

"Exactly what I said."

"Have you been able to connect Archibald Twain to Dinkins or anybody else?"

"I've told you all that I can."

"You've told me nothing."

"That's right," she said. "I am not going to compromise the integrity of the case by sharing information with a civilian. What I said outside Dinkins' house still stands, Bixby. This changes nothing."

Ouch. That had to sting. But Bixby was in too good a mood to start an argument. He held up his hands in surrender.

"Understood, Detective. I'm going back to the county jail."

"To tell Art what happened?"

"To give him a ride home," Bixby said. "I'll be waiting outside the front door. You'd better call the jail now, because I don't want to get a ticket for double-parking."

"We haven't actually proved his innocence yet."

"To a court," he said. "But you know it, I know it, Wally knows it, Sharon knows it, and so do those three lousy lawyers. Art shouldn't be in jail another second while you wait for the physical evidence to catch up with us."

Bixby didn't wait for an answer. He walked out, and I risked my life by giving McGregor a wink before I followed him.

We arrived outside that miserable, hellacious jail just as Art Malcolm was released. He looked a lot better in the sunlight. I opened the passenger door and got into the back seat so he could sit up front beside Bixby.

"I knew you wouldn't let me down," Malcolm said as he climbed in.

"I hope you don't hold your arrest against McGregor," Bixby said.

"I would never do that," Malcolm said. "She was doing her job. But she risked her badge by calling you in to prove her wrong, and again now by letting me go without solid proof."

"I'm the solid proof."

"No offense, Bixby, but nobody in law enforcement has been 100 percent convinced of that since you took a bullet in the face."

"But you were," he said.

"I *hoped* you were," Malcolm said. "There's a difference."

Bixby drove Malcolm back to his home in Simi Valley. The Cadillac's top was down, the California sun was out in all its glory against a cinematically blue sky, and the wind whipped Malcolm's wisps of remaining hair.

Malcolm tilted his head back, closed his eyes, and smiled, luxuriating in the moment. This was freedom. And with Alan Rook dead, maybe it was justice, too.

When we got back to Bixby's place, McGregor was there waiting for us, leaning against her car, holding an unopened bottle of champagne by the neck. To say I was surprised would be an understatement.

We got out of the Cadillac and she said, "CSU found Rook's blood between the blade and the hilt of Brooke Halsey's letter opener. She's singing like Beyoncé."

McGregor embraced Bixby, holding the bottle behind his back, and signaled me to shoo with a tilt of her head. I assumed she wouldn't be 5150ing him tonight. I wondered if there was actually a code to describe what she had in store for him instead. She was a complicated woman. But they all were, as far as I was concerned.

I left them to celebrate and went back to the guesthouse, where I checked my email and discovered I'd received a note from my agent about taping and uploading an audition for a commercial. It was for a new drug that reduced the inflammation of hemorrhoids so much that you didn't need to visit a colorectal doctor to remove them. The script was attached to the email.

I read the pages and discovered it was a nuanced role compared to most commercials, like those for breakfast cereals and banks. There was never any emotional depth for me to play in those parts. I ordered the free "emergency pizza" I'd earned on my Domino's app and settled in for the night to learn my lines, and define my hemorrhoid-afflicted character, before taping my audition the next morning.

When I got up around 7 a.m., I saw that McGregor's car was still out front and figured their celebration lasted long into the night. So I stayed away from the lagoon, had leftover pizza for breakfast, and recorded my audition for the commercial with my iPhone on a tiny tripod on the table. I had to dig deep into my reservoir of emotions to nail the character, to give him flesh and blood, but I thought that I'd achieved it.

I could have done the audition in just one take, but the sound of sirens passing by and helicopters flying low overhead kept ruining the sound. So I had to do it again and again. I finally locked a clean take and sent it off to my agent just as someone pounded insistently on my door. I opened it to find a weary, unshaven Bixby standing outside with his hair askew and dark circles under his bloodshot eyes. He wore a wrinkled polo shirt, blue jeans, and loafers without socks.

"You look like a zombie," I said.

Bixby stepped inside and headed for the box of pizza on my counter. "We went to bed early. I was exhausted. So was McGregor."

"Oh, stop it. I get it. You were training for the Sex Olympics. Congratulations to you both."

He helped himself to a cold slice of pizza and took a bite. "We were too bushed for that. We went to sleep right after dinner. Even with all that rest, I still feel drowsy."

"Finishing off a bottle of champagne between the two of you will do that."

"Two bottles, actually," he said between chews. "If it wasn't for her phone buzzing incessantly, we might both still be asleep."

"Was she called on a case?"

"Yes, and it's not even half a mile from here." Bixby finished the slice, wiped his greasy hands off on his jeans, and then took another piece. "So we have to get going."

"You must have really won her over by solving the Rook case if she invited you to look over her shoulder on this one."

He took another slice and went past me out the door. "She didn't."

"We're just going to show up?" I closed the door and hurried after him. "She's not going to like that."

"It's right up the street." He gestured with his pizza slice. "Everybody in the neighborhood is outside the house."

We walked up his driveway and down the tree-lined street. Or perhaps I should say up, since there was a gradual incline along the hillside to our left.

The houses on the hillside were set back, high above the street, at the end of long, steep, or winding driveways. Most of the usable acreage was in front of those homes, not behind like Bixby's. The homes to our right were below the road, their driveways sloping downward ever more steeply as we went up the hill.

I said, "Have you already forgotten her tirade in the screening room? Or on the front step of Dinkins' house? McGregor may never sleep with you again if you march into her crime scene to solve the case."

Bixby finished his pizza. "It's not a great love affair. It's a situationship, and I'm in a few others."

What was a "situationship" and why had I never been in one? I was thinking about that when Bixby added: "But what about you? Are you missing celibacy?"

"What is that supposed to mean?"

"I heard some of your audition before I knocked on the door. It's going to be a long time before your next erotic encounter if every woman you meet sees you as a guy with gigantic hemorrhoids."

"The point of the drug is that it cures you," I said. "I'd be a guy who no longer has hemorrhoids."

"And we all know that's irresistible to women. I thought we discussed being more choosy about your roles."

"I am. Pharmaceutical ads are the best roles in commercials. The characters have serious afflictions they have to cope with. That's an acting challenge. There are no levels in a guy looking for the best stain for his deck or wax for his car."

"But those ads suggest that you have a career and the money to afford a home and car," Bixby said. "That's more attractive than being the guy who once had bowling ball–sized hemorrhoids up his drain pipe."

"Nobody will remember me if I do those simple product ads because the characters are one-dimensional. People remember the roles I play because the characters have depth. I want to stretch my acting muscle, the same way you want to be challenged by perplexing mysteries, not easy ones."

"They are all easy," he said.

"You haven't nailed Caroline Crowley's murderer yet." It was a cheap shot, but he deserved it after ridiculing my acting and my sex life, which, for better or worse, were connected lately.

"But I know how it was done and who probably did it."

"What good is that if you can't get him?"

"I will," he said. "I always have."

He certainly did with those lawyers the day before. But perhaps Marcus Wilson's jab that nobody looking at that hole in Bixby's face would think anything he said was credible—and then what Malcolm said later, about cops doubting Bixby's abilities now—had gotten under his skin.

"And yet," I said, "here you are, in the meantime, rushing down the street to a crime scene without being asked, eager to score another win."

"It proves I haven't lost my touch."

At least he was honest. I wondered if the comment had involuntarily slipped out, due to his brain injury. But if he was embarrassed by the admission, he hid it well.

"Nobody is worried about that except you."

Bixby said, "Art Malcolm was."

I tried not to smile to myself. My psychological analysis of Bixby was spot-on. I knew that all of those hours watching *Dr. Phil* would pay off, except I thought it would be onstage, not in real life.

"Well, you got him out of jail," I said. "Why can't you be happy with that and leave this case alone?" I gestured to the scrum of police cars, a dozen lookie-loos, and official vehicles a half block ahead of us.

"It's how I stay on top of my game."

"But it might cost you McGregor, one of the only friends you have left."

"Nothing in life is free."

We got to the house a few minutes later. It was a ranch-style home below the street level with a sharply inclined driveway leading down to the garage. The front end of an enormous Monarch Bushranger SUV was smashed against the garage. The driver's side door and rear hatch of the Bushranger were both wide open. I noticed the SUV had dealer plates, so it was a brand-new purchase. Perhaps the owner still hadn't learned how to drive his new, monstrously large ride.

The garage door in front of the SUV was splattered with blood, the pattern reminding me of a water balloon hitting a wall. But I knew it wasn't a water balloon. It was a human being. That gruesome reality was underscored by the two ME guys pushing a gurney with a body bag up the driveway to a waiting morgue wagon.

Some CSU guys were busy photographing the area around the front of the SUV, where McGregor was hunched down, her back to the street, examining the point of impact. Luckily, she hadn't seen us and I hoped it stayed that way.

Bixby approached the CSU van, which was behind the yellow police tape. A heavyset African American woman in a Tyvek suit was outside the open rear door of the van, writing something on an evidence baggie that contained a stuffed puppy doll spattered with blood.

"Morning, Nan," Bixby said.

She spotted him and broke out in a warm smile. "Bixby, what are you doing here?"

"I live up the street. I'd like you to meet my friend Wally. He's a homicide detective visiting from Scotland." Then he turned to me. "Nan heads our county's crime scene unit."

I tried my best to sound like Sean Connery. "It's Nash, Wally Nash. Pleasure to meet you, Nan, though I wish it was under less tragic circumstances. I fear a child was killed." I let my voice trail off and nodded toward the bloody stuffed animal in her evidence baggie.

"No, no, thank God," Nan said, holding up the bag so we could get a better look at it. "The victim was holding it when he was crushed by his car."

Bixby said, "Does he have children?"

"He was single and lived alone."

Bixby glanced back at the SUV. "What do you think happened?"

"Last night the driver, Peter Welbeck, got out of his SUV for some reason, accidentally put his digital shifter into neutral instead of park, and forgot to set his emergency brake. He walked in front of the vehicle and it rolled forward, crushing him against his garage door. The ME thinks he could have been pinned there for some time, unable to call for help."

It was a steep driveway and I could easily imagine the accident and the agony that Welbeck endured. "What a horrible way to die. I guess he was unfamiliar with his new car."

I was very pleased with myself for noticing the temporary plates. I looked to see if Bixby noticed my brilliant observation, but he was still staring at the SUV.

"That's the weird thing," Nan said.

Bixby looked back at her. "What do you mean?"

"Welbeck was a salesman at the Monarch Motors dealership on Ventura Boulevard in Woodland Hills. It isn't far. He drives a different new Monarch home every night after they close at 10 p.m. The

Bushranger is their bestselling model. You'd think Welbeck would have been very familiar with it."

"Indeed." He looked back at the Monarch SUV.

It didn't seem so unusual to me. Sometimes I forgot how to open the gas tank of my Hyundai and I'd had it for years. "He must have been tired or distracted after a long day at work. What I wonder is why he got out and stepped in front of his car."

"I asked myself the same question, Detective Nash," Nan said. "But I know it wasn't to raise the roll-up garage door. I used the remote in the car to raise the door a bit so we had some wiggle room to remove the body."

Bixby asked, "When was Welbeck crushed?"

"The ME believes it was late last night," she said. "A neighbor walking his dog this morning discovered the accident and called it in."

Bixby turned, his face ashen, but I didn't think it was fatigue.

Nan noticed it, too. "Are you feeling okay?"

"Actually, no," he said. "I haven't been feeling right since I woke up this morning. I think I should go home."

"Take it easy," she said. "It was good seeing you, Bixby. I've missed you."

"Likewise, Nan." Bixby turned on his heels and we hurried back the way we came. He was in more of a hurry to leave than he had been to get there. He was moving fast for someone feeling ill.

"I'm surprised you're leaving so quickly and without talking to McGregor," I said. In fact, I didn't think she'd even noticed we were there. The CSU van had pretty much blocked us from view. "You must be *very* sick. Food poisoning?"

I hoped it wasn't the pizza, or I was a goner, too.

"That crash wasn't an accident," he said. "It was murder."

I was astonished. If Bixby was right, then he might have set a world speed record for homicide-solving, but there wasn't anybody around from Guinness World Records to make it official. This made his dash from the crime scene without informing McGregor of his discovery even more baffling.

"How do you know?"

Bixby answered in a rush that matched his speed-walking pace.

"Here's what happened. As Welbeck drove up to his house last night, he used his remote to open his garage door. He drove down his driveway and spotted a puppy right in front of him, frozen in fear in his headlights. So he parked the car on the incline and got out to pick up the puppy, but it was a stuffed animal."

"How does that make it a murder and not an accident?"

"The puppy was a lure," Bixby said. "The instant Welbeck got out to pick it up, the murderer dashed out of hiding and released the parking brake."

"How can you prove that?"

"The parking brake and the trunk-release buttons in the Monarch Bushranger look the same and are right next to each other. It's a documented design flaw, one that confused the killer, too, who opened the trunk by accident first, and then disengaged the parking brake. That's why both the driver's side door and trunk are open now. The digital shifter also has a design flaw. It's not clear when it's in neutral or park, which has caused a lot of accidents. Monarch is supposedly working on a fix, but they are still an accomplice to murder."

"You're brilliant," I said, and I meant it. His powers of observation were positively Sherlockian and made me feel stupid for being proud of noticing something as obvious as the SUV's dealer plates. "So why are you speed-walking away from the scene without saying anything to McGregor?"

"I'm trying not to run and call attention to myself."

"So you're leaving it to McGregor to solve this one for herself," I said. "That is big of you and, dare I say, a major personal milestone."

"It's self-preservation," he said.

"I don't understand. You aren't seriously worried that she's going to arrest you."

"Yes, I am." He lowered his voice, not that there was anyone around who could possibly hear us. "It was me, Wally. I killed Welbeck."

"Very funny."

"I'm not joking," he said, and I could see from the expression on his face that he was dead serious. "I killed Welbeck, Dinkins, and Caroline Crowley, too."

I believed him, or perhaps I should say I believed he believed it, but I didn't believe that. Does that make sense? "You must be *really* sick, because you're delirious. Do you have a temperature?"

"It makes perfect sense, Wally. Welbeck and Crowley are murders that only I could have solved because I'm the only one smart enough to have committed them. I saw it myself several times as we investigated the Crowley case and I said so."

He had. I remembered.

He'd even told McGregor, when he was trying to make her feel better about not realizing Crowley's death wasn't an accident, that he was *the only detective who could have seen that this was murder.* And what had she said? *It's a figment of your psychosis. It's all about you. You're still fighting for your parents, even after all these years.*

Was she onto something?

No, she couldn't be.

"You saw it, too," Bixby said. "When we left Bernheim Sutton, you told me that somehow only I saw the crime, that I'd exposed a murder nobody else would ever have noticed."

"But you've done that many times before Caroline Crowley was killed."

Bixby waved off my argument. "Even Archibald Twain saw it."

I remembered that, too. I'd even been impressed by how deftly Twain had turned Bixby's accusations back on Bixby and accused *him* of the murder.

What had Bixby said? *And I came here to let you know what I've done?*

And Twain replied, *Perhaps you just wanted to ease your guilt by indulging in a little confession . . .*

Bixby must have guessed what I was thinking, because now he said: "When I told you before meeting Twain that the likely number of people who had the skills and motivation to pull off a murder like this was at most one, I was right. But it wasn't Twain. It was me."

"That doesn't mean you did it."

"All of the clues point to me, Wally. I saw it myself from the beginning and did nothing. It's why I can't capture Crowley's killer. I've been looking in all the wrong places when I should have looked in the mirror."

"I can think of a lot of reasons why you haven't closed this case. You having a split personality disorder isn't one of them."

"Think of this objectively. I have a deep and abiding motive. Both murders are connected to Monarch Motors, the company that manufactured the car that killed my parents. Bernheim, Sutton & Associates was the apologist for Monarch's negligence and Welbeck was one of their car salesmen."

"Thousands of people sell Monarchs. Why would you kill this particular guy?"

We reached Bixby's driveway.

"Because Welbeck lives down the street from me and drives a car with two inept and dangerous design flaws that have received little media attention and that Monarch hasn't corrected. But now that someone—one of their own car salesmen, no less—has died a gruesome, horrible death because of those flaws, the media and the government will be all over it. Monarch Motors will face hundreds of millions of dollars in losses from the recall of their vehicles for retrofitting, lost sales, government fines, and the inevitable class action lawsuit. It could even drive Monarch out of business."

"You think you killed Crowley just to shame Bernheim Sutton again and you murdered Welbeck to draw attention to more Monarch Motors design flaws."

He stopped at his front door and faced me. "That's right."

"And you beheaded Dinkins to cover up the money trail that leads back to you."

"Right again," he said. "I led us there the next morning to throw suspicion off myself, or out of guilt, I don't know."

"That's insane."

"That could be my defense. I'm calling my doctor. I need to see him right now." Bixby took his iPhone from his pocket.

"Wise move," I said. "Is he a neurologist or a shrink?"

Bixby began punching in the phone number. "A general practitioner."

A GP wouldn't do, especially if Bixby was having some kind of stroke. He needed to see specialists. But I didn't want to panic him, even though he was already overwrought. I spoke as calmly as I could: "How about if we go to the ER instead?"

"Excellent idea." Bixby ended the call.

"I'll call 911."

"Drive me there instead. It will be faster. UCLA Medical Center in West Hills is almost a straight shot north on Topanga. When we get there, tell them I was delirious and babbling nonsense."

"It's the truth."

He led me quickly toward the garage. At least he recognized the urgency. "They'll take one look at this face, assume I have a neurological disorder that's become much worse, and immediately run a battery of tests. We could know in an hour or two who the killer is."

"I don't think there's a test that'll indicate if your personality was cleaved in half, like Dr. Jekyll and Mr. Hyde, when you were shot in the head."

"I'll know," he said, sliding open the barn door and revealing his large collection of vehicles. I knew which one we had to take.

"So what if you're right? Will you turn yourself in?"

"No, I'll let *you* solve the murders and deliver me to McGregor yourself," Bixby said. "You two can share the credit. But in the meantime, don't tell anyone about this."

"Considering that speed is of the essence," I said, "we should take the Bugatti Chiron with the bubble light."

"Absolutely," he said.

At least there was one upside to this crisis: I'd finally get to drive the Bugatti. It would be the one positive thing I'd remember from this day, assuming Bixby truly had lost his mind, and regardless of whether he was actually a killer who'd been tasked with catching himself.

But if he was the murderer, at least his record would be unbroken, even if McGregor and I ultimately got the credit for solving the crimes.

CHAPTER SEVENTEEN

It's very easy to drive fast when you are in a $3 million Bugatti Chiron. It was made for speed and, if you try to drive slowly, it fights against you, snarling and straining to be freed to melt the asphalt. I didn't have the strength or the courage to stand up to it. So I surrendered.

It wasn't until the Bugatti hit one hundred miles per hour that it really felt happy, moving with ridiculous smoothness, somehow making the speed feel natural and safe, even though everything outside, except what was right in front of me, was passing in a blur.

The cars ahead of us were moving so much slower than we were that they almost appeared to be stationary. I weaved through them, sometimes swerving into oncoming traffic on the opposite side of Topanga Canyon Boulevard to avoid collisions and blast through intersections.

The bubble light atop the Bugatti helped clear the way for us, but not as much as the loud siren that Bixby had installed, probably illegally, not that I was in any position at that moment to worry about that.

Bixby sat in the passenger seat with almost serene calmness, which was shocking given my reckless driving, the possibility of a catastrophic car accident, and the prospect that he had a grave neurological disorder that, at best, had impaired his thinking and, at worst, had turned him into a homicidal maniac.

I made a hard left on Sherman Way, nearly losing control of the car, then outflanked a racing ambulance in front of us to reach the emergency entrance of the UCLA West Valley Medical Center before it did. We came to a skidding stop outside the entrance to the ER. I got out of the car, grabbed a nearby wheelchair, and brought it up to the side of the Bugatti just as Bixby got out.

"I don't need one of those," he said.

"It helps sell that you need immediate medical attention."

"I really do. I'm not pretending."

"Then stop arguing with me, give me your wallet, and start speaking in tongues. A little drooling wouldn't hurt, either."

He gave me his wallet and I wheeled him through the automatic double doors, through the crowded waiting room, and right up to the admission desk, where a world-weary nurse sat behind plexiglass. Looking past her, I could see a lot of activity among the doctors, nurses, and patients in the exam areas. I had to cut through that human clutter and get Bixby treated fast.

"I'm Dr. Ross, this man's GP. He is having a stroke," I shouted. "He needs to see a neurologist immediately."

The nurse peered over the desk at him and, of course, noticed the gunshot scar on his face, which seemed even redder and bigger than usual. It might even have been throbbing. But Bixby didn't follow my advice about drooling or rambling. He just sat there quietly, hands in his lap, staring blankly ahead.

She asked, "What happened to his face?"

"What does it look like? A red-hot bullet blasted into his skull and played hockey in his brain. But he was clearheaded and coherent until an hour ago. Now he's babbling deliriously. We have no time for questions. Every second counts. If he goes another minute without treatment, he could be a turnip for life."

She said, "Does he have insurance?"

"The cards are all in there. We're wasting time!"

I tossed his wallet to her and pushed the wheelchair through the next set of double doors, aimed myself at the first ER doctor I could find, and practically ran him down.

"Listen up! Stroke alert. Start an IV, D5-W, and get his CBC, CMP, PT/INR, and blood glucose. This man needs a head CT stat, a full cardiac panel, and a lactate to rule out hypoglycemia or sepsis. Prep for a possible thrombolytic. But don't administer TPA until we rule out a bleed. Don't just stand there, *move*."

I had no idea what any of that medical babble meant, or if it was an even remotely accurate treatment for Bixby's condition. It was all dialogue that had stuck in my head after I'd heard it repeated multiple times during the shooting of a *Grey's Anatomy* scene while I was on a gurney in the background, playing a corpse.

I left Bixby with the stunned ER doctor and rushed out before anyone could argue with me.

The TV in the waiting room was tuned to MeTV, so I was able to watch Raymond Burr as Perry Mason browbeat a woman on the witness stand until she confessed to the murder that his client was charged with. This was one of the 270 times that DA Hamilton Burger and homicide detective Arthur Tragg had arrested and prosecuted an innocent person, only to be proved wrong by Perry.

How could two men as incompetent as Burger and Tragg have kept their jobs? It didn't make any sense to me. Surely Burger would have been voted out of office, and Tragg thrown off the force, after the first hundred times they'd railroaded somebody. On top of that, Perry could have made millions filing a class action lawsuit on behalf of his 270 clients against the City of Los Angeles.

All of which begged the question, Was Perry Mason brilliant, or did he just look that way compared to morons like Burger and Tragg? And why didn't those two learn, say after the 150th time, to listen to

Perry when he told them they were wrong? Even a dog learns from his mistakes.

Perry Mason and Edison Bixby were both great detectives with enormous egos who were confident in their skills. I believed Bixby was truly brilliant, and not because his colleagues were dolts, but because he was even better than the very smart and capable LAPD detectives he worked with. And before he was shot, they all knew it, too, and had learned to trust his skills. It was why McGregor had called him for his help in the case four years earlier that ultimately led to his tragic disability.

I'm sure most of those cops still believed in Bixby's brilliance after his injury, they just found his behavior impossible to deal with. Even McGregor set her ego and ambition aside to ask him to make sure she wasn't making a mistake with Art Malcolm. It would be a terrible tragedy if Bixby had unknowingly become a killer. He'd certainly made a strong and convincing case against himself.

I found myself wishing the doctors would find something wrong with his brain and determine that he was nuts. But hopefully *curably* nuts. Even so, it would probably mean that his career as a detective was over. And I would need to land that hemorrhoid commercial or face living on the streets.

I was still thinking about my possible fate when Bixby was wheeled out of the ER by an orderly after only two hours of tests and treatment. The orderly scowled at me and pushed the wheelchair in my direction. "He's all yours, *Doctor*."

The orderly marched back into the ER, leaving me with Bixby, who had a file folder in his lap. "They're releasing you?"

Bixby got out of the chair. "They think I'm a hypochondriac and that you are a drama queen."

"Did you tell them that you believe you've killed three people but don't remember doing it?"

"I didn't have to. I got my test results." Bixby held up the folder. "And they confirmed what I feared."

Oh crap. "And they let you go anyway?"

"They didn't realize what the results meant out of context." Bixby sighed, forlorn. "But I do."

I could see the pain on his face as he considered all the ramifications of his condition and the troubles that lay ahead for him. "And you still didn't tell them?"

Bixby shook his head. "But tomorrow *you* will. The whole world will know. I just want one more night of peace before you reveal the truth and everything changes."

I could do that. And then he told me exactly how. It gave us both the rest of the day, and the entire night, to prepare ourselves for the darkness that tomorrow would bring.

McGregor came over that night, presumably eager to share with Bixby the latest news about his neighbor Peter Welbeck's bizarre accident. Perhaps she'd even figured out for herself that it was a murder, but I didn't think that she'd made the connection to Bixby or she wouldn't have spent the night in his bed. She would have led him out right away in handcuffs.

But the moment of truth would come soon.

I had a sleepless night, which I spent rehearsing what I'd say to her and finding just the right clothes to wear for my performance.

The next morning, I was leaning against her car when she emerged from Bixby's house in the same clothes she'd worn the night before.

I was dressed exactly as I'd been on our visit to Dinkins' house in Bixby's old plain-wrap cop car. I was Frank Hellinger again, haunted by the ghosts of all the murder victims who wouldn't rest until they had justice. I needed to project that same kind of authority, world-weariness, and cynicism if McGregor was going to listen to me. It was crucial that I convince her.

"We need to talk, McGregor."

"I can't imagine what you'd have to say that I'd want to hear."

"I know who killed Peter Welbeck."

"There is no *who*. It's a *what*. His car did it."

"It was murder," I said.

"Yeah, yeah, I know. Bixby always says there's no such thing as operator error. It's always bad design," she said. "If the buttons weren't identical, and if they weren't next to each other, the mistake couldn't have happened. So the car did it or, more accurately, the inept designers did."

"That's what the killer wants us to think, but the design error had an affordance nobody anticipated."

She stared at me. "Affordance?"

"An alternative use."

"I know what it means," she said. "I've known Bixby much longer than you have."

"The affordance was murder. And it was committed by the same person who killed Caroline Crowley."

"I suppose you know who it is." Each word dripped with contempt.

"I do, but I need you to make the arrest," I said. "It will be a win for both of us. I'll become a famous detective and you can be my exasperated friend on the force. Every great private eye has one."

"Okay, I'll bite. Who did it?"

I nodded toward the house. "Bixby."

"You mean he solved it."

"I mean he did it," I said. "He killed them, and Dinkins, too."

She laughed sourly. "You've got to be shitting me."

"I wish I was. All the clues were there, you just didn't see them. It was practically a confession when he told you he—"

She whipped out her gun and shot me three times in the chest.

It felt like I'd been hit by a cannonball.

But unlike people shot in television shows and movies, I didn't fly back fifty feet. I instantly crumpled to the ground, curled into a twitching, breathless lump, experiencing my final seconds of life.

I didn't feel any pain. I didn't see a big dark tunnel to the next world. What I felt was a profound sense of unfairness, of being cheated out of the future I'd deserved, of all the roles I'd never play, of all the acclaim I'd never receive. My last performance on the stage of life would be shedding a few tears for myself.

McGregor was still holding her gun, and looking down at me with disgust, when Bixby ran out of the house.

"I heard gunshots—" And that's when he saw me dying, my shirt soaked with blood, a single tear rolling down my cheek.

It stopped him. He stood rigidly still, facing McGregor and me, his eyes disbelieving. *"Why did you shoot him?"*

"He was going to solve the murders." She turned with a sigh and pointed her gun at him, her back to me as my life ebbed poignantly, and unforgettably, away. "Can you believe that? It would've been even more humiliating than you doing it to me."

Bixby nodded, everything fitting into place for him now. "*You* were the woman in the nail salon and the woman in red."

"I was."

"You beheaded Mort Dinkins."

"Yep."

"You slipped me a roofie the other night, snuck out of my bed, and killed Welbeck."

"I did."

"Why?"

"Isn't it obvious? Because *I hate you*. I'm sick and tired of the endless humiliation. But if I put you in prison for multiple murders, not only will I destroy you and your reputation, I'll be recognized as the brilliant detective who outwitted Edison Bixby."

"What was my motive for killing Crowley and Welbeck?"

"To ruin Monarch Motors and get publicity, to become a celebrity and relevant again instead of a sad, forgotten, brain-damaged has-been."

"The frame won't hold up in court," he said.

"It will hold up in a casket. New plan, same result: I killed you and your flatulent monkey in self-defense when you both tried to stop me from arresting you for murder." McGregor aimed her gun at Bixby's head.

"Please don't shoot me in the face."

"I have to," she said. "I want to wipe that smirk off of it for good."

"That'd be a shame because—"

She fired.

He was still standing, no hole in his head.

She fired again. Same result.

He continued talking as if she hadn't just shot at him. "As I was saying, it's a shame because it means I put on all these squibs and bags of fake blood under my shirt for nothing."

Bixby opened his right hand to reveal the remote control he held that activated the bullet-hit rig we got from a special-effects guy I met on *NCIS*. Except Bixby didn't get to use his.

But I did. I had one of those rigs and remotes, too.

I sat up, my clothes soaked with stage blood, and smiled at Bixby. "At least now you can't upstage me with your death scene."

"It would have been a real tearjerker, too," he said. "I rehearsed it for hours."

McGregor glared at me, then at Bixby, as she began to process, to her dismay, what had just happened. "You knew I'd be so enraged at the prospect of Fartman stealing my glory and humiliating me that I'd shoot him. So you loaded my guns with blanks."

"I did it while you were snoring away in the afterglow of my spectacular lovemaking," Bixby said.

I could hear sirens approaching. If the gunshots hadn't drawn them, then Bixby's call to 911 before he stepped outside the house certainly did.

She stared at him in disbelief. "You knew I was the killer and you had sex with me *anyway*?"

"You hate me but you still slept with me. Repeatedly. For years. What's the difference?"

"Rage is an aphrodisiac," she said, getting into his face. "But you just wanted one more go-round for your sick gratification and to sabotage my gun."

He didn't flinch. "What you did was worse. You shared my bed just so you could frame me for murder. For months, while I was asleep, you used my devices, bank accounts, and credit cards to have the keto poster made, to send the chocolate magazines to the nail salon, and to bribe Dinkins to sabotage the step. You were creating the clue trail that would prove I was the killer."

Bees were beginning to swirl around me, attracted by the corn syrup in my fake blood. I swatted at them, eager to get this over with. "Is that really the moral issue you two want to argue about? You're a killer, McGregor. Bixby isn't. He wins."

She ignored me, as usual, and focused on Bixby. "How did you figure out that it was me?"

"Well, I certainly knew it wasn't me. Or at least I hoped it wasn't. So I had my blood and urine tested yesterday morning to be sure, because if it wasn't me, then I was being framed, and it could only be by one person. The tests came back positive for Rohypnol. You drugged me with a roofie the previous night so you could slip out and kill Welbeck when he got home at 10 p.m. It's the same story you were going to use to explain how I slipped out and killed him."

Her shoulders began to sag. "I suppose this little drama is all being recorded?"

I danced around, trying to avoid the bees. "Better. It's live streaming to Facebook, YouTube, X, and all over social media."

Now she looked at me. "No fucking way."

I wanted to grin at her, but that's when a bee stung me on the cheek, and I grimaced instead and maybe I shrieked. But those aren't important details.

Bixby said, "I don't want what you did to be covered up by the LAPD or anyone else. Now it can't be."

McGregor turned back to him. "It's against the law to record someone without their permission, and you didn't read me my rights."

"I'm not a cop. But they are."

He gestured to the two police cars screeching up. Four officers spilled out of the cars with their guns out, using their doors for cover.

One of them shouted, "Drop the gun, *now*."

Bixby continued to talk calmly to her. "You have a passing knowledge of architecture and design from observing me, but not the imagination or resources to come up with this scheme. You aren't that creative."

She just glowered at him.

The same cop shouted again: "Drop the gun or I'll drop you!"

Something occurred to Bixby in that instant. I saw it on his face. He said, "You're not the mastermind, are you? You're just the hired help."

McGregor dropped her gun, put her hands on her head, and slumped to her knees, never taking her eyes off him. "You sanctimonious prick."

Bixby smiled, as if that was exactly what he wanted to hear.

The officers ran up, placed the cuffs on her, and informed her of her rights. When they were done, Bixby took out his phone and used an app to shut off the hidden cameras that we'd installed yesterday afternoon and that had been live streaming her takedown.

I walked up beside him and we both watched McGregor being patted down. I know I shouldn't have withheld from you everything that Bixby told me after our visit to the ER, or how he enlisted me into his clever sting. But if I hadn't done that, you would have been robbed of feeling the shocking and emotional impact of my death. You'll learn just a few pages from now why giving you that experience is so important to me. Besides, it was a lot more fun for you that way, wasn't it?

Okay, getting back to our story now, at that moment outside of Bixby's house, I was very much alive and feeling great.

No, I was feeling more than that. I was *elated*. It was my best performance ever, despite the bee stinging my cheek. "I'm so glad you were filming this. My death scene was incredible. It's going to get me a lot of work."

"You've already played plenty of corpses."

"This was different," I said. "Nobody has ever seen me die."

We watched the officers lead McGregor back to a squad car and he said, "They have if they've seen your commercials."

"I didn't die in those."

He looked back at me. "Your love life certainly did."

The dig didn't bother me. My mind was already on more important things. I was mentally preparing myself for the media onslaught we were about to face. I was sure we'd already gone viral worldwide and that news vans with satellite-uplink capabilities from CNN and all of the major television networks, as well as droves of print journalists and vloggers, were already on their way to the house to cover our story.

But, to my profound disappointment, we didn't stick around for any of that, or even to give the police our statements for their reports. Bixby told the officers that the streaming broadcast was our statement.

We went back into the house, where we quickly removed our bullet-hit rigs and I changed into a fresh shirt. Then we went to the car barn, got into his Bugatti Chiron, and sped off, passing the parade of incoming media vehicles just as they were arriving. I looked at them longingly.

"Where are we going?" I asked him, my stung cheek beginning to swell and burn.

"To tie up the last loose end."

CHAPTER EIGHTEEN

The Central California Women's Facility, the second largest women's prison in the United States, was located at the intersection of Avenue 24 and Road 22 in Chowchilla, a few miles east of state highway 99. The street names were uninspired because there was nobody around to care. The prison was in the middle of a vast, seemingly endless expanse of flat land devoted to agriculture and livestock. This was the breadbasket of the nation. The 640 acres that the prison occupied was formerly a dairy farm. I'll let you ponder the ironic parallels.

We'd made the 251-mile drive up from Los Angeles in about two and a half hours in the Bugatti and we didn't get any speeding tickets, even though the supercar was highway patrol bait and Bixby was driving fast enough to change the rotation of the earth.

And yet, it didn't physically feel like we were going fast at all, and when I mentioned that phenomenon to Bixby, he said it was an illusion that was literally baked into the asphalt of America's freeways.

"The lane striping on highways can be anywhere from ten to fifteen feet long, and the spacing between the stripes is at a three-to-one ratio."

"I was never good at math. What does that mean?"

"They are enormous lines spaced far apart to make us believe we are going slower than we are. There's thirty-six feet of unmarked space between each strip. Even going the speed limit would be hard for our minds to handle without this trick and many others. They change how we experience the motion. Otherwise, we'd all be extremely disoriented and too busy vomiting to function, much less drive. It's all about how fast the retina can detect individual images and the brain can identify them. The stripes are smaller and the space between them is much shorter on city streets because the speeds we're driving aren't wildly outside the rate that human beings can travel on their feet."

"In other words, every road is manipulating us."

"Everything in the built world is doing that," Bixby said. "But nature does it, too."

"I don't see how."

"Have you ever asked yourself why an apple is bright red? It's to attract your attention. The apple, and all fruits, are sweet so you will eat them and maybe some of their seeds, too. And then you will take a dump, fertilizing the soil, and especially any seeds already in your poop, ensuring that more fruits will grow."

"I will never trust an apple again."

"You should have learned that lesson from Adam and Eve."

We arrived at the prison and, after going through all the security checkpoints, were led to a windowless interview room that might have been designed by the same uninspired interior decorator responsible for the Los Angeles jail, public park restrooms, and Target department stores.

Edith Gotsford was already waiting for us at a metal table. She couldn't get Botox injections anymore, so now there were wrinkles on her face, which was once tighter than the skin on a carrot. Her jewelry was gone and her baggy orange prison jumpsuit was the first piece of clothing that she'd worn in decades that didn't have a designer label. The only vestiges of her previous rich and pampered life were her collagen-plumped lips and haughty attitude.

Bixby sat down across from her and smiled. "How are you doing, Cruella?"

"This is a nice surprise. I've never had a chance to see my handiwork up close." She made a show of studying his gunshot-scarred face. "It looks good."

Bixby gestured to Gotsford. "She's the hag who shot me . . . right after calling me a sanctimonious prick."

Aha. That explained our little road trip. I sat down in the other chair. "You really know how to bring out the best in women."

Gotsford studied my face now, too. The bee sting on my cheek had swollen to epic proportions. It reminded me of a 1970s horror movie called *The Manitou*. A tiny bump on a woman's back kept growing until a reincarnated Indian medicine man burst out of her body in an explosion of gore and wreaked violent havoc on San Francisco. All that stood between an ancient evil and humanity was Tony Curtis. But he wasn't here to save us now.

"Who are you?" she asked.

"I'm Wally Nash."

"The actor," Bixby added.

"What have I seen you in?"

"I played a big role in the arrest of LAPD homicide detective Bridget McGregor for multiple murders."

"It's all over the news and the net," Bixby said. "In fact, it was live streamed."

"I haven't seen it," she said dismissively. "I don't have a TV or computer in my room. Or a decent toilet. I've complained to the front desk but so far, nobody has come to take care of it. I'm going to leave a very harsh review on Yelp."

Bixby said, "I hate to ruin the ending for you, but I tricked McGregor into admitting that she killed Caroline Crowley and Peter Welbeck."

"Should I know them?" Gotsford was a terrible actress.

"They were the innocent victims in your complicated scheme to frame me."

"I'm in prison. I'm in no position to do anything outside of these walls."

"But McGregor was," Bixby said. "We have the visitor logs. We know she came to see you multiple times since your incarceration."

That was a lie, of course. We had nothing.

Gotsford gave him a thin, wicked smile. "She likes me. We have shared interests."

That wasn't right, so I corrected her: "You mean a shared hatred."

Bixby said, "You read up on design while you've been imprisoned and McGregor was your avenging angel. But it didn't work. Here I am."

"With a bullet hole in your face and chunk of your brain missing," she said with smug satisfaction. "Now your cop friend, who is partially responsible for me being here, is facing life in prison. It might even be this one. Wouldn't that be sweet? I'd say I got even with both of you."

"Really? Because even with half a brain, I still outsmarted you. What does that say about your intelligence?"

Her face turned red and she bared her teeth. I wouldn't have been surprised to see fangs. The Manitou didn't look as menacing. It occurred to me that it wasn't Archibald Twain who was Bixby's nemesis, his Professor Moriarty. It was this woman, who probably still had her fortune safely locked away in secret accounts, waiting to be tapped by her evil minions to wreak havoc on Bixby's life.

She might have been thinking the same thing, because she said, "You don't want to insult me, Bixby. You never know what can happen."

"But I do." He leaned forward. "You will grow older and more haggard, marinating in your rancid bitterness, in a dank six-by-eight-foot concrete box while I continue to enjoy my wealth and freedom. The image of that future delights me."

The truth stung, and Gotsford wasn't having fun anymore. "Why are you really here? You didn't come all this way just to tempt fate by gloating."

"Of course I did." Bixby got up and looked at me. "She really doesn't know me at all."

I got up, too. "That's her fatal flaw."

He hit the buzzer on the wall to summon a prison guard. "Not just hers. There are a lot of other women in here with the same one."

"They should start a club," I said. "The Edison Bixby Appreciation Society. You could send them posters of your face with a target on it."

"That would be incredibly self-centered."

"You really don't know you at all, either."

The guard opened the door and Bixby nodded toward Gotsford. "It's her fault. She shot me in the head."

We walked out as she cursed us in our wake. I won't repeat the profanities, but some of it was quite clever, if often physically impossible to achieve, and involved an array of common objects and even some animals.

Once we were outside the prison, the earthy, pungent rotten-egg stench of fertilizer descended on us like a tarp. It was unpleasant, but it was also strangely satisfying, because I knew that sickening odor was what Gotsford inhaled every time she stepped into the prison yard for some sunshine.

Bixby turned to me and said, "Congratulations."

"On what?"

"You've officially outlasted all of my previous assistants combined. I think this job might work out for you."

"Don't get too used to this arrangement. I think Hollywood is going to take notice and some big roles are coming my way." The media firestorm was waiting for us in Los Angeles and I was certain it would propel me to overnight stardom.

"Based on what?"

It was a ludicrous question. Wasn't the answer clear?

"My fabulous death scene."

I knew with absolute certainty that every director in the movie business would see it, if they hadn't already watched it a dozen times by now, and would be floored by my gripping and honest performance.

"How do you know it was fabulous?"

"I was there."

We reached his Bugatti. "You should actually see it."

He took out his phone and showed the portion of the video after I was shot. All I could see in the frame were my ankles and feet twitching. Not one moment of my incredible death scene was captured for posterity. It was all about Bixby, who shone in his performance as the brilliant detective, taking down that wretched killer McGregor.

"You cut me out of it!"

"*You* did," he said. "You collapsed out of frame after you were shot. I saw it happen on my app from inside the house. There wasn't anything I could do. I was inside and you were outside, already dead."

"When you came out to see what happened, you could have dragged my body back into frame in your grief."

"Why would I do that? It makes no sense, and such a bizarre, unmotivated reaction would have tipped off McGregor that something was awry before she confessed."

He was right, of course. The motivation always has to make sense for a performance to be credible. "Aren't there other camera angles of my death?"

"This is it."

That is why, dear reader, I didn't tell you that we were setting up a sting on McGregor, because I knew you were going to be deprived of ever actually *seeing* my stunning performance. So I wanted you to at least feel the visceral horror of my sudden death for yourselves, which meant tricking you, too.

Alas, no matter how well I've described my death, or how vividly you imagined it, I guarantee you that my performance was even better than that.

It was one for the ages.

So you can understand why I was furious at Bixby for not having it on video for posterity. I thrust a finger at him. "You did this on purpose."

"You should have stayed on your marks," he said, referring to the pieces of masking tape placed on the ground to remind actors where to stand to be in focus and properly lit for the camera. The shots are framed to hide the marks, or after multiple rehearsals or takes, the actors become so familiar with where they are that they can be removed. If you watch TV shows or movies closely, you can often see an actor glance down at his mark as he walks into a shot.

"I didn't have any marks," I said.

"Whose fault is that?"

"*Yours.* You were the director. You were the one who scripted and staged that entire scene outside your house."

"But it's your job, as an actor, to always know where the cameras are and what they see." Bixby pointed his key fob at the Bugatti and unlocked the car.

"You did this just to keep me in your indentured servitude."

"I think you unconsciously sabotaged yourself because you don't want to leave." He slipped into the driver's seat of his Bugatti.

I was sure that I hadn't been betrayed by my subconscious, but he was right about one thing: I was in no hurry to leave the job. As infuriating as Edison Bixby could be, working on these cases with him had been the most exciting, challenging, and fun days of my life. I didn't want it to end yet, at least not until my shot at Hollywood stardom beckoned me away.

I got into the car. "The fact is, you need me to stay."

"I do," Bixby said and then, apparently stunned by what he'd just heard himself admit, smacked himself on the forehead. "That damned bullet."

It was great that he'd seemingly accidentally expressed how important I'd become to him, and I appreciated it, but I wanted him to know that I wasn't buying his act.

"I may not be a brilliant detective, but I'm a professional actor. And I know bad acting when I see it."

"What's that supposed to mean?"

"I think your traumatic corpo-poopsy or whatever it's called is an act so you have the freedom to behave like an ass."

"That's a very insensitive thing to say to a person with a crippling neurological disorder."

"I'm giving you fair warning, Bixby. All it takes is one good part and I'm out of here."

He started the car and drove back toward the highway. "Does that mean you didn't get cast in the hemorrhoid commercial?"

"I did, and although that might not be a big role, you should be worried," I said. "Bryan Cranston's breakout was in a Preparation H commercial."

"I didn't know you could break out down there."

"Very funny," I said. "But you won't be laughing when you're stuck with a juggler for an assistant and I'm the new Marvel superhero."

"Does that mean you've given up on the idea of writing a book about me?"

Edison Bixby's ego knew no bounds. "Dream on."

Author's Note & Acknowledgments

The character of Edison Bixby was years in the making and was inspired by a quote from architect Bernard Tschumi:

"To really appreciate architecture, you may even need to commit a murder."

The thought behind that quote is creatively explored in Tschumi's landmark work *The Manhattan Transcripts*, a series of drawings, designs, and photographs that show how criminal acts and architecture are inextricably connected, and then again in his book *Architecture and Disjunction.*

And now by me.

I read many, many books and research papers to enable me to see the world the way that Bixby does, and to figure out how he uses that particular knowledge to solve crimes.

The authors who educated me and shaped my thinking the most were Don Norman (*The Design of Everyday Things, Emotional Design, Living with Complexity*, and *Turn Signals are the Facial Expressions of Automobiles*), Paco Underhill (*Call of the Mall, Why We Buy*, and *What Women Want: The Science of Female Shopping*), Edward T. Hall (*The Hidden Dimension, Beyond Culture*), and Henry Petroski (*To Engineer Is Human, The Evolution of Useful Things, To Forgive Design: Understanding Failure*, and *Success Through Failure: The Paradox of Design*). I urge you to read their remarkable books. You will never look at buildings, roads, stores, or the devices around you in the same way again.

The following books were also enormously helpful and eye-opening. They were, in no particular order: *A Burglar's Guide to the City* by Geoff Manaugh, *Drunk Tank Pink* by Adam Alter, *Design for the Real World* by Victor Papanek, *Life Between Buildings* by Jan Gehl, *Ruined by Design* by Mike Monteiro, *City: Rediscovering the Center* by William H. Whyte, *Traffic* by Tom Vanderbilt, and *With People in Mind: Design and Management of Everyday Nature* by Rachel Kaplan, Stephen Kaplan, and Robert L. Ryan. I read many others that aren't listed here, and I am indebted to those authors as well.

There were also some key papers, newspaper articles, and research studies that stuck with me. They include "The Ecological Approach to Visual Perception" by James J. Gibson (*MIT Press*, Vol. 11, No. 3, 1978), "Smelling the Books: The Effect of Chocolate Scent on Purchase-Related Behavior in a Bookstore" by Lieve Doucé, Karolien Poels, Wim Janssens, and Charlotte De Backer (*Journal of Environmental Psychology*, Vol. 36, December 2013), "The Latest Traveler Kvetch: Hotel Lights Are Confusing" by Dawn Gilbertson (*Wall Street Journal*, April 24, 2024), "Landscapes of Fear and Stress" by Jack L. Nasar and Kym M. Jones (*Environment and Behavior*, Vol. 29, No. 3, 1997), "The Built Environment and Spatial Form" by Denise L. Lawrence and Setha M. Low (*Annual Review of Anthropology*, Vol. 19, 1990), "Public Space and the Situational Conditions of Crime and Fear" by Vania Ceccato (*International Criminal Justice Review*, Vol. 26, 2016), "Perception of Personal Safety in Urban Recreation Sites" by Herbert W. Schroeder and L. M. Anderson (*Journal of Leisure Research*, Vol. 16, 1984), "Fitting the Workplace to the Human and Not Vice Versa" by K. H. E. Kroemer (*Industrial Engineering*, Vol. 25, No. 3, 1993), "How Do People Organize Their Desks: Implications for the Design of Office Automation Systems" by T. W. Malone (*ACM Transactions on Office Information Systems*, Vol. 1, No. 1, January 1983), "Forget What You Know about Light Switches" by Michael McWatters (*Medium*, August 26, 2016), and four fascinating papers by David Kirsh: "The Intelligent Use of Space" (*Artificial Intelligence*, Vol. 73, February 1995),

"Distributed Cognition, Coordination and Environmental Design" (*The Proceedings of the European Conference on Cognitive Science*, 1999), "Problem Solving and Situated Cognition" (*The Cambridge Handbook of Situated Cognition*, 2009) and "Adapting the Environment Instead of Oneself" (*Adaptive Behavior*, Vol. 4, No. 3/4, 1996).

I am indebted to my brother Tod Goldberg, bestselling novelist, bon vivant, professor of creative writing, and founder of UC Riverside's Low-Residency MFA Program in Creative Writing for the Performing Arts, for downloading dozens of papers and studies for me from various online academic libraries and for being a sounding board for my ideas for this novel.

I also want to thank my good friend Phoef Sutton, the Emmy Award–winning screenwriter who wrote and produced the unsold 2011 CBS sitcom pilot *Vince Uncensored*, starring Michael Chiklis and Elizabeth Perkins, which likely inspired a key aspect of Edison Bixby's character.

This book is entirely a work of fiction. However, I was inspired by two *real* homes when I created Edison Bixby's personal wonderland, which, I suspect, some of you thought was *way* over the top and couldn't possibly exist in reality. If you were one of those people, you were wrong.

Los Angeles is dotted with wonderful examples of "storybook-style" homes, apartment buildings, and restaurants. They first started appearing here with the birth of the movie industry in the early twentieth century and would eventually spread throughout Southern California, the state, and even the nation (later, in the 1950s, LA would see an outbreak of Cinderella-style tract homes, but that's another story, one that I believe I touched on in one of my Eve Ronin or Sharpe & Walker novels . . . but I don't remember which one).

The Witch House is perhaps the most famous and enduring example of the storybook style. It was designed and constructed by movie art director Harold G. Oliver in 1921 as the administration building and dressing rooms for the Willat Studios in Culver City. Six years later, the building was moved to Beverly Hills and repurposed as a home. It's still standing today at 516 North Walden Avenue and was one of my inspirations for Edison Bixby's home. You can learn more about the house, and many others like it, in the wonderful book *Storybook Style: America's Whimsical Homes of the 1920s* by Arrol Gellner and Douglas Keister.

I was also greatly influenced by a unique property nestled in a secluded canyon in a remote corner of the Santa Monica Mountains. The home, the outbuildings, and all of the landscape features in the canyon were meticulously designed and hand-built over forty-three years by Gary Richardson, who was an architect, carpenter, furniture-maker, and contractor. This was his dream home, and it showed.

His house looked like a natural, organic extension of the trees around it, a tree house that wasn't in a tree, but was one itself, if you can imagine that. The theme continued inside, with his custom wood furniture, a bathroom featuring intricate inlaid timber, a living room dominated by a massive stone fireplace, and a cellar fashioned out of a preexisting natural cave.

The house would have been memorable and remarkable by itself, but the eight-and-a-half-acre property it was part of was also Richardson's personal wonderland. His imaginative work included elaborate gates, a bridge over a creek, a soap-maker's workshop, a carpenter's workshop, and an idyllic pond, fed by a seventy-foot-high waterfall that cascaded down a hillside and was a magnet for deer, mountain lions, and other wildlife.

For years, the Richardsons hosted an annual party on the grounds that reportedly was like a Renaissance Faire and that, in its final years, drew over four hundred friends and family. Richardson even built guesthouses that he rented out so others could enjoy his personal dreamland.

I wouldn't have known about this special place if not for my friend Shaun Prendergast, a UK-based writer and actor who appeared in *Fast Track: No Limits*, an action movie I wrote and produced in Berlin in 2007. Sometime after the movie wrapped, Shaun came to LA to see his sister Alison, who was married to Richardson, and stayed with them. So my wife and I, who lived not far away, went out to their home to visit Shaun. It was an afternoon that has stuck with us ever since.

Richardson was quite a bit older than his second wife, Alison, and if memory serves, he was in his late seventies, if not his early eighties, when we met. But he had the muscled body and boundless energy of a man in his thirties. Physically, he reminded me of a gray-haired Jack LaLanne (I know I am dating myself with that reference). He was a cordial host and was delighted to give us a grand tour of his property. I wish that I'd taken pictures, because the entire property was destroyed in 2018 by the devastating Woolsey Fire, the largest and most destructive wildfire in California history.

After that disaster, the Richardsons lived in a camper van on the desolate, blackened earth for two years before finally moving to a home in Tucson, where Gary died not long afterward at the age of eighty-nine. I didn't really know the man, nor am I a doctor, but I suspect that a broken heart was a contributing cause of his death.

I hope that my little tribute, in the form of Edison Bixby's imaginary home, keeps the memory of Gary Richardson's dream house alive for a while longer.

Finally, I couldn't have written this book without the enthusiastic support and patience of my wife Valerie, my daughter Madison, my publishers Gracie Doyle and Megha Parekh, my editor Charlotte Herscher, and my agent Amy Tannenbaum.

About the Author

Photo © 2024 Linda Woods

Lee Goldberg is a two-time Edgar Award and two-time Shamus Award finalist and the #1 *New York Times* bestselling author of more than sixty novels, including the Eve Ronin series, the Ian Ludlow series, the Sharpe & Walker series, and five books (and two novellas) in the Fox and O'Hare series, which Lee coauthored with Janet Evanovich. He has also written and/or produced many TV shows, including *Diagnosis Murder*, *SeaQuest*, *You're Killing Me*, and *Monk*, and is the cocreator of the Hallmark movie series *Mystery 101*. As an international television consultant, he has advised networks and studios in Canada, France, Germany, Spain, China, Sweden, and the Netherlands on the creation, writing, and production of episodic series. For more information, visit www.leegoldberg.com.